REVENGE KNOWS NO BOUNDS

Terry Barnett

Bondegard Press

LEBANON, INDIANA

Terry Barnett/Bondegard Press
104 Monroe Crescent
Lebanon, Indiana 46052

Publisher may be reached at: bondegardpress@gmail.com

Publisher's Note: This is a work of fiction. Names, characters, places, and incidents are a product of the author's imagination. Locales and public names are sometimes used for atmospheric purposes. Any resemblance to actual people, living or dead, or to businesses, companies, events, institutions, or locales is completely coincidental.

Cover Design by Meredith Federle

Editing by Susan Barnett and Cameron Steiman

Book Layout © 2017 BookDesignTemplates.com

Revenge Knows No Bounds/Terry Barnett. -- 1st ed.
ISBN 978-0-9986546-0-7

Dedicated to my family. The generation before me were mostly farmers. When my dad passed a few years ago many farmers came through the line at calling to tell me, "Your dad was a good farmer."

Prologue

Pacific Ocean off the coast of Chile

With the first leg of the flight from Rio de Janeiro, Brazil to Chile completed they were now back in the air and en route to Sydney. The thirteen-hour flight left Santiago International Airport at 7:37 PM local time to make the overnight flight to Australia. Captain Miguel Mulina was a long-time veteran in big aircraft and was edgy tonight as witnessed by his co-pilot, Luis. Luis had six years of experience and was still unsure of his future in this line of work.

"How you feeling Captain Mulina? Mind if I rest now and you get some later tonight?"

Miguel responded, "Yes, that's fine, please just sit back and relax."

Luis closed his eyes and reclined his seat. Miguel's sarcasm was crystal clear to Luis; the Captain was acting his age. The youthful spirit was long gone. He might want to mention his concern for Captain Mulina in the next psychological review they all had to endure. No potential flaw goes unnoticed, hypercritical bastard.

It was a clear night and the auto-pilot was programmed and in charge.

"You have another late night chasing the local senoritas?" Miguel asked.

This got nothing more than a small smile from his co-pilot. This young man had been living hard, and it was showing in his work and demeanor. Bags under his eyes and continuous yawning were hard to conceal. Luis was breathing deeply in three minutes.

Miguel shut the cockpit door and used the iron bars he smuggled aboard in the pullout handle of his carry-on to wedge into the grooves on the sides of the door. It was now securely and illegally locked. Luis was resting comfortably when Miguel pressed the small needle against his upper arm. It penetrated the skin and he barely stirred. Within two minutes Luis could not object to the new flight plan.

Miguel reprogrammed the flight plan to change course and set in motion a gradual decline in altitude to plunge them into the Pacific Ocean in a little more than 70 minutes. He turned off all possible electronics to make tracking difficult. His research had given him the best area to have minimal coverage by radar and satellite. Miguel removed his captain's hat and lowered his head.

"God please forgive me and please take care of my daughter."

He thought to himself how would God forgive him for taking all these innocent lives for the sake of one life. Miguel felt a trickle of sweat moving from the hairline on the back of his neck into his collar. He loosened his tie and pulled the picture of his daughter from his shirt pocket.

The flight attendants had started the mundane task of offering refreshments. Passengers were settling in for the long overnight flight. Amy was good with people and enjoyed leading her crew.

She found it interesting how some people could be asleep so fast while others read and others stared blankly; deep in their own thoughts. Maybe they were praying or already missing someone left behind. Several years of experience in aircraft left her with an internal set of guidance controls and a small buzzer was going off in her head. They were now at cruising altitude, but it seemed she was feeling a change.

"Maria how are your ears?" Amy asked her partner in a low voice.

Maria responded with a quizzical look, "Popping a little."

Amy glanced toward the closest window knowing there was nothing to see flying over the ocean at this time of evening. She decided to give it a few more minutes to see if the feeling persisted.

After serving several more rows of passengers the alarm buzzer was going off in Amy's head. She looked at Maria with a face that showed she was on edge.

"Go check with Captain Mulina and offer him a cup of coffee," Maria said.

Amy nodded and turned toward the cockpit. Rather than following normal protocol and use her intercom to the Captain, she knocked softly with no response and then knocked a little harder. She could barely hear Captain Mulina's response and she attempted to open the door. It was locked, she again called for Captain Mulina and tugged harder on the door. This was very unusual; mentally she was heading for crisis mode.

Miguel had planned for a possible call to the cockpit and had prepared a message to send to the flight attendants and passengers. Internal speakers crackled to life.

"We are approaching some unexpected turbulence, please keep your seat belts secure. We have changed course and altitude to keep your flight smooth."

This gave Amy a feeling of relief, now knowing the pilots were working on getting around or through some rough air, but she would make a note of the door being locked. That was highly unusual.

Miguel was having "what the hell have I done" thoughts as minutes passed slowly. He wondered why he had not just given himself an injection as well and ended his life before the crash. He thought of a million things, but knew this was his only choice. Thoughts of his daughter came rushing to him. First steps, playing soccer and seeing her in a formal gown.

"She's beautiful," Miguel said to himself.

The last thought Amy had before the 777 hit ocean water was how the altitude was affecting her ears. At impact, thankfully no one on board except Captain Miguel Mulina knew what happened. He kept his eyes open and could feel the crushing blow of the water as the cockpit windows were blown inward.

Santiago, Chile

As minutes turned into an hour, Chilean air traffic controllers were quickly going into crisis mode.

"How can we lose a Brazilian 777?" the controller in charge said to no one in particular.

It had been a quiet evening with normal flight operations and no apparent weather problems. Controllers called their counterparts to the south hoping it was just a glitch at Santiago and they would have them in the filed flight plan, but this was not the case. Finger pointing began almost immediately, there was no Brazilian airliner on anyone's screen.

Operation managers calculated where they should be and kept trying to contact them on the radio. Knowing the time of last confirmed contact by radio, the planned flight speed and altitude along with the planned flight pattern gave them the best guess of where they should be. This location was over a thousand miles off the coast of Chile and available military aircraft from three countries were vectored to the area. Initial searches found nothing. A detailed search plan was started using a grid pattern of the "best guess" area.

News traveled fast as word of the missing 777 rolled around the world. The bigger news soon became how with all modes of radar and satellite information available there was no idea where the plane went down. But that was the case, no one had a clue. As bits and pieces of information were accumulated and woven into a timeline and possible flight pattern the countries who had the means sent planes and ships to begin the search. Hours became days with still not a clue. How could a jet from a country in South America with 278 passengers and crew totally disappear with no wreckage to be found, not even an oil slick? No fireball was ever determined with any of the sources and this meant a lot of jet fuel should show up somewhere. It also meant this huge plane went straight into the ocean with no explosion. This raised many questions about this not being an accident but a planned attack.

Besides all the planes and surface ships that were being shown on major international networks, submarines from three countries were also tasked to the area. Submarines value their stealth to an infinite degree thus no discussion of the underwater world of the search made the news. They also dislike being tasked to any area with subs from two other countries. Not good. Submarine stealth includes a lack of communication with their mainland navies. Submarine Captains have varying discretion in what they can do and how far they can change from the original mission. There is no other way with limited communication available. Above all they are tasked to bring everyone back alive.

With all the international outcry over the missing airliner, an underwater explosion detected by the United States Navy out of San Diego and groups of scientists from Columbia to the southern tip of Chile went virtually unnoticed. The United States Navy was happy to keep this information from the public as they suspected the worst. They always do. The South American scientists attempted to get this information to New Zealand and Australia fearing a possible tsunami. Hours passed with waves only two feet higher than normal, this became a blip on the radar and quickly forgotten.

The United States Navy would never know exactly what happened to their nuclear submarine. The USS South Carolina had been tasked to aid in the search. They would never know a deep undercover jihadist was on the crew. A plan which was years in the making had ended in an underwater disaster costing many lives.

Calls from the high brass were made from the west coast to the Pentagon of possible problems with one of the nuclear submarines that had been vectored to the southern Pacific. It was well known it would take time to get any information in this part of the globe. Patience was not a virtue in military operations, patience is overrated!

London, England

A meeting of jihadi supporters in London had been planned for months pending good news from the Pacific. They still did not have full confirmation, but wanted to discuss their next move. The leader of this secret organization was named Asis.

"The U.S. will take this very hard," Asis said. "The American public will be outraged they were kept in the dark. This attack is the biggest since 9/11, it will not be visible to the world but very deadly in the loss of life and equipment to the American military."

Others around the table nodded their agreement. Asis was very aware the American people had developed a total need to know philosophy in this new world of the internet and instant gratification. Many times the information now provided on the nightly news proved invaluable to organizations like Asis had put together. The American people seemed not to care this *extra* information put their troops in more danger. They expected their organizations like the Central Intelligence Agency and Homeland Security to tell everything, the politically correct term was *total transparency*. This sounded like a good thing, but usually it was only good for people like Asis in the long run.

Asis had skin in the game. His nephew, Babur, had been groomed all his life to become an important jihadist in the war against the United States.

"My nephew Babur gave his life to further our war on the infidels. He completed every step of the plan."

Babur had gone to the right schools in the U.S. and then was accepted into the Naval Academy. His performance was excellent and his engineering degree put him in the correct line to have his hands on the S9G nuclear reactor in a United States Virginia Class submarine. Babur was in the exact place his mentors had wanted him. Only three years ago the plan became clear how to make this all happen and drive the biggest possible sword into the hearts of the infidels. Asis always knew it may have been more luck than precision planning to get his nephew in the right place at the right time. Communication with his nephew was less than sporadic and always a huge risk, but when it happened, they were able to time the jet crash to give them the best chance. It had worked and Asis was feeling fabulous about himself. Losing his nephew was just part of the greater good, no more no less.

Pacific Ocean

The search for the missing airliner had not turned up one shred of evidence. This was not only a huge disappointment to the world it was a huge embarrassment as well. It was inconceivable the largest navies and air forces in the world came up empty. Several times they believed there was a lead on the black box but time quickly ran out on the pinging it generated. Ninety-five percent of the deployed assets were called off within ten weeks of intensive searching by all the countries involved. This left it as one of the biggest, if not the biggest, cold cases since World War II.

The United States Navy was ready to make an official call on the loss of their submarine. Another sub sent to the area had located wreckage, it was verified there had been a powerful explosion on board the USS South Carolina. There had been little debris left which made it clear it was from the nuclear reactor. It would be made public very soon, there would be many families to notify and a lot of questions to answer from the press. Questions to which there were no answers. Losing a nuclear submarine is an extremely big deal. Sailors manning a submarine represented many years of training and technical expertise. It is also a huge financial loss and could be a catastrophic loss of intelligence if a sub was ever taken intact, this was not the case here. This submarine had such a devastating explosion that all was lost. One hundred thirty-four men including officers had been killed. No one except Asis and his small group knew this included one murderous traitor.

Chapter One

Greenville, Indiana

Mike Baker grew up on a farm in Hampton County, Indiana, the county seat was Greenville. Indianapolis was the biggest city in Indiana and the closest big town to Greenville. As a young boy, Mike's family occasionally traveled to Indianapolis for shopping, but did most of their business in Greenville.

Greenville had several nice stores owned by the locals and Mike's parents wanted to do as much business as possible to support their community. It was a community that valued agriculture, the local farmers were a big part of the commerce. On any morning you would see more pick-up trucks parked on the downtown tree-lined streets than cars.

Mike loved the spring, but it always seemed as if everyone in his business loved the fall. This was understandable since the fall is when the crop was harvested and money would come to you and not the other way around. Spring is the time of everything turning green and brightening up from the gray winter months. Leaves could never get back on the trees soon enough for him.

"C'mon son, back on the tractor!" his father hollered.

Mike smiled to himself as he considered how the roles had reversed. As a boy he was saying the same thing to his dad. His father did all the planting when he was a boy and did a fine job.

His dad would start every field with the same procedure, get off the tractor numerous times to go back and dig in each row to make sure the seed was being planted at the correct depth and the correct spacing between seeds. Mike wanted him to get going so they could get more acres planted. Dad was more interested in making sure it was done right the first time. Years later Mike had taken over the planting and the digging and the being meticulous part.

"Got to make sure this planter is working right," Mike yelled over the noise of the tractors.

His dad waved and went on tilling ground ahead of him, smiling to himself. Fathers and sons go through a rite of passage all over the world.

Another thing Mike liked about this time of year was the smell of the soil as it was being worked. It has a certain smell. No need to describe it, you either know it or you don't. Most people feel that way about freshly mown hay in the field or grass in their yards. Smells good.

Mike was born the oldest of two sons to Gordon and Jean Baker. He didn't realize until now how much he enjoyed being a farmer. It seemed farming had a lot more risk than reward and as a younger man he wanted to be in another industry. He had nothing against agriculture, he liked to eat as much as anyone, he just didn't want to be a farmer. This led him to Purdue University to study Building Construction Management or BCM. He loved his time at Purdue and kept his agricultural ties by living at Farm-House Fraternity.

A successful four years studying BCM led him to a job with a contracting firm in Georgia. The heat in the summer was worth it to have less cold in the winter, and he enjoyed being asked if he wanted sweet tea whenever he stopped at a restaurant. Most didn't ask, it was just assumed; you had to let them know if you didn't want sweet tea, the "Wine of the South." Being a lifelong Atlanta Braves fan led him to many ballgames while working in Georgia. His dad tried to make at least two games each summer with Mike. As Mike would venture out to job sites, he would wear his Atlanta Braves hat pulled down over short-cut brown hair instead of the hat issued by the company. This was overlooked by company employees, seemed they all were Braves fans. Mike even put a Braves "*A*" on his hard hat. At five foot eleven and one hundred ninety pounds Mike had been a decent baseball player in high school, Mom and Dad were his biggest fans.

Mike remembered the call from his mother like it was yesterday.

"Mike, your dad is in the hospital."

"What happened Mom?"

"He's had a heart attack. They have him stabilized and he's resting, but he'll need surgery."

"How soon?"

"They're not sure yet, depends on how quickly he regains strength but they want to do it as soon as possible."

"We'll be home soon Mom."

"There's nothing you can do Mike."

"We can be with you, and Dad needs all the support we can muster."

"Don't take the kids out of school Mike."

"Okay let me worry about that. I'll talk to Sandy and let you know our travel plans."

"Thanks, Mike, love you all."

"Love you too, Mom. Bye for now."

This call from his mother came when he was 39 years old. They had quickly realized Dad's heart attack would cause him to either quit farming or slow down to a point he could no longer do it alone. Until that point Dad at age 68 had still been in good shape and going strong. Mike thought he would get back to his old self, but no one knew for sure. It seemed Mike should come back home to take over the business. Days of not wanting to be a farmer were quickly becoming a lot more blurred at this point in his life.

He could still have sweet tea in Indiana if he asked for it and he was old school enough to enjoy listening to the Braves on the radio. The decision was made and his family moved north. Dad recovered from bypass surgery to a point where he could help Mike in the field and with the books. That had been seven years ago and Mike had not looked back. His wife had rapidly acclimated back to her Indiana roots and life was the right pace for now.

Mike had met his wife at Purdue. Sandy was a dark caramel blonde with blue/green eyes and the love of his life. Mike said she'd put on a jean jacket and walk into a room like she was going to a suffrage meeting. She was also a dyed in the wool Purdue person and was glad to be back closer to her family and Purdue. Campus was different from their days there, but in many ways the same. Maybe their kids would be Boilermakers. Their oldest child was a seventeen-year-old son named David, their youngest was a fifteen-year-old daughter named Sarah. David and Sarah were growing up and had made an easy transition back to Indiana. Mike was pleased he still heard "Y'all" come out of David's mouth, it sounded right. Mike and Sandy were glad their children had spent their first few years in the south, both still talked about friends from elementary school and kept in touch with a few. Mike still wanted to keep some roots in Georgia.

A spring storm moving in late this afternoon was likely to keep Mike and his dad out of the field for a couple days so they pushed on working later than normal to finish the 80-acre field. It felt good to pull out of a field and let Mother Nature take over for the next six months. You can have all the latest equipment costing hundreds of thousands of dollars including GPS systems to fine-tune fertilizer and herbicide application but if Mother Nature was not working with you, nothing mattered. Mike understood this, that's how it had always been. That little knot of "weather uncertainty" in your stomach was always there. This was not from his lack of faith, just knowing things can happen. Mike had much more faith in Mother Nature than he had in a lot of other things going on in the world today.

Rain moving in overnight led him to send a text to his good buddy, Brian Miller, to meet for breakfast.

His response was *see you there*.

Brian had been a friend for many years and was always interested in hearing a story and not shy about telling one. Brian was a graduate of Wabash College in Crawfordsville, Indiana and a career employee with the Indiana Department of Natural Resources (DNR). This career had provided Brian with the fodder for many stories; Mike thought at least 75% of them might be true!

Mike was up early to have coffee at home before heading to town. While making coffee he found a pair of clean jeans Sandy had folded out of the dryer and pulled on an old Purdue sweatshirt over his t-shirt. He stepped into his work boots as he headed for his truck.

Mike opened the door to the Skylight Diner and immediately saw Brian sitting in a booth, Brian waved him over.

"How you doin' buddy?" Mike asked.

"I'm good, how's planting coming?"

"Good, it's nice to have a couple days' break. This gives us time to make some repairs and let Dad catch up on some needed rest."

The waitress stopped with ice water and coffee and asked, "The usual boys?"

They both nodded yes looking forward to biscuits and gravy with hash browns on the side.

"Any spring birding trips planned?" Mike asked.

Mike often referred to Brian as the "Bird Man". Brian was a lifelong lover of Mother Nature and one of those guys who kept a Lifer List. This means he kept records as to time, place, conditions and whatever else was pertinent to the sighting of a bird. This life list had grown to 696 species from all points in the United States and areas of Canada, Central America, and South America. Brian's wife not only understood his love of birds, but shared his passion for science and wildlife; he counted this as one of his *top of the list* blessings! Pam had accompanied Brian on many of these birding trips. Brian always had a birding trip in the planning stage.

"Pam and I have a trip planned to Brazil next February," as Brian had a bite of biscuits and gravy.

Mike sent a fork of hash browns down at the same time while wiping extra gravy off his moustache. Facial hair of other sorts had come and gone but the moustache had always stayed. Sandy had threatened a messy divorce if the moustache went away.

"Have you ever been to Brazil before?"

"No," Brian said after taking a drink of coffee. "The birding trip is a 25th anniversary present to ourselves."

"You dog," responded Mike. "Maybe Sandy and I can spend a weekend in Atlanta watching three Braves games for our 25th in six years!"

Brian gave him a grin that Mike saw as recognition to *You Dog*. They knew each other well and would always be friends. Brian was eight years older and Mike thought of him as an older brother. Brian and Pam cared deeply about the environment and would never back away from trying to protect the earth. This was one of many things he admired about them. With breakfast finished and the waitress paid; they both stood to leave. They went on their way with a handshake and a pat on the shoulder that meant, take care.

Three days later the fields had dried to a point they could get back to planting. They finished planting corn and then started with soybeans. They had switched from planting soybeans in rows like they did when Mike was a boy to using a drill. This meant the beans were planted thicker and there were no rows to drive down later to cultivate the weeds out. The new herbicides available made this possible.

When Mike was a boy Dad would call him to go to the bean fields to cut weeds. Dad had purchased three weed cutters that were nothing more than a wooden handle with a steel hook on the end. He sharpened them between trips to the field. The process was grabbing a weed by the top and cutting its stem down by the soil, then drop it between the rows to dry up and die. Looking back this was environmentally friendly and in Mike's memory blistering hot and tiring on the back. Dad, Mike, and younger brother, Scott, would head to the field mid-morning. Each would take two rows and go up and down the field until Mom either hollered for lunch or brought it to us in the Ford F150. Mike would often let himself daydream back to times like this. Seeing Mom in that truck was a beautiful thing. She could make lunch or dinner on the tailgate of that old truck seem like a feast fit for kings. Mike would always think the tea out of a Mason jar was the sweetest tea of all. Maybe it was, Mom probably had made it sweeter to bring to the field. It didn't matter, all that mattered was the great memories of the family working together on the farm. One of them would sit on the tailgate, two would grab folding lawn chairs out of the truck and Mom would be up and making sure the three guys had all they wanted to eat. She'd eat last and Mike hoped she had been nibbling as she was preparing.

Mike always thought of his dad wearing bib overalls. That's what he wore. There was always a pencil in that narrow middle pocket. There was always a small notebook sticking out of one of the pockets by his pencil. Seed corn companies gave these little notebooks to their farmer customers. Dad filled these notebooks with information that would be kept on a computer hard drive today. It was filled with farm things describing what had been planted in each field that year, bushels per acre produced and number of pigs per litter. There may have been a page listing the birthdays of his grandchildren. There was always a pair of pliers in the side pocket on his right leg because Dad was right handed. The other thing you could count on would be a red or blue bandana in the back right pocket. Those bandanas had wiped a lot of hard-earned sweat off the brow of this farmer over the years. Mike used to tie a bandana around his head while baling hay in the hot months. Seemed like a very Bruce Springsteen thing to do.

They finished planting beans on the 16th of May which was Dad's birthday. This pleased him to no end and they went out for dinner to celebrate and returned home for birthday cake. Sandy always made his favorite since Mom had passed and Dad had taken the spare bedroom. Now that spring planting was finished it was time to let Mother Nature take over. They'd clean up the equipment and get it put away for next year.

Chapter Two

Greenville

With kids in high school it was not uncommon for the Bakers to have a visitor at 9:17 PM in the evening. It was still light this time of the summer. Light enough to still be outside, but not dark enough to enjoy seeing lightning bugs yet. Mike answered the door to greet two men in Class A White Naval uniforms, who were looking a lot more solemn than he would have preferred. After a brief introduction, the Chaplain delivered the news of Mike's brother, Scott's, death onboard the USS South Carolina last February. Nearly five months to the day to get news they had put in that back corner of their minds where no family ever wants to go, but news they were somehow expecting. The two officers sat with Mike and Sandy for nearly thirty minutes and were then on their way with an overwhelming sense of condolence. Few facts were delivered because of the ongoing investigation. It was now up to Mike to deliver this news to his father who was already asleep.

"Should I wait until morning to tell him?"

Sandy said, "That would be a mistake."

Mike knew she was right. He heard every step creak as he slowly climbed the stairs and tried to compose the right words.

Mike's gentle knock on his father's door did not get the job done the first or second time so he eased the knob to let himself in. Sandy followed close behind to support both men she knew so well. Family was everything to Gordon and she knew this news would devastate him.

"Hey Dad, Dad." Mike gently touched his shoulder.

"Son?"

"Dad, I need to talk a minute."

Dad rubbed his eyes and reached for his glasses.

"Turn on the light, Son."

Mike pulled the chain to turn on his table lamp. Dad was getting himself in a sitting position.

"Dad I've got rough news."

Dad looked at him and then at Sandy and was feeling that tightness in his chest that immediately arrived at times like these.

"Two naval officers just came to tell us about Scott. He and the entire crew of the USS South Carolina were lost at sea last February. It has taken months for them to get enough information to tell us.

As they expected, Dad was devastated. Tears flowed for all three of them, talk did not. It is amazing how anger, shock, grief and absolute despair can all bubble out at once when death strikes a child before a parent. No parent ever wants that, ever. Never ever. It is everyone's worst nightmare and one that Mike knew Dad had worried about ever since Scott had joined the Navy after college. Scott was determined to serve his country aboard a warship that spent its time under the sea not upon the sea. This is hard for a parent but probably the toughest is the total loss of communication for months at a time.

This is one of many wartime stories that never let a soldier or parent say goodbye. Mike had been having a nagging worry for a few weeks as the current deployment of the USS South Carolina should have ended several weeks prior. He also knew it wasn't uncommon for these deployment returns to be delayed due to changes in international circumstances such as the hunt for the downed airliner last February.

No one slept that night for more than a few fitful minutes. They all looked haggard the next morning as to be expected, especially Dad. Mike felt his father had aged ten years overnight, not good because his health had been teetering on the edge, anyway.

Dad had nothing to say except, "Thank you Sandy," as he sat down at the table and Sandy brought him a cup of coffee.

Mike could see the shake in his hands as he carefully brought the mug to his lips. No one knew what to say. It was fine that way with all of them.

Dad broke the silence to ask, "What do we do now?"

Mike just shook his head not knowing himself and said, "The officers told us that more information will be coming. They also said no remains were recovered from any of the crew, the explosion was fierce enough to render all but parts of the hull totally gone."

Death would have been instantaneous, which is a little relief. Suffering in any form of death is so hard to fathom and get out of your mind.

Mike said, "The Navy will honor the crew in a service at Arlington National Cemetery where the President will be on hand to speak and the Navy will also provide Officers to attend private services at each sailor's hometown."

The outpouring of support for Scott was incredible later in July. The support from Scott's friends from high school and college was overwhelming. Grief turned into a celebration of life which was awesome for everyone, but grief takes its hold again when everyone goes back home. That night after the service Dad, Mike, Sandy and their kids, David and Sarah, were all sitting in the family room.

Dad said, "I feel like I've lost a piece of myself, like I did when Mom passed. It's kind of weird how I'm relieved that Mom is not here to be part of this loss. Selfishly I'd like to have her with us to hold during this time, but more importantly I'm glad she greeted Scott into heaven. What would we do without faith?"

Sarah walked over and knelt beside her grandfather to hold his hand. Sarah could feel these were hands that had worked hard.

Dad then said, "Ok listen to this while I'm baring my soul. Strangely I feel relieved Scott didn't marry and start a family of his own. They'd now be grieving his loss like we are. Then I'm also sad for the same reason. I mean Scott didn't have the chance to be a father and all that goes with it like me and your Dad as he looked down at Sarah and then over to David. I have always said I loved being a farmer but being a dad was the best job I've ever had. I could not imagine what life would have been like if I had not been a happily married man who was blessed with two children and two more grandchildren."

Everyone just sat for a long time, Mike thought his dad had summed up his life better than anyone. They all let that emotion soak deep into their hearts. David realized at eighteen years old he was somehow older that day.

In the months that followed Gordon felt what can only be described as a full body numbness. He counted his blessings for each day he spent with Mike, Sandy and his grandchildren on the farm but he fought back tears daily when that realization of Scott's death hit him like a ton of bricks. He wondered if a day would ever pass when he didn't think of Scott. Part of him longed for that, another part hoped it would never happen.

London

Asis had waited to tell the world they had successfully blown up a United States nuclear submarine. Cells in the U.S. were reporting the military was delivering the information to families. This gave Asis his final confirmation their plan had worked. He wanted to let the world know at the same time the U.S. government was telling the families to make them look bad. He called a meeting of his London group.

"It is time for the world to know what we have done. Can you imagine the speculation there will be about how we did this?"

They looked at each other in silence amazed that it had worked to perfection. Part of this look was the realization that they would now become the most hunted men in the world. Several around the table felt a chill going up their spines not knowing what their futures might hold.

The following day Asis watched the video the world was seeing. This video was filmed in Syria, men with covered faces told the world that jihadists had blown up the USS South Carolina nuclear submarine last February off the coast of Chile.

"All infidels aboard were killed; this is only the beginning of a step up in the Holy War."

"From your twin towers in New York to a United States Navy submarine no American is safe."

"We can hit you wherever we want and whenever we want."

As Asis and his group imagined, the press around the world lit up the airways. The lines of communication between the Pentagon and the Department of Defense were jammed with speculation. The White House was forced to immediately make a statement to the American people concerning this possible terrorist attack. It had taken four months for the Navy to confirm the loss of the submarine in the Pacific due to the explosion. Now this terrorism claim had reopened the wound. Angry protests of citizens asking why it had taken so long for the truth to be revealed began immediately.

Unofficially, employees of the Pentagon, Department of Defense, National Security Agency and the Central Intelligence Agency all smiled inwardly because they now had a target. This terrorist organization had put a big bull's eye on themselves and every agency was ready to drive a stake right through it! It seemed everything came from Syria these days but the jihadists with covered faces always had a British accent. London was a hot spot for international activity and it had a huge Muslim population. The CIA would have to step up their activity in that area, someone would talk eventually. They'd spread some money around, that usually did the trick.

Greenville

Mike could see as harvest came to an end that fall happiness was not evident for him or his family. Yes, life must go on but it would never be the same for the Bakers. The weather had been mostly agreeable with harvest conditions this year but it seemed like an early winter was in the offing. Cold air was diving down from Canada earlier than normal. Mike never wanted to hear the term *polar vortex* again, but that was being said; another winter of potentially brutal cold and lots of moisture. He was getting to that age when winter was not fun.

Mike had planned an end of harvest breakfast with Brian to learn about his and his wife Pam's trip to Brazil coming up in February. Brian was very talkative for two reasons. One being he was excited to share information about their trip and new birds he hoped to add to his life list, reason two; he knew Mike needed space to listen and be taken away from here for at least a few moments. Mike took in most of what Brian had to tell him, he also took in all his biscuits and gravy. They agreed a full debriefing would be in order next February over another breakfast.

When Brian got home Pam asked, "How was breakfast with Mike?"

"He didn't have much to say Pam; in all fairness, I didn't give him much chance."

"Did he seem happy with harvest?"

"He didn't seem happy much at all," Brian said.

Brazil

Three months later Brian and Pam landed in Brazil with the anticipation of the explorers they were. Both had a strong faith in God and loved to explore any part of the world they could get to. This ten-day trip turned out to be all they'd hoped for and included some new additions to Brian's lifer list. One day of the ten proved like none of the other. They had traveled inland about 250 miles to a region that promised a chance to see a species Brian had never seen before. Along the way they saw a large flock of birds named Scarlet Tanager that Brian recognized as migratory from North America to Brazil. These birds are also seen in Indiana. Two things. These birds were not normally this far into South America and secondly; they didn't look right, he couldn't put his finger on it, but they didn't look right. They looked sickly. He'd file this away for future thinking, Brian was like that. Brian stopped the old Jeep along the side of the road.

Pam looked over at Brian and he pointed past her.

"This does not look right," he said.

There were large numbers of the birds within fifty feet from where he parked.

"They look somehow sick, lethargic. Like they could care less about our presence," Pam said.

"Do you recognize the species?"

"Scarlet Tanager," Pam said.

"Exactly, they do migrate here from the Midwest, but not this far inland. I know enough about them that this is not normal."

They both snapped some photos and Brian put the Jeep back in gear. They ended up seeing one more group of the same species with the same mangy look to them. Brian made notes of the type of birds, time and place they had seen them.

They had a great trip with lots of sightseeing and good food. The English language was usually not a problem with many in the hotel and restaurant business. They had rented a car and drove around enjoying the countryside and wildlife. Brian added ten species to his life list, this was always a treat to do. The trip was well documented with plenty of digital photographs and many journal entries. Brian and Pam had a book to write in their future about their travels.

Greenville

Upon arriving back home Brian and Mike met to discuss the trip. Brian shared all information about life list additions, beautiful scenery and great food. Brian made one offhand comment during breakfast that stuck with Mike.

"One afternoon as we were traveling inland we came upon several large flocks of birds that looked sick."

"How did you know they were sick?" Mike asked.

"They were not holding their heads right; you know not like a healthy bird would hold its head. Feathers looked wrong. They were Scarlet Tanagers from this part of the Midwest and they're normally pretty to see. These looked sick."

"They sure travel a long way," Mike said.

"Yes, and that's the other thing, they were not in the area where they normally migrate. Way too far inland."

"I see why that caught a trained eye like yours."

"Just weird," Brian said.

Tickets paid, they shook hands and headed out the door.

Mike thought about their conversation as he drove home. It seemed like another strange phenomenon happening with a lot of other strange shit going on in this world.

Often the national news would bring up the airliner that was lost in the Pacific. It had been one year with not one shred of evidence. This incident along with the submarine explosion crossed Mike's mind frequently. There always seemed to be something about these terrible events that just nagged at Mike like a dull headache that wouldn't go away.

Chapter Three

Greenville

In the last four years since Scott's death Mike had watched farming spiral downhill at an alarming rate. It was one of those times when everything that could go wrong in an industry went wrong, primarily in the mid-part of the United States, which Mike considered the breadbasket of the world. Weather problems that were loosely based on the El Nino effect involved dramatic moisture swings. Two years of crushing drought followed by flooding that devastated huge areas. Thousands of acres were never planted due to flooding. Federal crop insurance helped farmers but proved to be a Band-Aid that just prolonged the economic agony to follow.

The poor crop production caused commodity prices to soar, the supply and demand charts Mike's fraternity brothers studied in Ag Econ at Purdue were working to perfection. High priced corn and beans did not mean a damn if you didn't have a crop to sell. If you were diversified and raised livestock, you couldn't afford to feed the high-priced grain. This made the economic pain even worse.

There was also trouble with livestock herds. Unknown diseases had ravaged many animals. Again, everything that could go wrong, did. Many herds were being liquidated. Dairy herds kept producing but the price of milk was dramatically increasing, this was being felt by all consumers.

American companies were importing agricultural products from South America, specifically Brazil. The Brazilian Ag economy was booming.

Mike was the eternal optimist, but he couldn't find anything in agriculture to be optimistic about after the last few years. He had always been a good numbers person and with Sandy's help they were a formidable team in many respects including Ag finance. This was one of those times you knew in your gut where you stood but not wanting to admit it to yourself or your banker was a far easier road to take. Each year had eaten away at the solid foundation they had built over several generations of family, this made things all the worse. Mike had shared some with his father but not a lot of details, it didn't matter because Dad knew very well about the problems. He could see what was happening.

One gray, blustery morning the week before Christmas, Dad put on a coat and hat and found Mike on his way to the barn. It was one of those mornings when the breeze out of the northwest chilled you to the bone and the weather was as dreary as their mood. They walked around the corner to get out of the wind and Dad said, "Mike where do we stand with the bank?"

Mike said, "We're at a point where we can't pay interest this year and definitely no principal reduction. The first week of January is our appointment and I'm worried, there's no cushion left."

Dad nodded and again felt that helpless feeling he had experienced when they lost Scott. Total helplessness.

Christmas came and went. Mike and Sandy prepared their information to sell the banker on giving them more time but truth be told neither of them had faith they could overcome the last four years. Mike kept thinking to himself you never want to quit fighting but digging deeper may get you past the point of salvaging anything.

The day of their appointment finally came, and they arrived early to wait their turn.

Sandy said, "I feel sorry for Melissa, she has stress trying to figure out how to help us all."

Mike nodded his understanding of what her job must be like. He wouldn't want her daily negative stress. Everyone felt helpless to know the next step in farming.

"Yeah, she is probably wondering why she wanted to be an ag lender," Mike said.

Several neighbors had come and gone through the lobby to see the tellers while they were waiting. Mike noticed the general feeling of despair from the public.

"Everyone has their head down," Mike said to Sandy. She had noticed it as well; it was as gloomy as it could be for a January day. Both inside and outside the bank.

The clock made it to 10:00 AM and they sat down at Melissa's desk. Melissa looked as stern as they had ever seen her, she was normally good with a story or a quick laugh to settle your nerves and stomach. Not today. All business. She showed no surprise as they laid out their financial statements, there was nothing there Melissa had not expected. After some silence as she poured through the numbers she looked up and took off black rimmed glasses that furthered darkened the mood.

"Mike, Sandy; I have no answers for you, the bank cannot go on financing your operation. You can tell me that you have no choice but to push on, that worked last year but not this year. It's time to put the land up for auction and get this debt off your back."

Even though they had expected it, it still hurt more than you could ever explain. It wasn't like losing a job or learning the company was moving its operations to Mexico or India or wherever. Farming is a way of life, you live and work on your business and in their case, it was the same land and house where two generations of Bakers had done the same thing.

Mike said, "Melissa there is so much land on the market in the coming months we'll never get close to the value we should, it's crazy to sell now."

Melissa nodded her understanding, "We have no choice Mike. Our Board of Directors say we must move forward to collect the loans. You're not the only farm family in this situation."

Mike stood and Sandy followed, "We'll be in touch Melissa." They turned and headed for the door with papers in hand. A dark and blustery day matched their mood. No words were spoken as the pickup truck headed for home.

The thought of not telling Dad until tomorrow hit Mike as they were driving home, the same feeling as when they received the news about Scott. He gave Sandy a quick glance.

She said, "You must tell your dad".

Mike just looked ahead at the familiar road that led to home. Who knows where home would be in the next few weeks, but for now, they headed home.

Mike needed some strong coffee for what would happen next. After getting that first hot cup, he was ready to drink it and then decide how to tell his father the news. He seemed to make that cup last longer than normal. He would have taken all day to drink it if he could have. Upon finishing, he went for cup number two and off to sit with Dad.

Even though she'd offered to go with Mike, he'd asked Sandy to let them have this talk in private. She respected his wish and asked Mike to let her know how it went when finished. Mike went to his dad's room and found him reading the paper and having a cup of hot tea. Dad had taken to hot tea after Mike's mother passed. He had also been a coffee man while mom was a hot tea drinker. He was not sure if Dad changed to tea for a reason involving remembering mom? Probably yes.

Mike said, "Morning Dad."

"Morning son."

That was their greeting each day for as long as Mike could remember.

"We met with Melissa this morning at the bank", Dad nodded and laid the paper in his lap. Eyes alert as old eyes can be but also watery as old eyes can be.

"I've been waiting for you to come up those stairs son, I heard you come up the drive."

"Been calming my nerves Dad."

"I figured as much, give me the verdict."

"The last three years have brought us to a point where the bank says it's time to stop," again a nod came from Dad.

"No final decision was made but she told us to be thinking about putting the farm up for sale."

This caused Dad's head to drop a little in resignation and he said, "We both knew what was coming, I say you call the auctioneers and set a date. You could fight it, get it pushed back but with all farmers in similar circumstances waiting will likely get us less."

Mike had to agree with this thinking, this common sense that his father always employed. "Agreed", Mike said.

"You okay Dad?"

"I'm not any more okay than you are son. I can't get over all the strange events that have led us to this point after decades of farming this ground. Something is going on. Can't just all be bad luck."

Mike just nodded, his thoughts had been wandering along that same path. Mike got up to walk out and closed the door leaving Dad to think.

Sandy looked up as Mike came in the kitchen, "How'd it go?"

"He knew what was coming, he said we should just make the call and get the auction scheduled."

"What do you think Mike?"

"I think I agree. If we just get it scheduled it'll get the worry of this decision off our minds."

Sandy began searching for auctioneers and they narrowed it down to two companies that Mike knew were good and had been involved in a lot of land sales over the years. He'd been to sales handled by both companies.

Mike made two calls and they decided on their first choice. The auctioneer suggested a date about four weeks out to give the auction company barely enough time for advertising and all the things that must happen before the sale. The date was set. This date would allow the new owner time to plant a crop, waiting later would have further depressed the value of their land.

Mike asked Sandy what she thought about going ahead and selling all the equipment at the same time which would get them to a point where they could keep the house and buildings. She agreed, and secretly had been hoping Mike would see it that way. They could lose the land but she still liked the idea of keeping their home and continuing to live in the country. Who knew, they may someday have an opportunity to get the farm ground back. Sandy may have been the biggest optimist in the family, she loved farming and the land.

As the weeks passed and the day of the sale approached, the local papers from many communities had more and more sales showing up. Mike wondered who would buy all this land?

Chapter Four

Missouri

Janet Knight was spending this day like the rest of her days for the past couple years, finding ways she could add to her fortune by making money in the commodity markets. Events leading up to problems for agriculture had created opportunities to make money in the grain markets as well as livestock futures. Prices had whipsawed about for months on end, each movement created winners and losers and she had ended up on the winning side most of the time. As she watched the midwestern farmers continue to fail, she smiled knowing it was all coming together. The perfect storm that would make she and her brother, Roger Knight, very wealthy. Her years as a registered representative in the investment business had given her lots of seed money to put her plan into action. She didn't care who she stepped on to make it happen. She always smiled to herself when she read how they were supposed to care for their clients, she only cared about money and she'd get it from whoever was dumb enough to trust her pretty face. There was a never-ending line of people to do just that. It was all about trust and she only trusted in herself.

Janet never looked at herself as a greedy person, but a practical you-better-take-care-of-yourself person.

Indianapolis

Roger Knight was spending his day reading reports coming in from their branches all over Indiana. This would be the year of the farm sale and he was ready to see it happen. He hoped all this planning would at long last pay off.

In school, Roger had been one of those boys who'd been bullied by classmates and was thought of as a nerd. A successful high school career led him to college on the East Coast and then on to England to finish a Master of Business Administration at Kingston University.

Roger had returned to the United States and worked his way up the corporate ladder at an up and coming regional bank. He was an excellent salesman and a very shrewd lender. He always met his sales quotas and clients always seemed to end up with a bigger loan than they initially wanted or a second mortgage they didn't want. Nothing illegal in the process but it was wrong as it could be. Roger knew it was not in the best interest of the borrowers, his superiors knew it as well but they were making loans and banks wanted to make loans. It wasn't just Roger's bank; it was happening from large to small banks all over the United States. It was amazing how companies turned a blind eye in the name of profits. The housing market bubble had burst in 2008. That sent banks scrambling to stay afloat and keep the regulators and auditors at bay. The stock market lost 40 percent of its value in less than a year and it now showed we have not learned a damn thing because it was still going on nearly a decade later.

Agriculture had not had a defining moment since the excesses of the 1970s played out in the 1980s. Land inflation and leveraging the land using debt worked great in the 1970s. The 1980s saw the first decrease in land values for years and this caused that bubble to burst. Farmers sold assets to stay afloat, most kept some of their land and didn't lose it all. Roger hoped this cycle would be much worse.

Fort Meade, Maryland

Steve Bradshaw was an up and comer at the National Security Agency based in Fort Meade, Maryland. Recruited out of the University of North Carolina five years ago he wanted very much to make a name for himself in the agency. He was part of a team that had been tasked to gather all information possible about the submarine explosion. Month after month had gone by with nothing new. That was normal in this business, you kept looking for leads of any type. On this day, something came along that piqued his interest.

They had decided early in the investigation to look at the families of the pilots of the lost airliner. Nothing had shown up until today. A daughter of one pilot had recently moved from her modest home in a small Brazilian village to a very nice oceanfront home. Not illegal on the surface but why not dig a little? Steve made the request for specific help from the analyst section specializing in researching financial transactions. Sure enough the pilot's daughter had come into a sizable amount of money. Steve's first thought was life insurance proceeds; he'd make a note to see if this could be verified.

No one could ever understand what happened with the airliner that had crashed. That's why the USS South Carolina had been sent to the search area. Many ideas had been passed around the lunch table by other analysts trying to connect the dots. Nothing ever made sense connecting these two catastrophic events.

The jihadists had taken credit for the submarine explosion but made no claims about downing the airliner. They normally claimed anything and everything about events such as these, thus not claiming downing the airliner was a red flag to Steve even if they had nothing to do with it. This may be some kind of reverse psychological thinking but why not? Nothing about these adversaries ever made sense anyway.

The search functions of the huge mainframe computers at Fort Meade were humming along and working overtime. They had been working overtime since September 11, 2001 and as far as Steve could tell they would never quit. The global war against the jihadists was ongoing and he could not see any conclusion to this problem ever. The world had changed for the worse.

As bits and pieces of information were flagged to search from different sources, progress could be made. They needed the bad guys to make mistakes, subtle mistakes were good enough and all you could hope for.

Delphi, Indiana

Disease in the swine, beef and dairy herds had caused problems for Charles Summers. He was as good a livestock man as you could find in Indiana. A graduate of Purdue's Veterinary School and many years of experience with a large animal practice in Carrol County, Indiana had let him see pretty much everything, he thought. This last year he had been trying to help farmers with diseases that seemed to come out of nowhere. He had sent blood samples, tissue samples, fetal samples, fecal samples and every other kind of sample to several land grant schools. They came back with ideas but none fit the circumstances.

Charlie was working as hard as he could because that's how he did things, but truth be told he was wondering if he'd have any farmers left to help or animals to treat if this kept up. It had reached biblical proportions.

Illinois

White Oak Real Estate Holdings was a shell company. A subsidiary of a subsidiary that was set up to do things that needed to be hidden and out of the public eye and owned by people who wanted to be hidden and out of the public eye. The parent company was owned by Roger Knight and Janet Knight and the holding company was set up to do one thing, buy and sell farmland. This holding company was doing that as fast as they could flow money into it and then leverage the farm ground it held as an asset. Land values were being driven down by all the sales and this completely played into the hands of the owners.

Nothing illegal was happening with all this but there would be public outcry when the amount of land being purchased came to light. This would take a while to become public. Roger was facilitating bank loans to the holding company which was not illegal but as close to stepping over a line as possible. It was amazing how questionable things could be pushed to the edge when extra profits were involved.

A representative of White Oak would approach the auction companies and give them a maximum bid for each farm sold. They were making it high enough to drive legitimate buyers away and still getting land bought for less than the appraised value. It was working like a charm.

The only thing not working as well seemed to be a difference of opinion between Roger and Janet as to how long this would go on and how much they would buy. Janet knew the value of diversification in a portfolio. Roger's idea of diversification was not owning all the land in one township, just most of it. They had amassed thousands of acres in Central Indiana. Janet felt it was enough that different people and/or organizations would take extra notice. Janet had made a call to Roger to check in and make her thoughts known.

"Roger, we must consider saying enough is enough, we don't want to make such a splash to get ourselves on the radar instead of under it!"

Roger understood her worry, "Give me a day or two and I'll get back to you."

Janet said, "Please do," and ended the call.

Roger called his employee at White Oak.

"Jason, you doing okay?"

"Yes Mr. Knight, things are going great."

"I've decided to let things cool off for the time being. Let's talk before the sale next week to see where we stand."

"Sure thing Mr. Knight, everything okay?"

"Yes, all is fine, just evaluating where we are. Have you contacted the farm management firms?"

"We are looking at two different firms with a presence in central Indiana and should have a recommendation by the end of the month."

"That sounds good, thank you and your people for your hard work." Roger ended the call, smiled to himself. It all worked!

Chapter Five

Greenville

The morning after the farm sale Mike was up early. He felt very fortunate the land and farm equipment had brought enough to clear their debt load at the bank. He stood in the shower deep in thought. Warm water turning cold got his attention. He knew he needed to move on but he had a fight building in him like he'd never felt before. As he shaved he knew there were forces at work that had led him to this day. He could accept weather cycles. He'd read about the dust bowl times and seen parts of "The Grapes of Wrath" but this was different. He felt this was a calculated plan to hurt the American way of life, hit the farmer and then kick him while he was down.

Sandy stuck her head in the bathroom door, "How does bacon and eggs sound?"

Mike replied, "Just right. Sandy, would you put on the tea kettle full of hot water. I'll be down shortly."

As bad as this was he somehow felt relief this morning. The weight of the growing debt load was suddenly off their shoulders.

A few days later Mike went in his dad's room to check on him as he did every morning. This morning Dad was still in bed.

As he came around the bed, he felt a huge dread overcome him. As he tried to shake him awake there was no response.

"Sandy," he yelled and she came down the hall. Mike was kneeling at the side of the bed in tears as Sandy entered the room. She knew Gordon was gone and came around to hold Mike. They stayed there for several minutes before either one of them could talk or move.

"This has killed him Sandy. All this has taken down the strongest man I ever knew."

Sandy agreed with Mike, and feared for him as well. Suddenly losing his brother Scott to terrorism, and now his father was maybe more than Mike could bear.

They made the call to 911 and explained what had happened. Less than fifteen minutes later an ambulance was in the driveway and the EMTs were at his bedside. They began the process of preparing to take him.

As they took Gordon away Mike felt as hopeless as he thought a man could feel.

"Sandy would you call David and Sarah. I don't think I can do it."

Mike had come through the last three years masking anger over the terrorist organization that had allegedly blown up the sub. That anger was barely below the surface. He had a feeling in his gut this could be something more. It was eating him up.

Mike was also having old feelings of guilt he'd always kept to himself. He had thought for many years that he and his brother would sell the farm after Mom and Dad were gone. They'd get a big price and move along with their lives. He had never spoken of this to anyone, not Sandy nor Scott. These thoughts came when he was in his twenties as he began a nice career in Georgia. He was mad at himself and the whole situation that had transpired. It now seemed so far away and long ago. His folks were now gone and the farm was gone as well.

The funeral happened like all funerals happen. He appreciated all the friends and acquaintances who came to visit and reminisce about a farmer's life well lived in Gordon Baker. Mike knew he had more blessings than he could ever count and felt God would help him search for some answers. If something bad was going on with the American farmer, Mike felt God wouldn't be happy about it either.

Mike knew his dad would want him to move on with his life. He'd been asked to drive a school bus for the local public school, he'd work between bus routes for a local construction firm. The construction business wasn't great, but still active. Sandy would substitute teach at the same school and waitress in the evenings at a local restaurant. They would make ends meet until they could sort things out. It was not what they wanted but a lot of financial stress had been lifted from their lives.

Brian and Pam were sitting around the dinner table having a beer and talking about the Bakers. They were both concerned about their friends and everything they had been through over the last three years.

"They've gone through a total change of life," Pam said.

"You know that list when someone has experienced a life-changing event? Brian asked. It seems they've gone through the entire list except for Sandy getting pregnant! The adage, 'God won't give you more than you can handle' thought must have them questioning everything."

Pam shook her head, raised her beer and said, "To the Baker clan!"

Brian clinked his beer against hers and they both took a long drink.

Brian said, "I just read about a vet who was doing research on the new diseases that popped up over the last two or three years. He said some of these diseases had to be delivered by air and one mention was made about birds."

"And?" Pam said.

"I'm going to search for this guy's number and call, I'd like to know more, maybe I can help."

"Okay Bird Man you should follow that lead, now let's head to bed, it's getting late."

A few days after the funeral Mike was in his dad's room cleaning. He found a box under the bed he had not seen before. He sat it on the bed and opened it to find a 1911 Colt 45 handgun. Mike had no idea his father had the gun or the story behind it. He carefully lifted it out of the box and checked to see if it was loaded, it was not but there was a box of 45 shells in the bigger box. There were cleaning supplies and Mike found a small piece of paper. He opened the paper to find a short note in his dad's handwriting addressed to him and Scott.

Boys if you're reading this my intention is that I'm not around. I bought this gun and learned how to use it when you were both in grade school. Your mother never wanted it in our home. I respected her wish and it never was in our home while she was alive. I was honestly always about half afraid of it myself, but felt I should have a way to protect my family. I never wanted to use it and as I'm sitting down to write this, I never have. Only thing I ever killed was several paper targets. One of you take the gun and learn to use it, then keep it well hidden for your own safety. Love, Dad

Although Mike was surprised this sounded very much like Gordon Baker. He respected his wife and wanted to protect his family. He carefully folded the paper just as Dad had left it and put it back in the box. He repacked everything and thought about where he'd hide this in the barn.

About two weeks after the funeral Mike and Sandy received a call from Melissa at the bank. She expressed her sympathy over Gordon's passing and asked if they'd meet her for coffee on Saturday morning at the Starbucks on 86th street.

Sandy said, "We'll see you Saturday."

They made the thirty-minute drive without many words, mostly lost in their own thoughts. They walked in, saw Melissa and all ordered a Grande. They had known Melissa for several years and these last three had aged her. She never felt like the enemy even though she sat on the other side of the desk, this morning she sat at the same table and truly felt like a friend.

Melissa said, "Mike, I'm so sorry about your father."

Mike responded, "I think he was just drained, the past few years sucked the life out of him."

Melissa nodded her understanding. Melissa had grown up on a farm in western Indiana and had also seen her family struggle the last three years.

"I came to the funeral and sat in the back, I'm sorry I didn't get to speak to you both. It was a wonderful celebration of his life."

Mike said, "Thank you, yes it was. The hardest part for me was losing him like this. He had a blessed life and he knew it, we talked about it."

Melissa again nodded in agreement as she thought about this possibility with her dad and a wave of sadness washed over her. "I asked you here because I care about you both and have enjoyed working with you. I have something I want to say and you can do whatever you wish with it, but please don't mention it came from me."

"Sure Melissa, go ahead."

"As you know I've been lending money to farmers for several years. I go to ag lender meetings around central Indiana and as usual you oftentimes learn more between meetings while talking to other bankers. We're competitors, we know that, but we care about our farm customers and agriculture."

For the next thirty minutes Melissa told a story that was hard for the Bakers to hear, but listened intently.

"I've noticed a trend over the last couple years. Other bankers tell stories about how their banks have bent over backwards to help their customers. They negotiate work-out plans to set up a partial sale of farm ground to lessen the debt load, all kinds of things to save the family farm. I sit and listen and realize my bank is doing none of this. My bank drops the hammer on everyone to completely sell out."

Melissa said, "It seems they want to guarantee all our customers are out of business and I cannot in good faith work this way anymore. I for sure need a job, but I feel like the grim reaper."

Melissa caught herself.

"Mike, I'm sorry I said that."

Mike waved her off knowing she'd made no reference to his family.

"You're saying you're being told to work like this?"

She nodded yes and said, "We send in ideas for work-out plans and every situation is a little different depending on someone's level of debt, but we're sending in plans to keep farmers on their farms. The loan committee then sends back a short statement saying due to the prospects of a further decline in the agricultural economy we recommend a full liquidation. I'm not so naive to know sometimes this is the only way, but surely not in every case and probably not in your case."

Mike and Sandy had little to ask, they were not expecting this discussion and it was difficult to hear. This meeting with Melissa ended with hugs instead of handshakes like a normal business meeting.

"Melissa take care of yourself," Sandy said.

"Thanks for listening to me, I care about your family."

"We can tell," Mike said.

Chapter Six

Greenville

The White Oak Holding Company was ready to begin hiring the local farmers. The farmers needed work and this was just another way to take advantage of the bad situation and rub salt in the wounds. Hire them at a poor wage and make further profits for the holding company.

Mike Baker got his letter in the mail and read it at their kitchen table. It was a slap in the face as far as he was concerned but he also felt he'd rather be the one operating the equipment on this land rather than someone else. He'd discuss it with Sandy and decide, they were supposed to give this White Oak Holding Company an answer within the next week. It was apparent they controlled all the shots. If Sandy was on board he'd ask the construction company if they'd allow him some time off to plant the crop.

Twice a year the local Ag Extension office would have a professor come from Purdue to talk about the farm economy and current trends in the industry. Mike had always enjoyed the camaraderie of these meetings that were held at the county fairgrounds. You always learned something, saw other farmer friends, and ate well. Mike's dad used to say, "if you have nothing good to say then it might be a darn good time to be quiet." Mike was thinking about this when the professor got up to speak. What on earth could he have good to say? The answer ended up being, not much, but he didn't mince words either. There was a lot of talk and a lot of questions. The professor said the consensus from the academics was that the weather pattern would be back closer to normal going forward. Many felt too little too late, but they'd hang on to every bit of good news he could tell them.

It also seemed the livestock disease problems were coming into check. There were still no answers on this mystery disease, and everyone wanted to make sure this did not happen again.

There were questions raised about who had bought all the land. It was evident not much was known about the holding company. Mike had not forgotten their talk with Melissa, and he made a mental note to check in with her again to see if she had anything new.

The professor ended the meeting talking about alternative sources of income. He discussed the need for farmers to raise hops for the growing craft beer industry. This sparked Mike's interest. It seemed like the demand was well ahead of the supply. Mike decided he'd discuss this with Sandy. The small parcel of land they'd been able to keep around their home and barn could support hops production. He would do more research but he knew you had to build a structure that supported wires in a vertical fashion. Hops grew up the wires. These vines were cut back each year and grew again, he was not sure how long it took to get the plants established. It was good to leave the meeting with an idea to percolate on.

That evening over dinner Mike discussed the meeting and mentioned the idea of growing hops. Sandy liked the idea and agreed to do some research. They were both hanging on to anything to keep their hands in agriculture.

Mike also spoke to Sandy about taking the job to farm for the holding company. He took no risk to do this work, he didn't own the machinery and provided no inputs. He was just being paid a nominal wage to run over ground he saw as "their" home farm. It also let him keep his hand in farming. Mike was an eternal optimist and would always keep that inner hope of reacquiring the land back someday.

He signed the employment agreement and sent it back to the holding company in Illinois. They would contact him with further details shortly. He felt his father would have liked knowing Mike was tilling this ground instead of someone else, or would he? He might have encouraged Mike to gather up his family and move back to Georgia and work in the construction industry and get his Braves tickets back. Mike knew his father loved farming but working this land for someone else would leave a sour taste that would never go away.

Regardless, for this year and until there were more answers he would stay here and keep watch over the farm and the surrounding area. There were a lot of other friends in the same predicament. Mike received an email announcing there would be a meeting on the north side of Indianapolis sponsored by the holding company to discuss details of the upcoming planting season. All employees were to be there. It was very curt and to the point, he'd grit his teeth and go.

Indianapolis

Mike attended the meeting on the north-side of Indianapolis with about seventy-five other farmers. Many he knew or had seen at other agricultural events. They were meeting in a hotel that made them feel like ducks out of water. The gentlemen who spoke seemed to be a nice enough guy and laid out the plan to get the job done. It did seem like just a job when you listened to him. The joy or the satisfaction you get from farming the soil was replaced with a very businesslike tone. He was beginning to second guess himself as the evening wore on. It did turn his stomach as another speaker was letting them know how great this was and how they were doing the farmers a real favor by allowing them to still farm. There were several grunts and the muttering of "bullshit," and several other muffled comments Mike couldn't make out. He agreed with the BS comment himself. This guy was too cosmopolitan for this crowd of flannel shirt and jean guys.

The discussion of farm equipment came up, and they learned they would share equipment with each other. The holding company would let you know when you were getting the planter, etc. and you'd deal with that. They'd monitor the weather and get equipment to places that could be worked if other farms were too wet. Mike was now thinking this plan sounded like an ill-conceived idea. It made sense economically, but they forgot the common sense of how this all works. He wondered if anyone in charge had any successful farm experience under their belts.

There was one interesting character in the back who never came up front to talk. One of those guys who just looks out of place, thinks he's pretty important and just gives you a bad vibe.

At the end of the meeting Mike made his way closer to this fellow. He was talking quietly with the two other presenters and ignored everyone else. Mike was feeling just enough contempt for the whole damn situation that he wanted to see what role this man played. As he approached and was in proximity to hear the conversation all three men looked up at him. It was awkward; they didn't say a word or smile or anything. Mike felt they just wanted him to move along. After a few seconds, he shook his head and did just that. He gave this arrangement one year with no certainty after that.

He came home to let Sandy know how the meeting went and how it ended. She could tell it was awkward and her female *something's not right* meter was going off.

She said, "Wonder who that guy was?"

Mike knew in his gut he needed to find out. He called a neighbor he'd seen at the meeting and asked, "Fred, did you see the guy at the back of the room?"

Fred said, "He's a banker from Indianapolis, he works for Indiana Constellation National Bank."

Mike thanked his neighbor and hung up, he turned to Sandy, "That fellow works for our bank!"

Sandy said, "You need to talk to Melissa."

Greenville

The next morning after the bus route Mike stopped at the bank to see Melissa. He told her about the meeting the night before. She was aware it was happening from some other customers and knew the public was not invited. It was a private meeting. He told her about the awkward moment he had at the end and then also about the conversation he had with his neighbor, learning the guy in question was an employee of the bank.

Melissa said, "Describe him," and Mike did so. Melissa's eyes narrowed as she knew immediately this was Roger Knight.

"Mike please step into my office", she pulled the door shut. "Mike this fellow is our top credit person over agriculture. Keep it between us, he's a real jerk. I personally blame him for most of the auctions that have happened around here. He has no empathy for the plight you were all going through. He wanted full liqui- dation for customer after customer and no work-out situations. I'm not saying I ever saw anything I felt was illegal, but it didn't feel right. Many situations warrant a work-out plan not just total liquidation."

Mike asked the man's name again and made a note of it. He thanked Melissa and told her to take care.

When it came Mike's turn to have the equipment, he needed to start planting. He had missed good day after good day waiting his turn at the tractor and planter. This probably makes good fi- nancial sense to do it this way, but it is agonizing for a true farmer who wants to be out working. He did his best to get that smell of the soil in his nose, that familiar smell a farmer knows well, thrives on it. His only consolation was thinking about his dad. That was hard and brought a few minutes of tears in the tractor but was worth it. His father was a true optimist and Mike was just like him. You can find good in anything like the old joke of the two little boys. One boy was sitting in a room full of toys with a frown on his face and unhappy because he hadn't gotten the extra toy he wanted. The other boy was sitting in a room full of horse manure, happily throwing horse shit all over the place with a total look of glee on his face. When the person observing him came in and asked what he was doing, he answered, "With all this horse shit, there's got to be a pony under here somewhere!"

Mike wanted to be the boy with the horse shit, but today it was just shit. No damn pony in sight.

Farming his own ground for someone else would be harder than he imagined. He pushed through the next few days and the planting was done on this land. He would watch Mother Nature take over as he always did. The new owner, the holding company, held all the cards but Mother Nature was still in control and to that he smiled to himself.

Sandy Baker was true to her word. She wanted to learn about raising hops for the craft beer industry. She had been doing research since last winter. Starting with Google and ending with trips to breweries in Indianapolis and Lafayette. Nothing she found deterred her from thinking this was not something to try.

One evening Sandy looked at Mike over the top of reading glasses to make sure she had his attention and continued, "Hops is a great idea. The initial investment is not that great and we're not relying on it for income so why not try? Craft breweries are popping up everywhere."

Mike was her biggest fan. They ordered the materials they needed which consisted of posts and wire and began construction. Posts were erected and wire strung to give the hop vines a place to climb. They can grow up to twelve inches a day and up to maybe thirty feet. They bought cuttings to plant as opposed to seed for a quicker start and a hardier plant and were on their way to hop production. Brian and Pam Miller offered to trade their labor for some of the hops. Brian brewed a batch of beer occasionally and was looking forward to using these hops and naming a batch after Sandy and Pam!

Sandy had been searching for a daytime job and leaving the part-time waitress position behind at the local BBQ restaurant. She'd been looking since the farm sale and had received an offer. She was excited to start a new job with a business that specialized in corn genetics. This company had been in business for a long time and was well established internationally as a corn breeder. This kept Sandy close to agriculture with a company doing research to keep the American people fed. She'd continue to help on weekends at the local BBQ restaurant.

Chapter Seven

Brazil

A group of Brazilian farmers had scheduled a meeting in their town's local coffee shop to discuss their good fortune and the events that had been happening in the United States. This group of men were very excited for the prosperous times they had experienced, but were worried about their northern neighbors. They had been taught to farm much more profitably by agronomists from the United States who came to them in the 1970s. Soybeans was the crop they initially put into production and they would always remain grateful for it. One professor from Purdue University had spoken fluent Portuguese and had remained a lifelong friend of the Brazilian farmers. Dr. Sutherlin stayed in contact with them over the years and made several trips to make sure they were abreast on the latest science of farming.

The U.S. Department of Agriculture made low interest loans to the Brazilian farmers to get them started and was involved in the clearing of land to expand the area to farm. It was amazing how bad a rap the U.S. got for flexing their muscles around the globe. Some of it they deserved but in this case they had dramatically improved the lives of many farm families and this had a very positive effect on the Brazilian economy. The meeting broke up with the consensus thinking they'd be happy to help the American farmers in any way they could, and they would contact their old Purdue friend to let him know they were available to help.

Lafayette, Indiana

With three clicks of the mouse Brian Miller found the number for Charles Summers and called him.

"Dr. Summers my name is Brian Miller. I know you've been doing research on the livestock problems we've been facing and I have a couple ideas I'd like to share with you."

Charlie ran requests like this through his mental *waste of time* filter but felt like giving this fellow a chance to talk. He didn't sound bad on the phone, and his research was not going anywhere new the last few weeks anyway. They agreed to meet the next morning over coffee on the east side of Lafayette.

Brian took everything he had gathered including notes and pictures he had taken while in Brazil. They sat down and he gave Doc Summers some of his background including his time with the DNR and being known as the "Bird Man".

"How many on your life list?" Doc asked.

Brian was impressed with the question and gave an answer that got a smile.

"That close to seven hundred different species is why you earned your nickname, very impressive," Doc said.

Knowing he was with a busy man Brian jumped in to show and tell him what he and Pam had seen in Brazil. He added that Pam being a science teacher had caused her to notice this as well, giving it more credence in Doc's mind.

"There was something not right with this flock of Scarlet Tanagers. I felt they were not healthy."

Doc studied the pictures and they did not appear to be healthy birds. Their heads were not held quite right, and their feathers looked mangy. That didn't prove anything but they both knew something about birds and they both had the same gut feeling.

"Did you say anything about this to anyone else?" Doc asked. Brian shook his head no. He had no one else to mention it to other than Pam.

"Brian, I appreciate you bringing me this information. I want to do some thinking and I'll get back to you. I have an old buddy at Purdue who has had close ties with Brazil since spending time there helping their farmers in the 70s. He stays in contact with them so I'll call him and see if he might help us."

Doc knew his friend was not working full-time anymore and would love to have a little mystery to check out.

Brian left his cell number and email, they shook hands and went on their way. Dr. Summers said he'd buy next time and Brian agreed with a smile saying, "I'll look forward to it."

Brian called Mike to see if he'd like to go see the Colts game on Sunday and Mike said, "Sure would!"

They stopped for a quick lunch on the way and got to the game 15 minutes before kick-off. Finding their seats, they settled in to see the Colts and Andrew Luck light up the big Lucas Oil scoreboard.

Brian shared with Mike about his meeting with Dr. Summers and the background that led Brian to make the call. Mike was always hungry for more information to help all of this make sense.

"I also learned Doc Summers has a professor friend with ties to Brazil. This professor still keeps in touch with farmers there and could be a good source of information."

"That's amazing, I'm sure I know who he's talking about. I've known Dr. Tom Sutherlin for years."

"Small world," Brian said.

Mike said, "I'd like to sit in on your next meeting with Doc Summers and hopefully Dr. Sutherlin."

"Yes, we'll make that happen."

It ended up not being a great game to watch, the Colts won easily. It was one of those games where they got a big early lead and then just played hard enough to stay ahead in the second half. This gave the boys time to admire the cheerleaders.

When Mike got home he gave Dr. Sutherlin a call to let him know he was a part of this fact-finding mission.

"I've already heard from Charlie Summers. He told me enough that I want to help. It'll be good to see you and I'm looking forward to meeting your friend, Brian."

Doc Summers called Dr. Sutherlin to request a meeting time at the Student Union on campus. An email was sent to Brian and the meeting was set.

Mike and Brian drove to campus and found Dr. Sutherlin and Doc Summers at a table in what used to be called the Sweet Shop when Mike was a student.

"Being in here brings back great memories," Mike said.

"Me too, said Doc. "Learned to drink coffee here."

"Speaking of which, I need to get rid of some and get some more," Mike said.

Five minutes later they were back at the table with fresh coffee in hand. Brian told the story of what he and Pam had seen and photographed in Brazil adding additional information he had gleaned over time. The professor listened intently and took notes.

"I'll be happy to help. I'll think about how I will ask my Brazilian friends without looking like I'm accusing anyone of anything."

"Any information to add Dr. Summers?" Brian asked.

"Let me stop you there. I answer to Doc or Charlie."

"Sure thing Doc."

Dr. Sutherlin added, "I needed something like this to work on, give me a few days boys."

Charlie knew that would be his response, he'd never back down from this situation.

Charlie asked, "Is your Portuguese still fluent?"

Dr. Sutherlin responded, "Sim."

"That Portuguese for yes?"

"Sim!"

Professor Sutherlin had an old farmer friend, Carlos, in the area where Brian said the photos were taken. He'd start with him. After exchanging pleasantries and inquiring about families (Dr. Sutherlin had stayed in his home many times on trips to Brazil and this friend and his wife had been to his home in Lafayette) they got on with business. The professor took him through his notes and the reason they were asking due to the proximity of what had been seen.

With a slight hesitation, Carlos said, "I have an idea but I'm not sure I want to say."

The professor assured him it would be held in strict confidence where he got any information and with that his friend said the name, "Alberto Mulina."

Carlos spun an interesting tale of Mulina and how he was always dealing with things and people on the fringe of the law.

"There is still a lot of talk in our town of how his brother went missing." Carlos said.

"What do you mean?" the professor asked.

"His brother Miguel was one of the airline pilots on the missing Brazilian 777 that was never located in the Pacific."

The professor had certainly heard of this.

"Also, just recently Miguel's daughter, Alberto's niece, purchased a huge villa on the ocean and is living like a princess. I've heard there is no proof of any wrong-doing, but it's all very questionable."

"He does sound interesting."

"Dangerous too," Carlos added.

"Well please be careful and let me know if you hear of anything." Dr. Sutherlin said.

Carlos agreed to keep his eyes and ears open for additional news on Alberto Mulina and to pass this along if anything came up. Mulina was one of those guys you never trusted and never fit in and didn't want to fit in.

Brazil

Things were tight knit in Brazil. People looked out for each other. Carlos decided to put the word out he was looking for information on Alberto Mulina. Two days later he received a call with some information about Mulina working with birds and a day after that he got another call concerning Mulina putting together the deal for his niece. The deal for the niece involved some strong-arm tactics that ended up getting the villa purchased at a very favorable price. The caller had personal information on the strong-arm tactics Mulina had used and was glad to pass this along. He'd like to see Alberto put in his place once and for all.

Carlos called Dr. Sutherlin to tell him what he knew which wasn't much, but involved birds and his niece. Dr. Sutherlin thanked him and they agreed to talk again soon. Two days later, a call came in from his old friend's number. Upon answering it was not Carlos, it was his wife.

"Dr. Sutherlin, Carlos has been in an accident and was killed."

"Maria, I'm so sorry."

"They say his car was too close to the edge of a drop-off. He's driven this road all his life."

Dr. Sutherlin could tell she was extremely upset.

"Carlos didn't tell me what you and he talked about. I think he was asking the wrong questions on behalf of you, Dr. Sutherlin. Please don't contact me again."

With that she hung up. Dr. Sutherlin was stunned.

Alberto Mulina had heard a local farmer was asking questions about him and with a little digging, decided this was not good. It was easy for people to have accidents in this part of the world and the local authorities did not do an extensive investigation as in other parts of the globe. They did not have the expertise or funding or the inclination to stick their noses into places where it might get taken off. This farmer had close ties to people in the

United States and Alberto could not be sure what had already been said or what he knew. When he learned he was asking about birds that was enough to stop this in its tracks. The widow would not prove a problem; she was not as diligent or brave as her husband. The message would be clearly sent.

Mulina was close to leaving this part of the world. Everything was in place for a new life except for Mulina feeling he needed more money for all his work. He sent an encrypted email to his friend Asis in London making his plea for more money. He gave Asis information on what had just transpired and demanded five million into the account they had used before.

Asis did not take this request well. Mulina was a dangerous man who'd proven he didn't mind getting his hands dirty, but there was no way he was sending five million his way. Funds were not as plentiful. He needed Alberto to remain quiet and also have him available for future plans. If he persisted with his demands for more money, then he'd also meet with an unfortunate accident. Alberto certainly knew how this worked. Alberto's new home in Portugal had been purchased by Asis, so Asis would know exactly where to find him.

Lafayette

Tom Sutherlin was ready to turn the cavalry loose on this man named Alberto Mulina. He called Doc Summers and his former student Mike Baker to meet. Mike said he'd bring his friend Brian, the Bird Man, and they all agreed on this meeting of the minds.

They met in Lafayette and Dr. Sutherlin brought them up to speed on the news he'd received from Carlos' wife about his accident and how Carlos had confirmed two days prior that Mulina had something going on with birds and that Mulina's brother was one of the missing pilots and Mulina's niece had come into money and a very nice new home. Way too many things happening to not raise suspicions. They all agreed and began thinking of how they could help or what needed to be done. Consensus was they needed help from the authorities but wondered who should that be? It seemed logical to turn all of this over to the FBI in Indianapolis. The FBI was on the domestic side of the issue versus the CIA on international. This situation had aspects of both, but there were no local CIA offices.

It was agreed to let Dr. Sutherlin write this up and send it to each of them to make sure he hadn't missed anything vital and after hearing from each of them he'd send a final draft to the FBI. Brian agreed to check state employee contacts for an FBI contact. It was evident Dr. Sutherlin would not back down on this investigation after losing his Brazilian friend. He knew in his bones this was no accident. Carlos had been murdered by Mulina or one of his goons.

Within forty-eight hours everyone had reviewed the notes and added a couple small changes. Brian had found a good contact at the regional FBI office in Indianapolis who would listen to their information. The email was sent and now they'd let the FBI use their powers to push this investigation in the right direction.

Indianapolis

Natalie Jackson, known as Nat by her friends at the Bureau, was very interested in the information that came to her in the email. It talked about a man in Brazil, Alberto Mulina, who may have poisoned birds that migrated to the U.S. and caused disease in midwestern livestock herds. This seemed farfetched but she would dig. What was not farfetched was the other piece of information that Mr. Mulina was a brother to the missing Brazilian pilot and an uncle to the pilot's daughter who had recently come into a small fortune with a fancy new house on the ocean and plenty of money. This was worth some phone calls; she would have to decide who to call first.

She knew there were turf battles that happened between government agencies, this had the makings for one. She knew she'd need help and was not worried about asking another Federal agency. Nat forwarded the email with some cover information of her own and hit send to the NSA. She thanked Dr. Sutherlin for sending this to the FBI in Indianapolis and agreed to keep him in the loop as best she could with anything further that came of it. Now she would wait.

Greenville

Sandy could not wait to get home to tell Mike about what she had learned at work. The corn genetics firm where she worked announced they are working on strains that will be more resistant to drought and disease. The disease that had killed so much live-stock also seemed to have caused the corn crop lots of trouble. They still had no direct tie between the two but had a lot of circumstantial evidence as to how the two phenomena had started at the same time. This corn would be fed to livestock and then consumed by our population. That alone sent up plenty of red flags worthy of investigation. Sandy was glad her firm was on the cutting edge of this research.

Chapter Eight

Chicago, Illinois

The terrorist cell in Chicago had all the technology they needed to do exhaustive research on targets in Indiana. Asis had provided them with ideas and venues to research. From schools to shopping malls to sports arenas, they were all workable choices. They had two truck drivers in the cell. These guys drove all over Indiana and funneled back information. They had pictures, videos and timing information on traffic patterns of people and types of vehicles. This group had been trained they could leave nothing on the planning table and live, they were thorough. Frankly, Asis was not concerned if they lived or died in an attack, but preferred death over capture for new recruits. He did not want new recruits being interrogated. Losing an entire established cell was a different matter. That would set operations back years. Asis had sent an encrypted email with the final touches on his plan. He told them to move forward and start the process of setting up a base. He would send a signal when it was time.

Greenville

School was back in session and Mike was once again driving his bus route. The beginning of school always seemed such a natural course of business. After about two weeks they would get back in the flow and it would all run smoothly.

As Mike waited for his kids to board the bus this afternoon, he thought about the meeting he attended in Lafayette last month. All but one of this group had Purdue ties to each other. Mike decided he would call this group the Boiler Club. They would stay in touch and try their best to find answers.

With fall here and harvest just getting started, Mike decided this wasn't how he wanted things to be, but things were not as bad as he had imagined either. He knew he'd jump at the chance to own this farm again but for now he'd count his blessings. It seemed the tide had turned on the terrible years of crops and livestock problems and that was good news for every American, not just the farmer. His main responsibility this fall was to provide the labor to run the combine. He'd cut the soybeans and shell the corn and the holding company truckers would haul it away.

The best crop this year was the hops that Sandy had planted by the barn. Those vines grew as advertised in the good topsoil and produced a fair amount of hops for year one. Brian had taken the female flowers with the promise to bring back a new brew to share.

Western Hampton County

Nine members of the Chicago cell had made their way to central Indiana. One of the cell members had rented a farm house with a pole barn on a gravel road which was not well traveled. The house and barn were on a farm owned by the White Oak Holding Company. Cell members had traveled and moved in over a one-week period. Cameras had been installed to monitor anyone getting close and two men were always on watch. The barn was secured by making sure all windows were covered with black cloth that was not visible from the road.

Only two of the nine members were outside at any one time. The two females in the group did most of the shopping. Trips to town or anywhere were kept to a minimum. Cell members were hoping this plan would play out quickly, before a neighbor noticed anything unusual going on here.

It was easy to locate the fertilizer and fuel oil needed for the explosives. It was also easy for them to get their hands on an old school bus from the back lot of a local school bus supplier. The place had dozens of old buses sitting around waiting to move south. Many old buses were sold and moved to Central America. The day arrived for cell members to pick up the bus. This bus had been purchased by a company in Texas. Paperwork was already in place and after showing fake drivers licenses they were on their way within minutes. The sellers didn't notice the driver turned north instead of south when getting on the Interstate. The bus was driven to a secure location and then driven to the farm under cover of darkness and backed into the barn to be reconfigured.

Weapon grade C-4 had been stolen months before and was carefully moved from a cache outside of Chicago. This would add to the magnitude of the explosion. Cell members installed additional fuel tanks under the bus and the original tank was altered. They only needed a small amount of diesel fuel to drive the bus to the location of the attack. The rest of the fuel capacity could be used for the explosion. They carefully stacked bags of fertilizer under all bus seats to spread the load and its force upon explosion. They took care to make sure the bus could still maneuver while being driven to the target area. The tires were upgraded to make sure they would handle the extra weight. Detonation was set to be handled either from inside the bus manually which was the least favorite choice of the driver or by a remote control from another cell member. This would only be determined when they arrived on site.

Timing was critical to insure the largest loss of life. This would happen at the end of the day as students were leaving the building. Preparations were nearly complete.

Hunting season was underway and three good friends were out scouting for places to go. The old Hinkle place was somewhere they used to go but had not been there for a few years. This farm had sold along with many other farms. There was word in the neighborhood that someone had bought or rented the house and was living there. They stopped to ask if they might hunt back in the woods.

One man and one woman were on watch this late afternoon. They were surprised when the pickup pulled into the driveway and was heading up to the house. Cameras showed three men in the truck. They didn't appear to be any form of law enforcement but they could take no chances. The truck came to a stop on the driveway east of the house and two men got out and were heading to the door. Maria was the fairest skinned of anyone in the house and went to the door. Three men hid armed with silenced pistols, one behind the door and two in the next room.

Maria opened the door just as they were approaching and said, "Hello, may I help you?" She immediately realized she sounded nervous and much too formal.

They each introduced themselves and said, "We used to know the Hinkle family who lived here and Mr. Hinkle would let us hunt back in the woods. We were wondering if you would allow us to hunt?"

"My husband is not well. We need peace and quiet so I appreciate you asking but I will have to say no."

One man said, "We understand, we won't bother you at all."

This time Maria was more forceful as she imagined the tension behind her on the triggers escalating, "No. The answer is no!"

She then backed up and closed the door. The two men looked at each other, shook their heads and turned for the truck.

Back in the truck the third man asked, "What did she say?"

"She said her husband was not well and they wanted peace and quiet and the answer is no."

"Not neighborly," said the third man.

The other two agreed. He put the truck in reverse and backed up, turned and left.

"Good job, Maria," said one of the men as they were putting down the guns. "You think they'll be back?"

"I hope not, we need to be out of here soon, we are too far off our own turf. I prefer Chicago," which brought nods from everyone else.

"Let's head back to town and get something to eat."

"That was weird, don't you think?"

"Yeah, but times have changed."

"Mr. Hinkle had no problems with us."

"Did she look familiar?"

"No, not at all."

"Your wife drives this route Jerry. Do they have kids riding?"

"No, I asked her yesterday if there were any kids at the old Hinkle place."

The next morning Jerry was eating breakfast in Greenville and saw one of his buddies, a sheriff's deputy.

"Hey Earl, do you know anything about the new family at the old Hinkle place? We stopped there yesterday and the wife won't let us hunt."

Earl shook his head no.

"Just wondering, it was kind of weird for folks around here."

Chapter Nine

Greenville

Earl kept the *kind of weird* comment in the back of his head the rest of the day. Near the end of his shift, he mentioned it to one of the other deputies and they took a drive in Earl's patrol car. It was about a 15-minute drive out to the old Hinkle farm. They drove slowly down the gravel road and pulled left into the driveway and started toward the house. The man on watch saw the sheriff's car and alerted the others including the men in the barn. It was quickly decided that Maria would answer the door like she had the night before. The three men took up the same positions as the evening before, guns in hand.

Earl and Tom got out of the car and headed for the house with their side arms holstered. Earl knocked on the door and Maria opened the door.

"Good evening ma'am. We're checking to make sure all is fine with you. We understand your husband has been ill."

Maria said, "Yes, he's doing better, thank you for checking on us."

"Do you mind if we have a look around?"

"Well…. Is there a problem?"

"No ma'am, not that we know, we just want to take a look."

They both turned and headed for the barn. Maria closed the door and looked at the other men. They were already on the radio to the men in the barn. If the deputies opened the barn door they would have few choices.

Earl and Tom walked to the barn and noticed the windows were blacked out from the inside.

"Hey Earl, look at this."

"That's odd."

They walked to the front and Earl reached for the handle. He gave a hard pull on the sliding door and stepped in to be nose to nose with an International School Bus.

"What the hell," Earl said, "Hey Tom look at this."

What the hell was enough for Tom to unholster his service revolver. As he stepped in, gun in hand, he was shot in the side of the neck. Earl watched his friend drop and instantly stepped back for cover and dropped to a knee. He was able to draw his gun, getting off two shots before being hit in his right side by another man behind the bus. As he spun from the impact of the first shot, he was shot again by the first shooter. This shot hit his Kevlar vest and drove him back but not down. Earl got off another shot at the first shooter but was hit again in the side of the head.

Everyone in the house was on a dead run to the barn. They heard seven shots in about that many seconds. The first one to the door entered slowly, gun first, and saw both sheriff deputies on the ground with blood everywhere. He called to the other cell members. They answered one by one. One had been shot in the leg and was losing blood. Everything had changed dramatically. They took their injured friend to the house to get him bandaged and inspect his wounds. They were not sure if the bullet was still in his leg. There was not a clear exit wound. Maria poured antiseptic on the wound and bandaged it tightly. They all knew this was all the medical care he was getting for now.

Two of the others pulled the still running sheriff's car into the barn and shut the door. The car was searched for cell phones and anything else including the on-board laptop that should have GPS capabilities. Cells phones were smashed along with the laptop. They brought Earl's handheld radio into the house to monitor department transmissions. It was now 5:40 PM.

They all sat at the kitchen table and their leader said, "We have to decide what to do. It's only a matter of time before the Sheriff determines two of his own are missing."

The original attack date was planned for Wednesday afternoon as school was dismissing before Thanksgiving break. This was Tuesday afternoon and school had already dismissed. They checked the school website to see what activities were planned for this evening. There was a high school basketball game scheduled. That would have to do. The first game started at 6:00 PM.

One man said, "The second game will start about 7:30 and that's when the most people will be there."

Nods all around agreed that would be the best they could do. There would be no way they could wait until tomorrow.

They decided to leave the farm at 7:40 PM for the eight-minute drive to the school. They'd park the bus at the front door and head north to Chicago.

By 6:50 PM the radios were buzzing about two officers not reporting in to dispatch. Maria was listening intently for any radio traffic that might tip anyone off to their location. No one knew where they had gone and no one had seen their car. Earl and Tom were not answering their radios or cell phones. Dispatch had also sent emails to both men with no response.

The bus was wired and ready to go. They had tested the switches multiple times. The juice for the firing devices was supplied by the bus battery, this bus had a main battery and a backup. There should be nothing to stop this explosion. Once the bus was in place, they would leave it running as drivers often do in the cold months and walk away to the waiting car.

Preparations were happening in the house and barn to leave no evidence. The two dead officers and their car would be discovered soon enough, hopefully they'd be in northern Illinois by that time.

The first SUV left the farm at 7:30 PM. They pulled into the high school parking lot at 7:38 PM and took a slow drive around. People were still coming to the game but the lot was full. The area by the front doors was open according to fire code. They'd park behind the visiting team's bus. A cell call was made to say, "*it looks like a good game tonight*," and the school bus pulled out as planned with the other vehicle trailing behind. They pulled in at 7:48 PM and slowly drove to the front door. The driver parked and turned off the headlights leaving only the parking lights. He was very relieved when he got the signal he could leave the bus due to no security presence in the parking lot. He opened the door and walked around the bus and then made his way to his ride. They drove out of the lot and onto the road leaving the school. Both cars gave one last look as they turned west to head for the Interstate. It was agreed to set their cruise on 59 miles per hour and leave Hampton County a much different place than they found it a few days ago.

Mike Baker was pissed off. He was a basketball fan, and he'd been looking forward to the game for several weeks. It was a long-time rivalry game that was always played before Thanksgiving. He and Sandy arrived in plenty of time, but a call from the holding company about his hours worked this fall during harvest had him still in the truck. Sandy had gone ahead to find seats. As he was arguing with the person about his hours at 7:48 PM for crying out loud on a Tuesday night, he noticed something that seemed strange.

A school bus had come into the parking lot and parked at the front door. The other school was already here and the varsity game was under way. The bus had the school name blacked out on the side like they do when buses have been sold. He saw the driver get out and walk around the bus one time and then walk to a waiting car and leave. That was weird. He decided it was worth a look. He was a bus driver so why not?

Mike walked about a hundred yards to get to the door of the running bus. He pushed and the door came open.

"Hey, anyone here?"

No one answered, he climbed the two steps to look in. He was met with a smell you do not find on a school bus. He smelled fertilizer and fuel oil. He was a farmer and these are distinct smells. It had been about four minutes since the man left and Mike's heart was in his throat. This bus was a bomb!! Everyone had heard about Timothy McVeigh using fertilizer to blow up the Federal Building in Oklahoma City years ago. About twenty things went through his mind all at once including thinking of Sandy and several hundred other students and parents just inside those front doors.

He jumped in the seat, flipped on the lights, put it into gear and gunned the engine. Thank God there were no students walking in the parking lot. He gained speed as he drove south through the lot banging off a pickup and a small car. He drove into a grassy area between the lot and the state highway in front of the school and decided he'd drive south into the field on the other side of the road. He hoped he could keep getting it further away from the school. As he made it about a quarter mile into the field, the bus sank enough to be hung up, he took it out of gear and hit the button to open the door. The door opened slightly but not all the way. It must be jammed from the rough ride he'd just given it plus corn stalks in the field. He hit the door with his right shoulder and stumbled out, fell to the ground and got up to run as fast as he could. He had no idea of time but it couldn't have been over five seconds when he felt the shock wave hit his back. The sound was instantaneous with the shock, the flash and the heat. His knee hurt as he was going down on a corn stalk when all went black.

The Chicago cell members were nearly five miles west when they all saw the flash in their mirrors. It was done.

"Death to the infidels," said each driver.

"Inshallah Allah!" came from their riders.

Everyone in the school and within a mile felt the rumble. The high school principal looked at the athletic director and said, "What the hell was that?"

The athletic director shook his head and was heading for the gym door with the principal right behind. They came out the gym door to see students pointing out the front door of the school. They ran to the door and could not believe their eyes. There was a huge fire in the field south of the school. It looked like a few cars on the highway were also on fire but who could tell? Cell phone in hand, the principal called 911. When dispatch answered, he was told they had already been called by the sheriff deputy on duty at the game and units were on the way.

She asked if they needed ambulances and the principal said, "I don't know. It looks bad," and ended the call.

Parents and students were spilling out doors. School officials were yelling for them to remain in the building until law enforcement arrived. Some people complied, and many did not. The sheriff's department had extra people on road duty due to the fact they had two officers not responding to repeated calls. Sheriff and state police cars arrived in just a few minutes to the country school. They set up a perimeter around the school and the fire in the field. It was too early to tell what had happened but the initial guess was some type of explosion. They had not identified any credible eye witnesses yet.

Sandy came out the door as well, looking for their truck and Mike. The last she had seen Mike he was still sitting in it on the phone with the holding company. A deputy stopped her as she made her way to the truck. She explained that her husband was in the truck so he agreed to accompany her. Mike wasn't there. She thanked the officer and said she'd go back inside and look for him. She called his cell phone as she crossed the parking lot and it went to voice mail immediately. She thought that was odd unless he was in the school far enough to not get a signal. There were parts of the building where this happened. She was concerned but not ready to panic.

More emergency equipment arrived on scene including water trucks to put out the blaze and a light truck to illuminate the blast site. At this point it was hard to tell anything, but it appeared what was still burning was the remains of a school bus. This made no sense at all. Soon they could get closer.

About fifteen minutes later emergency personnel were getting closer. They were now at a point where they could see part of the hood of the bus, but there were no school markings on it. All they could see was a conventional school bus that had apparently blown up in the field across from the school. Deputies were now talking to two witnesses who confirmed the bus had been parked close to the front door behind the visiting teams bus and someone had driven it through the parking lot and through the grass and over the road into the field before it exploded. They could then find the tracks in the grass and see where more than one vehicle had been hit as it sped through the parking lot. Witnesses said there had been three or four other vehicles moving around at that time but there were no descriptions on any of them.

The search began for the driver. They were not hopeful due to the magnitude of the blast and the short period of time between it going into the field and the explosion.

Sandy now had some serious dread setting in. She had asked everyone she knew if they had seen Mike but they had not. She found a deputy and asked to speak to the Sheriff. She was told he was very busy, but she persisted saying her husband was missing. As of now no one else had been reported missing. This got the

Sheriff over to her because that was the first he'd heard of a missing person. Sandy was standing with her hands clasped in front of her chin. Her eyes showed real fear.

"Dan, I cannot find Mike; he was in the truck on his cell phone when I last saw him!"

"Have you tried calling him?"

"Yes, but it went to voice mail."

"Okay we'll tell all the first responders out there to look for him."

Sandy thanked him and he assured her he'd get her info as soon as he could.

"Please stay close, Sandy." She agreed.

Dan got on the radio and relayed the message to all responders to expand the search area looking for Mike Baker. Many of them knew him or knew who he was. Many exchanged concerned glances. Why Mike Baker? The Sheriff wondered if Mike might have noticed something from his truck and checked it out and found something bad. That was the only logical explanation. He radioed to say to concentrate the search to the west of the burning bus. If Mike made it out that would have been the direction to flee from the bus door.

It was not five minutes later when the call came in. They had located a person laying in the field. EMTs were working on him and he appeared in bad shape but still alive. His coat was burned and his face was bloody. The closest ambulance was making its way through the muddy field to get him transported. The Sheriff had a deputy locate Sandy to tell her they had found a man in the field but they didn't have an identity yet.

"Please let me go to him," she pleaded.

Dan said, "I'll take you."

They were there in three minutes and Sandy could see it was Mike. EMTs had an oxygen mask on him and were hooking him up with every wire imaginable. He did not have his eyes open.

"He has not regained consciousness since we got here. His vitals seem strong for the trauma he's endured. We'll take him directly to Methodist Hospital."

Sandy punched Pam Miller's number on her speed dial as the EMTs lifted the stretcher into the ambulance.

"Hi Sandy."

"Pam, I need your help. Mike has been in an accident. I'm getting in the ambulance now."

Her breathe heaved in and out. Focus, I must focus.

"They're taking him to Methodist."

"Sandy I'm so sorry. We'll head that way. See you there."

"Thank you Pam. We need prayers."

Pam told Brian, and they were heading towards the door.

Forty minutes later Pam had her arm around Sandy and Brian was listening intently to Sandy telling what she knew which wasn't much.

"Please sit with me while I call the kids."

Sandy made both calls and kept as calm as possible. Sarah first and David second. They both said they'd head to Indianapolis instead of home. They both had planned on leaving after class tomorrow for Thanksgiving anyway. She made both promise to take their time.

"There will be a lot of waiting. Dad will be fine."

As she clicked off with David, she burst into tears. Pam held her tight. Brian walked with his hands stuffed in his pockets.

Chapter Ten

Indianapolis

Information was coming into Indianapolis law enforcement including the State Police and FBI. A colleague of Natalie Jackson called her cell to fill her in on what they knew. This ended with the name of Mike Baker and she shook her head. She grabbed her coat and headed for the door.

London

Asis was up early as usual scanning the internet for world news. He'd been watching Indianapolis to keep in touch with any possible problems ahead of the planned attack on Wednesday. Everything was in place and he was anticipating the news. What he was not expecting was news of an explosion at a school north of Indianapolis that happened about 7:55 PM Eastern time. It was 6:00 AM in London, thus this happened about five hours ago. Pictures were showing burning wreckage in a field south of a high school. Preliminary reports showed no loss of life but one man critically injured.

This could not be. It was not the correct day. This school and everyone in it was not supposed to be standing as of this afternoon. Reports were very sketchy. He would wait and check in later. First light in Indiana would be about 1:00 PM his time. He would not attempt to contact the Chicago cell. He would give them time and see if any of them made it back to Chicago.

Greenville

The investigation went on through the night but daybreak was a welcome help. The blast area could now be seen clearly. Helicopters from the Indianapolis news stations buzzed overhead taking pictures. News reporters and anchors had already started using the words terrorists and terrorism themselves even though no law enforcement agency had confirmed this assessment. It gave everyone a chill to wonder what the scene would have looked like if it had blown up next to the high school as it was intended. It appeared the bus had been configured for the blast concussion to be concentrated out from each side of the bus. Investigators surmised this allowed the *terrorists* to park the bus facing whatever direction was available at the time. The loss of life would have been terrible. Early reports talked of a local school bus driver who had been critically injured in the explosion. They had not released a name, but he had evidently driven the bus through the parking lot and into the neighboring field. He was found less than 100 yards from the site of the explosion. They agreed he drove into the field and ran from the bus before the explosion. He was in critical condition in an Indianapolis hospital and the news crews were awaiting further information and would broadcast when available. The term "hero" had already begun being used.

Indianapolis

Sandy could see Mike for five minutes each hour and only Sandy was allowed in. Close friends waited with her in a large room set up for family members by hospital staff. It had been a long night, and it would be a long day. They faced the possibility of weeks of long days, but Mike was alive and in Intensive Care. It did not take the news reporters long to determine he was at Methodist Hospital and they were there to get a story. Hospital staff kept them at bay outside the hospital, promising to keep them up to date as soon as possible and protecting the families wishes for privacy.

Chicago

The terrorist cell members had made it back to Chicago by midnight. They were back to their three different apartments by 1:00 AM and had turned on CNN. The story they were hearing was confusing. They were seeing video of a huge fire in a field close to a rural school in central Indiana. This was not right, they should be seeing a huge fire engulfing a high school in central Indiana. They found the same reports online. Apparently a yet unnamed hero had driven the bus full of explosives away from the school in the last possible seconds to avoid a catastrophe. They were all in shock. This should not be, but there was no doubt the attack had failed. As of now there was not one death, except for the possibility of the unnamed hero. A nationwide manhunt was under way to bring the persons responsible to justice. This was attempted murder of hundreds of innocent people attending a high school basketball game.

Not one of them wanted to report this news to Asis even though they knew he already knew. They had done everything according to plan except for the date and time. He would be very disappointed.

Greenville

The investigation of the blast site would last for several days and was headed by members of the FBI and Homeland Security. It was easy to determine this was an Oklahoma City type scenario because of the diesel fuel and fertilizer used. Local authorities were going door to door looking for their missing deputies. On day one after the explosion they found the now abandoned farm house and barn. In the barn, they found the bodies of the officers and enough evidence to determine these killings were related to the attack on the school. It was apparent the barn and house had been well sanitized in a hurried fashion, mostly clean but not completely. They had not attempted to hide the bodies. They were just pulled to a corner of the barn. There was blood spattered on the doors and the west wall of the barn. Blood samples taken from the scene later was determined to be from each officer and one other unidentified person. Slugs were taken from each officer showing two different weapons being used.

The search moved into the house. Officers began the tedious process of trying to get finger prints or anything else that may contain DNA evidence. One of the FBI agents located the basement door and made his way down looking for a light switch. As he hit the switch, the explosion was instantaneous. The house was fully engulfed in flames within a matter of two minutes. Three officers at the entrance to the kitchen from the side porch were able to get away from the house. Four other officers inside died instantly. At the same time, another explosion was triggered at the back of the barn. No one was working that far back at that time. The concussion of the blast plus falling debris caused a serious laceration to the shoulder of one female agent. Local fire departments were called, but they could do little to save either structure upon arrival.

The only useful evidence that had been gathered was the small blood splatters in the barn and the recovered bodies of the two fallen deputies. A community's anger over the attempt on their school was now ramped up after learning of the death of two Hampton County deputies and four Federal agents. It seemed no one had considered the house might be rigged with explosives. Life was different now. All law enforcement was in a battle with professional criminals. They could underestimate nothing at this point going forward.

Questioning in the community determined a man with two friends stopped at the former Hinkle house and asked to hunt in the woods but were turned down by a lady who came to the door. This had led the search to this farm. Records showed the farm was now owned by a holding company out of Illinois named White Oak Real Estate Holdings. The farm was purchased at auction a little over a year earlier. Representatives of the holding company had rented the house two weeks earlier to a woman and her husband. The entire transaction had taken place by phone and online, thus no one had seen either the wife or the husband. Two of the three hunters had spoken to the woman and gave a general description of her but nothing definitive enough to use with facial recognition software. Continued processing was happening at the residence and the barn to search for further DNA evidence, but the explosions and fires left little hope.

Indianapolis

Mike remained unconscious through the crucial first night and well into the next day. Testing determined he had bruising of the brain resulting in a mild concussion. He had a laceration on the forehead resulting in 22 stitches, a broken collarbone and burns to the back of his head. His heavy winter coat saved him from additional burns to his back and upper legs. The concussion of the blast had catapulted him forward causing the injuries and then the intense heat had passed over him. His good physical condition had saved his life along with his ability to sprint across the field, that would have wowed his high school coaches even more than when he was in school. An old distance runner could be a sprinter when he had to be.

Mike regained consciousness late on day two and immediately wished he had not. He had the most intense headache of his life and was in severe pain from the injuries. They told him due to the concussion he could not have the strongest painkillers, but they would do what they could to keep him comfortable.

Mike told Sandy, "I'm not comfortable! I feel like I've been run over by a herd of bulls."

Testing showed that he had no loss of motor skills or brain function. He needed time to heal. The lead doctor was Graham Moore, and he was making certain Mike was staying on track with continued testing and keen observation of where he should be as each day progressed.

Natalie Jackson had been to visit more than once and was now asking Dr. Moore if she could ask Mike a few questions. Mike had already told Dr. Moore he wanted to talk to officials before Dr. Moore allowed it. On day four in the hospital Agent Jackson came to see him with another representative of the FBI from Washington and another gentleman from Homeland Security named Morris Keane.

Mike was remembering everything up to the blast.

Dr. Moore told Sandy, "This is an excellent sign. A severe concussion can easily cause short term memory loss. Mike is not showing it."

Mike heard their conversation, they were not out of earshot.

"Are you saying I've got a hard head, Doc?"

"Basically, yes and your hearing seems to be intact as well."

Mike gave him thumbs up, Sandy was happy he'd used his thumb. With this Dr. Moore agreed to let Mike talk to his law enforcement guests.

"If he gets tired have them come back," Dr. Moore told Sandy. She nodded.

"Mr. and Mrs. Baker my name is Natalie Jackson, I'm a Special Agent working with terrorist activity in the Indianapolis field office.

Mike said, "We're glad to meet you in person. You received information from my friends about the poisoned birds. I remember your name."

"Yes, that was me. I'd like to introduce FBI Agent Rob Cook with our Washington D.C. office and Morris Keane from Homeland Security."

Mike extended his hand as did Sandy.

"Mr. and Mrs. Baker were…."

"I've got to stop you Agent Jackson, we're Sandy and Mike."

"Fair enough, call me Nat. We're here to hear your story."

"I keep playing this through in my head. I saw a school bus come into the lot and remember the side not showing a school name. It was blacked out. I watched the bus park behind the visiting team bus."

"Where were you at this point?" Nat asked.

"I was sitting in my truck finishing a call."

"Go on."

"The driver got out, walked around the bus and got into an SUV. The white SUV immediately pulled away and left the lot. This was odd. Why would a driver bring a bus and then leave? I decided to go look. I got out of my truck and walked to the bus. I pushed open the door and asked is anyone here? No one answered so I stepped inside to the smell of fertilizer and fuel oil. I could see bags of fertilizer under the seats and knew this was bad. All I could think of was Oklahoma City. I won't lie I thought there is no way this could be happening but I got in the driver's seat. It was running so I put it in gear and turned away from the school."

Mike stopped and reached for his ice water. Sandy handed it to him and he took a drink.

"You okay honey?" she asked as she held his hand.

"Yes, I want to tell this. I remember being thankful there were no kids or parents in the parking lot. I know I hit more than one bumper as I gained speed. I knew I needed to get it as far away from the school as possible. I drove right across the highway through the ditch and into the field south of the school. I just kept going until I buried it. Ground was too soft. I got out of the seat and thought I was done for sure when the door jammed."

Sandy sat on the side of the bed motionless.

"I hit the door with everything I had and it popped open, I jumped out and fell, then ran like hell. Guess I got far enough, how far did I get?"

Natalie said, "208 feet."

"How fast did I run?"

"We don't know, yes we do, just fast enough for an older guy."

Mike managed a weak smile. "Any ideas on who is responsible?"

"We're examining all evidence but it's not much. At this point we have very few leads."

"Anything I can do to help?" Mike asked.

She smiled, "You already have. You saved countless lives." Natalie knew more than she was telling, but didn't feel he needed to hear everything yet. Details of the farmstead explosion would raise his blood pressure and he was in no shape for this yet.

Morris Keane asked Agent Jackson if they might go back to her office to talk. She made the twenty-minute drive to her office on the north-east side of Indianapolis. They showed badges, made their way to her office on the second floor and closed the door. Keane sat while Jackson walked around her desk and sat down.

"I'd like to know more about the poisoned birds Mike Baker mentioned Agent Jackson."

"Let's start by you calling me Nat."

"Then you call me Moe."

"How long have you been with Homeland Security, Moe?"

"Long story but I started in March 2003 when the Department was created."

"What were you doing before 9-11?"

"Retired from Marine Corp and working at the Pentagon. Tell me about the poisoned birds."

Nat printed a copy of the email from Dr. Sutherlin and handed it to Moe.

"This is all I know and there's some very interesting coincidences here. Mike Baker and three other friends have developed some theories. It's all here."

"Thank you."

"Will we approach this attack as domestic terrorism like McVeigh or as foreign?" Nat asked.

"It's too early to tell, but I want to get everything we have to NSA."

Nat agreed to get this all sent according to encrypted protocol. Moe stood and shook her hand.

"There's a car waiting to take you to the airport." Nat said.

"Thanks, I'll be in touch. Here is my card."

With that Moe was out the door and Nat was left in her thoughts. Violence had come to them. They won this one thanks to quick action by Mike Baker. Thank God for a strong citizen with his eyes open. Nat was also thinking about Moe Keane from Homeland Security. He had an air about him that left you feeling you were damn glad he was on your side.

Mike was released from Methodist Hospital on the morning of the 6th day after the attack which was much sooner than anyone expected. He was given strict orders to take it easy for the next couple weeks then return for more tests. The 35-minute ride seemed considerably longer. He wore sunglasses because of some light sensitivity. Pulling into their driveway was the best thing he'd ever seen. Sandy helped him in and he was ready for his favorite chair. He had a stack of cards in a basket next to his chair and he went through the well wishes one by one over the next few days. He also spent a lot of time looking at family pictures around the house. Sandy screened his calls and let a few through. This was the same for visitors. Brian and Pam came to visit about every other day. Brian had kept Dr. Sutherlin and Doc Summers updated on his progress throughout the ordeal. They wanted to come see him and sit down for a visit. No one imagined he'd be released in six days. Mike was a tough dude.

Sandy heard from Nat more than once and Mike was asking for a meeting where she would give the Boiler Club a briefing.

"What is the Boiler Club?" Nat asked on the phone.

"Brian Miller, Dr. Sutherlin, Doc Summers and me," Mike answered.

"So, you have a name for your group!"

"It's my doing, I came up with it. I was inspired by one of my favorite books, *Camel Club by David Baldacci*."

"I like it," Nat said. "You are the Boiler Club!"

This request was out of the norm but she felt they deserved the briefing, Mike had earned it. There would be information to present that would hit Mike hard and for this reason everyone would want to make sure he was up to hearing it both physically and mentally. The other guys understood this and were always supportive.

Chicago

Members of the cell had heard and read the story about the local hero that had driven the bus away from the school. All nine members had different thoughts ranging from the guy got lucky to let's go back and kill him. Planning a murder like this would cost them more than it would gain the cell. There was talk of hiring someone else to do it. This thought was at least still on the table. None of them approached Asis with these ideas, and wouldn't. He approached them, not the other way around. It had not yet been two weeks, and they were all keeping their heads down and going about their normal business in Chicago

Chapter Eleven

Greenville/Brazil

Brian Miller had been working on home projects and was still feeling newly retired. There had only been one out of state birding trip with his brother since the Brazil trip with Pam. He was ready for another trip and he still had his part of the Boiler Club on his mind. He had his computer browser set on a site that was always searching for last-minute flight deals and this morning an email appeared about flights to Brazil. This was one of those times you tell yourself you'll kick yourself if you let this pass by.

He mentioned it to Pam, and she agreed but said, "I will pass on this one Brian. You should find a buddy to go with you."

After lunch Brian hit on a winner of an idea. He would call Dr. Sutherlin to see if he would give him the names of some of his Brazilian farmer friends. He'd contact them while he was touring around looking for birds and maybe get some clues. Brian found his number in his cell; they had all traded last time they met. He got Tom Sutherlin on the phone. Brian told him of his trip to Brazil after finding one of those fares you couldn't pass up. He asked if he might send him some contact info of farmers in Brazil he knew. He'd like to make contacts himself.

Tom asked him, "How about some company?"

"Well, I was planning to go alone this time. My wife, Pam, is staying home."

"I'd like to go with you. It has been a few years and I'd like to see my friend's widow to pay my respects in person."

Brian thought about two seconds and agreed this was good for them both. He gave Tom the link and the flight number so he could get his ticket booked.

Tom called Brian back, and it was all set. They left in three days for a ten-day stay in Brazil. Brian then emailed Mike and Charlie to let them know two of the Boiler Club were going to Brazil. Brian was glad to be part of the Boiler Club even if he was a Wabash alumnus. About 30 miles separated the two schools north to south connected by State Road 231 in western Indiana. Both guys wished them a safe trip and wished they were going along. Everyone promised to meet for coffee and details of the trip upon their return.

Tom picked up Brian early on the morning of their flight and they headed for Indianapolis International. They cleared security and got settled in for their bonding adventure. It was good both of them had been there before. Tom knew much more about the country and culture and Brian had just been there months earlier. The fourteen-hour flight went well including one stop in Houston before they landed in Brazil. They checked in for the night and both got some needed rest.

The next morning, they drove to the village where Tom's friend lived and they asked around to find his widow. It did not take them long to learn she was in the same house Tom remembered from his visit years before. They came to her door, and she immediately recognized Dr. Sutherlin. She began to cry as she gave him a hug and invited them inside. She still blamed him in part for her husband's death but she also knew her husband would have told her to not think badly of the good Dr. Sutherlin. He had worked tirelessly to help them many years ago and had improved their standard of living many times over.

She invited them in to talk and made coffee. She offered to fix something to eat, but they declined. They knew she was being cordial but still grieving the loss of her husband. She relayed little information except she believed it was no accident. She was fearful for her life and her family and was not overly excited for their visit because of this. She told them how deeply her husband had appreciated everything the professor had done for the farmers in their country. It sounded to Brian that Dr. Tom Sutherlin was close to sainthood in this part of the world. One last hug and wishes of safety before they left, and they were on their way.

It would come as no surprise that any foreign travelers would interest Alberto Mulina. He was on full alert along with his small team who protected and worked for him. News of the visitors traveled quickly to Mulina, and he'd sent men to watch her home. Sure enough they reported two men had visited her and stayed about forty minutes. They were now leaving.

"What should we do?"

Mulina told them to follow at a safe distance, "Let's see what these gringos are up to."

Greenville

Mike was enjoying driving the school bus route again. It had been four months since the school attack and he'd been cleared to drive. It was amazing to see the sunrise each morning. It was true there were never two the same. He saw deer in the fields and occasionally he'd see a fox. He couldn't wait to get leaves back on the trees each spring, which never happened soon enough for Mike. He always thought it would happen by the first of April but it didn't, it was the end of April. The transformation from the gray dingy winter to vibrant green was always welcome. His time in Georgia was good in that this transformation happened sooner. He missed that. There was something about Indiana in the spring though. Local papers were full of basketball news from high school to college that lasted until April and then they were all ready to report on the opening of the Indianapolis Motor Speedway for the *Greatest Spectacle in Racing* in May.

Driving a school bus was very important work. He knew drivers were important. His own kids had been bus riders for many years and he knew they were safe on the bus. The school had several drivers who had been working for years, and he knew of one couple in eastern Indiana where the husband and wife had each been driving for fifty years! That was incredible. They were now driving a few great grandchildren of some of their first student riders. Most families appreciated the drivers. Only few families caused problems. Thank goodness, most families were appreciative and helpful when you needed them.

After the route this morning, Mike gave Nat Jackson a quick call to see if she might share any news. She told him all information had been sent to Fort Meade and Washington and was awaiting an update.

"Maybe my friends Brian and Dr. Sutherlin will bring something useful back from Brazil."

Nat said, "What do you mean?"

"Brian and Dr. Sutherlin are in Brazil. Brian is doing some birding and Dr. Sutherlin went along to pay his respects to the widow of his friend and try to find out if there is any new information on his death."

Nat was surprised to hear they had gone to Brazil and was immediately sending up mental red flags.

"Where are they staying?"

"They're staying in the same village his friend lived."

More red flags shot up! Nat understood these guys wanting to help but they may get themselves into a dangerous situation. She thanked Mike for calling and hung up to think.

Indianapolis

It didn't take Nat long to decide to call Steve Bradshaw. Steve had a direct link to Moe. When she told Steve the two men were in Brazil he gave a quick, "Oh shit, you've got to be kidding!"

She responded, "No kidding. I learned this from Mike Baker."

"I wish they would have bounced that idea off you before they left," Steve said.

"They probably didn't even think about it or didn't want to hear my answer."

"I'll let Moe know they've gone to Brazil. He will probably arrange to get eyes on them."

The phone conversation between Steve and Moe was short. Moe was trained to expect the worst, and this had problems written all over it. He called his friend in the CIA and was told they would get to the village as soon as possible and locate them. It was easy for the CIA to find where they were staying. They had checked in under their own names. No reason they shouldn't. Three hours later two CIA station personnel visited the hotel and discovered that after a quick breakfast, Brian and Dr. Sutherlin left the premises.

The CIA had information where the widow lived and this was their next stop. Feeling confident they were not being followed, they had a short visit to learn Dr. Sutherlin and Brian had been here this morning. They felt good they were not followed but not being watched is an entirely different thing. There could be many neighbors being paid to watch her home. The trail was now cold. They would have to spend time in town and ask around being as discreet as possible. They were both Brazilian and fit in, but the locals would know they were not from there. Information would not come easily and they knew it. There were ways, but you could not burn too many bridges along the way.

Brazil

Tom and Brian had taken a road north out of the village to go to an area Brian had read about. Brian was hoping to see a bird he could add to his life list and Tom was enjoying the countryside of Brazil. He loved this country and had a lot of his life invested here. He'd spent many months on and off over a five-year period.

Alberto Mulina had not needed this unexpected visit from the Americans. He did not see it as a huge problem but he couldn't take it lightly either. He was making final plans to leave Brazil and wanted nothing to interfere. The farmer who he had killed had been asking too many questions and these fellows may follow along that same path. Killing two Americans would start a shit storm of activity. What he needed now was time. A kidnapping would also start activity, but not for a couple days especially if the local authorities did not announce it was a kidnapping.

His men had a place where they would take them. They controlled the area for a few miles in each direction plus they had experience with this type of thing. If this place could talk, there'd be hell to pay. They needed to get them before they came back to the village. Alberto made the call.

Brian slowed and stopped as an older man in a beat up old Jeep Cherokee gave him a wave. He had an uneasy feeling, but it did not look like anything to be alarmed about. He was wrong. The two men who jumped out of the back raised automatic rifles. Brian and Tom froze. They were ordered out of their rented SUV and into the Jeep. They were cuffed using plastic ties and hoods were put on their heads. They pulled away and Brian felt fear grip him like he'd never known. Pam will never know what happened to me he thought. Tom, being older, was also afraid but a little more prepared for this adventure. It was surprising, but he felt adrenaline like he had not felt in many years. He wanted to fight but also wanted to learn what kind of rat bastard does this kind of thing and knew it would be the same SOB who killed his friend. There was nothing to do but go for the ride.

Upon arriving at their destination, they were taken inside and seated on chairs. It was hot and musty. The hoods were pulled off to reveal their captors wearing masks of their own. The air was as thick as a dusty old hen house, maybe it was a dusty old hen house. Furniture was sparse, a few wooden chairs and one old table with a kerosene lantern. No electricity.

Tom said to Brian, "I don't think the air conditioner is working."

This earned Tom a hard backhand from one of the men. He spoke harshly in Portuguese and asked if Tom spoke Portuguese. Tom shook his head no and shrugged his shoulders which got him another slap to the face. Brian could see a slight smile from a bottom lip starting to swell. A small amount of blood ran from Tom's nose. Brian thought, *this is one tough old bastard.* Brian knew full well he could probably speak Portuguese with a better flair than their captors but if they didn't know this, then Tom may pick up some important intelligence. Tough old son of a gun. Brian was quiet to keep whatever strength he could muster. It might come in handy.

Mulina was informed that all had gone according to plan. He told his men to sit tight and not hurt either of the men for now. If they tried to escape, they had orders to kill them both and make sure they'd never be found.

As darkness came to the village and there was no sight of the Americans, the CIA men sent a report to their superior. He sent it up the food chain to his boss and he informed Moe Keane.

"Shit, I knew this wouldn't be good," he said to himself as he read the flash report. He called his CIA contact, and they agreed it was still too soon to report an international incident but they also both felt this is what they had on their hands.

"Can you have your people push some of the locals a little harder?" Moe asked.

He was given a "Will do. I'll be in touch as soon as I know anything."

Moe thanked him and ended the call.

This message was sent to the men in Brazil. It was what they had expected and had already been making plans to do. They made their way to a couple local watering holes and bought drinks and did a lot of talking. They turned up nothing of value. They took turns keeping watch until first light and were back out to see what they could learn.

Chapter Twelve

Washington D.C.

Moe Keane was growing more worried by the hour after a sleepless night. He checked in with his CIA contacts to verify nothing new had turned up. He then decided to go public after calling Nat Jackson in Indianapolis. He gave Nat enough time to notify the families of both men and reassure them they were doing everything possible to find them. They had been missing for nearly twenty hours. There were no ransom requests so no foul play was assumed at this point. They may have had vehicle trouble and spent the night hoping for a local to come along and give them some help.

Pam Miller was very upset as was Dr. Sutherlin's wife. They both had been worried about this trip but had been assured by both husbands they would be safe and travel on the main roads. Pam had times in her life when she had a feeling of helplessness and this was like none other. Thousands of miles away and not knowing was unbearable. She was a woman of strong faith and she was drawing on this faith now. She was praying it would come to a peaceful solution soon.

Pam called Mike and Sandy and they were over to her house immediately, she relayed what she knew and asked for prayers.

They all knew it would be released to the National Press by the time of evening news and her phone would ring nonstop. Sandy asked to stay with Pam and help with the calls or whatever else she could do. Pam appreciated the support and thanked her for being a great friend.

Mrs. Sutherlin called her family and had the closest children there in an hour with two others looking for the quickest flight to head home. They knew Tom had lots of friends in Brazil, hopefully ones who could get him home in one piece.

When the news broke that two men from Indiana had gone missing in Brazil, it made both national and local news. Word got around fast in both of their communities.

Brazil

Brian and Tom had a long night tied to the chairs. They both were as stiff as boards by morning. Amazingly, both men had gotten a little sleep. It seems you can get so exhausted the body will sleep even if the mind is going a thousand miles an hour, processing ideas and thoughts and escape plans. Tom was glad he'd lied about his language skills. The captors spoke in Portuguese and he could hear it all. This was both good and bad. Bad in that he could tell these guys were used to killing the people they captured. Good in that their boss was hoping to avoid it this time. Tom would take any positive thoughts he could get right now. He could not relay this info to Brian; they were forbidden to talk.

Mulina was confident that no one from the village would talk. He had been informed there were two Brazilians poking around asking questions. It would be so easy to have these investigators killed, but then he'd have troops coming his way immediately. Better to just let them nose around and not turn up anything. If he could get the time he needed, the Americans would be released and end up looking a little bruised and battered but alive. By then he'd be heading to another country and a new life with his fortune and the extra five million he'd demanded from Asis.

He called his men at the farm house to learn all was fine. The detainees were not making it hard on his men or themselves. They'd been given water and two energy bars. It seemed funny they were giving them energy bars, probably all they had. He planned to leave under the cover of darkness tomorrow night, in a little more than 24 hours he'd be on his way.

Lafayette

When the news arrived at Purdue that one of their own was missing in Brazil the campus was abuzz. All kinds of stories started about the professor from students, former students, and other faculty.

Sam Ryan, the Director of Security for Purdue shook his head and said, "I'll be damned."

The official announcement which was emailed to all staff had a phone number in Indianapolis to the FBI. It was a direct line to Nat Jackson. Sam called the number and gave her some quick information concerning Dr. Sutherlin. Nat got his number asked him to stay by the phone. Fourteen minutes later his phone rang, it was Moe Keane with the Division of Homeland Security. They had a quick conversation and Sam agreed to email the information for Dr. Sutherlin immediately. Sam hung up and sent the email. "I'll be damned," he said again.

Fort Meade

Moe Keane made a direct call to Steve Bradshaw and relayed the information he had just been given by Sam Ryan at Purdue.

Steve could not believe what he had just been told.

"That sounds like something a university like Purdue would mess around with. They train men to go to the moon and build spacecraft that can go to the moon, why not experiment with something like this?"

It would later come out the idea for this came from the Purdue Vet School.

Steve took the information from Moe and ran it through their software to program the satellites to triangulate his position. In a matter of minutes, waiting for the satellite flight paths to progress in the southern hemisphere, he had the information. A blip was showing up on his screen. There was Dr. Sutherlin and hopefully he was alive. At least the chip implanted in his shoulder was working as planned.

A quick call back to Moe with the coordinates and the information was on its way to the CIA agents in Brazil. Steve agreed to keep monitoring the coordinates and immediately relay any change of location.

Brazil

When the email came over their secure line, the two CIA agents looked at each other. This was amazing. Some days you got lucky. Night was approaching, and they had what they needed to go forward with their mission. They began to ready themselves and their equipment. This location was not far at all but it would involve some hiking through rough ground. They could use a vehicle for part of the trip but wanted to take no chances on being seen. They had been handed a gift as their world goes and they could not screw this up.

They left at about 12:50 AM for a twenty-minute drive followed by what should be a 75-minute hike. The drive went according to plan. They hid their four-wheel-drive Range Rover off the side of the road in brush and trees. The hike was difficult and slow. In about an hour they had a visual on the farm house. Night vision goggles allowed them to see one man guarding the front of the house. Circling around showed no one else in the back. Their biggest fear at this point would be the possibility of any booby traps or trip wires to set off alarms or worse. Claymore mines buried underfoot were a known enemy of both men who were former Special Forces. They had seen more than their share of friends who had lost legs, arms, and their lives from those things. Not much they could do about this with just two of them and working at night in unfamiliar territory.

It was now 2:55 AM and all was still. They wanted to wait to watch for any other movement before taking the farm house. The sky was as clear as it could be. Lifting the night vision goggles revealed a sky full of stars but only a sliver of a new moon, this was on their side. Giving a look at the sky had a calming effect on a soldier, it was the same sky loved ones back home would be enjoying as well.

They decided at 3:07 AM to move toward the house. They were armed with the same rifles used by Navy Seals, very accurate and extremely silent. Rifles were set for two shot bursts. The pfft, pfft of two quick shots to each bad guy was the method of kill. Red laser sights were used to assure accuracy and avoid focusing on the same target.

They moved forward in an agonizingly slow manner to stay as safe as possible. When they were within 40 yards of the first guard one man put the laser sight mid chest and one quick burst dropped him to the ground. They moved quickly at this point. Another guard came out the front door. He was taken out as well. One CIA agent entered the house and was fired upon by a third guard. He jumped back and the other agent took out the third guard through the side window. This guard was hit in the shoulder, thus not killing him instantly. He was bleeding out and was willing to say the name Alberto Mulina before he died. They had not even tried to interrogate him. Tom felt this last guard had not wanted to be part of this. His blurting out the name, Alberto Mulina, may have been his way to point a finger at the man who had ultimately cost him his life. The agents entered and cleared the house in a quick fashion. There were only three rooms to check.

This had all happened so quickly that Brian and Tom were wondering what had just happened. With the two agents being dressed in all black they were not sure if this could be a rival group. The two agents immediately identified themselves as U.S.

and they were here to get them home. Brian looked at Tom amazed at their bad and now good fortune.

One agent said, "Thanks for letting us know your location Dr. Sutherlin."

Brian looked at him puzzled. Tom had shown an uncanny steadiness through this thirty-hour ordeal. Brian thought it came from him being an older man and just calm about his life.

"Brian some people have a chip on their shoulder, I have one implanted in mine. Worked like a charm. Led these guys right to us."

"Are you kidding me?" Brian said.

Tom said this was an idea from a professor in the Vet School for faculty who traveled internationally. It had never been utilized as far as anyone knew until now. It was the same technology they had been using for people's pets for several years only with a chip that was stronger. It could be located using satellites.

Brian said, "Don't you feel funny with that implanted in you? Like Big Brother is watching or something?"

"Yes at first, but then I just felt like a lab rat. I started eating more cheese."

Brian looked at him funny and Tom laughed out loud.

They located the keys for the rental vehicle Brian and Doc had been using. Brian was secretly relieved because the rental was in his name! The four of them drove to get the Range Rover. One agent drove it back to town while the other agent followed with Brian and Tom in the rental. A call to the hotel had their contact clearing their room and bringing their belongings to the airport. A plane was fueled and waiting. They'd have them out of Brazil and into international airspace as soon as possible. Neither man protested. They were ready to go home. The CIA jet had enough fuel and cruising capabilities to get them to Keesler Air Force base in Biloxi for refueling and the last leg home. Once in the air the agents called their handler with the good news.

He said, "I'll be here to debrief you all tomorrow afternoon at Langley, good job gentleman."

This news was passed through channels and Moe Keane got the call just as he was getting out of bed. He called Nat Jackson in Indianapolis and asked her to call the families. She was thrilled to be tasked with these calls after fearing it would be worse news. Pam Miller was the first call and Nat could tell it was terrifying for her to answer this call. Nat immediately told her Brian was safe and in the air on his way home. Nat could tell she was relaying this information to other family members with her. Nat was glad Pam was not alone.

"I'll call you back as soon as I know the details of when he'll be home."

Pam thanked her and then thanked her again. Nat then had the same conversation with Mrs. Sutherlin. She too had family with her and relayed the good news to them. Nat hung up the phone and felt so relieved they had dodged a huge bullet and another tragedy.

Word of the rescue found its way to Mulina by early morning. He wondered how in the hell they found them? His network might not be as tight as he thought and the timing was such that they'd just taken off the airstrip. Info just a little quicker could have had the two Americans killed. Let them go he thought to himself, he needed to leave the country tonight as planned. He spent a long day in a safe house. That night he boarded a yacht in the nearby harbor and headed out to sea.

Local police had spent time at the crime scene during the day to collect three bodies and process the scene. Information had been sent detailing this was the scene of a kidnapping and rescue. Local authorities knew of the group involved, there would not be a lot of time spent on trying to piece together what had happened there.

Local authorities did not work aggressively at trying to find Alberto Mulina for two reasons. One, they feared what he'd do to them if they put him behind bars. Two, several if not all were on his payroll. Turning their head was the easier road. Most hoped he had fled the area. All his activities up til now seemed to always involve local people. He was the local bully and played the part well. This scrape with the Americans and whatever American organization had been sent to rescue the hostages put him higher on the bad guy list.

Late the following day, the yacht was in the shipping lanes in the Atlantic and met up with the cargo ship. Alberto was ready to board the rusty old ship that would take him north to Europe and maybe he could settle things with his old friend, Asis. For a bad looking old ship, the cabin they'd prepared for him looked like five star accommodations. He had a bar which was stocked and a king size bed. "How did they get a king size bed in here he wondered?" Who cares it looked good. He had his own bathroom and satellite television. This eight-day trip was looking better and better. He settled in and prepared himself for a new life.

Chapter Thirteen

Washington

Much to the disappointment of their families, Brian and Dr. Sutherlin spent a day and a half in Washington as guests of Moe Keane and Homeland Security. There were questions which needed asking. The two men felt this sense of responsibility plus they wanted to give all the information they could to help stop Mulina. They both felt Moe Keane was ready to cut loose on them about traveling to Brazil and getting into this predicament, but he never did. Knowing the worry they put their families through was punishment enough. They were glad to be going home alive.

Moe was involved in the questioning along with several other Homeland Security people and two agents from the CIA. They also called in Steve Bradshaw from the NSA. Steve had been working on piecing things together and hopefully would be more help in the future. The two men each told their story separately several times and then told the story together. They were assured this was not because they were under any suspicion of not telling the truth, but to make sure all details that could be remembered would come to light. This was exhausting to both men after what they had just been through, but they were glad to help and glad when they were told they were heading for home. It was agreed to keep information concerning the chip in Dr. Sutherlin's shoulder confidential. Brian and Dr. Sutherlin agreed and understood it could help someone else someday.

They were on a late afternoon flight going home and seated in first class. Brian said, "Do you think you'd ever go back to Brazil after this?"

Tom said, "Yes I will, I won't allow it to end this way."

Brian could tell Doc had already thought about this and he meant every word.

Brian said, "I'll feel a lot better when we know Alberto Mulina is behind bars for life before you buy a ticket to go back."

Tom nodded his head in agreement and said, "Me too, he's in his element there and we're not."

He added, "We'll have a beer together when we get the news this prick is in jail or better yet, if he's been in one of those accidents he likes to orchestrate."

Brian raised his hand as if offering a toast.

Doc clinked his imaginary beer to Brian's. "Cheers!"

The direct flight to Indianapolis was uneventful and quiet. Both men got some rest knowing they would be met with happy families and a late evening. Next thing they knew the fasten seat belt tone was happening, and they were about to land. They stepped off the plane and made their way down the corridor to where people waited. They both could not believe the number of people there to greet them, it was quite a thrill. There were smiles, tears and cheers. Brian thought he should announce himself as a candidate for mayor, seems like he might have been elected that night. Tom's family was a little more subdued but just as happy to see him. Tom said a private goodbye to Brian and said, "See you soon."

He was then off with his family to Lafayette. The University had sent its most comfortable coach bus for his family to ride to the airport and then back home.

Brian's family and friends headed back to Greenville and several of them ended up at his home. Pam and Sandy had prepared things to eat and there was cold beer. This group didn't break up until about 2 AM when Brian was ready for more sleep than he had on the plane. He and Tom had been cleared to tell most of the story, they were not to talk about the men who rescued them with the exception to say they were former military men. The stories were starting locally and would no doubt be embellished and get bigger over time.

As Brian awoke the next morning and lay there in his own bed, he had a weird sensation come over him. Going through this ordeal he had definitely been scared and worried about how it would turn out. But thinking of the homecoming he and Tom had been given last night made him realize that almost everyone around home had not expected an outcome this good. He had a chill down his spine as it became apparent how close they were to never being found again. With Pam lying next to him his bed felt better than it ever had. He wondered if he should ask Tom if he had similar thoughts. On one hand, the ordeal made you appreciate this safe return home, on the other hand your own brush with mortality and someone taking life away from you was daunting. These were thoughts he'd share with his friend Mike. He could empathize well.

All Central Indiana had been following the news events of the past few days. The safe return of the two Indiana men who had been held captive gave everyone a huge sigh of relief. The name of Alberto Mulina was in all the stories. This mysterious character made for great speculation.

Greenville

Mike was glad Brian and Tom were home safe, but inside he was burning like never before. His best friend had been abducted and held hostage. Something was going on, something sinister. One Brazilian farmer had been killed for just asking questions and his friends could have been numbers two and three.

He was also having bad feelings about the banker he'd seen at the meeting, the one Melissa told him about. This guy just didn't look right to Mike. And why would a banker be at a meeting put on by the holding company to discuss employment with farmers, Many of whom had been customers at his bank? It didn't feel right.

The text from Brian for breakfast tomorrow morning was answered with a *see you there*. Good friends didn't need to ask where and when. They got a booth and asked for coffee and cream. Mike was looking forward to everything about this visit except for the crappy coffee in this breakfast place, a place that should have great coffee. They needed a huge Chemex.

"How you doin' old buddy?" Mike asked.

Brian said, "I've been counting my blessings and saying thank you prayers since I got home."

Mike shook his head and Brian told him about the stone-cold realization he had lying in bed the first morning back.

"This was my first real brush with mortality, you think you've faced mortality when you lose a parent but not like this. I was lying there thinking "what am I going to get up and do today?" Whatever it is it will be more appreciated than ever before. I'm sad I had to have this ordeal to get this appreciative, but it worked this way. I have always been a man to count my blessings and always will, but this punched me right in the gut."

"How'd the debriefings go?" Mike asked.

"It was intense! If you'd been going through that as a bad guy it would not have been any fun, they were very thorough. We hope that it'll help the authorities bring the bastard to justice who killed Tom's friend. Before we were captured, we spoke to his friend's widow and you could tell she was afraid to talk to us. I'd say everyone was afraid to talk to us and then we learned why the hard way. They play hard ball and the bad guys are in control in lots of places."

"Did Keane tell you much about what they know?" Mike asked.

"Very little, he mentioned the ongoing investigation and how certain information could put us and our families in more danger. I'm not sure if that's true or not but it got our attention."

Raising his eyebrows and a slow nod showed Mike's agreement.

"It seems like we want to know more but maybe not," Mike said.

Breakfast was set in front of them along with lukewarm crappy cups of coffee. They ate mostly in silence. Brian was thinking the biscuits and gravy were better than he remembered in the past. This ordeal had even improved the taste of the food!

Delphi

Doc Summers had been keeping busy with his vet practice over the past few months. He had never given up on his quest to learn more about the diseases that had plagued the large animal herds over the last three years, but the trail had gone cold. One day he received a letter in the mail from a private company with information about the disease. This was a surprise since he had only shared information with midwestern universities with vet schools. One of them must have passed it on to this company. The letter confirmed the disease was a new strain of an old disease harmful to livestock and carried by birds. He read through the letter digesting the technical information but the *carried by birds* was the main thing he wanted to understand. Hopefully this would be the link to tie the birds in Brazil to the problems in the Midwest United States.

He wanted to speak to Dr. Sutherlin and Brian Miller after their ordeal in Brazil. This was a good reason to get together with the Boiler Club. A group email was sent and a date was set for lunch in Lafayette.

Lafayette

The Boiler Club sat down for lunch with the talk going straight to Tom and Brian being taken captive in Brazil. Events were relived and stories told amidst shaking of heads and gaping of mouths. It was incredible they were in a place where it was not a big stretch to be hijacked right out of your vehicle and taken to an abandoned house with a bag over your head. It seems this happened more than just in a movie or television show.

Discussion of Alberto Mulina and his whereabouts left lots of wondering if he were still in Brazil and how everyone there feared him. Tom took it very hard that people he cared about had been wronged by this man and that his friend had lost his life trying to help.

Tom wanted to see this end with Mulina in jail or worse, he said it out loud, "I hope he's shot running for his life."

"He deserves much worse I'm sure," Mike said.

Tom added, "That kind of fear from people comes from terrible wrongs."

Mike said to Doc Summers, "What do you have new to tell us Doc, you called this meeting?"

Doc produced the letter and read the parts that were not the technical stuff.

"So there is now proof the disease was spread from birds," Brian said.

Summers shook his head and then read the second page where this lab had recovered some of the actual birds to tie the disease to them. This was big news.

"Well it looks like we have to send this letter to Nat Jackson so she can feed it up the intelligence chain. We can now say we feel certain these birds were intentionally infected with this disease in Brazil. The birds migrated back to the Midwest and transferred the disease in their droppings to livestock which killed off millions of dollars of these herds. This is a huge criminal undertaking."

"Who would be behind all of this?" Mike asked.

"I can't imagine this Alberto Mulina thug would do this on his own volition, anyone else?" Sutherlin asked.

Heads shaking no all around the table.

"Then who would stand to gain from large amounts of our livestock being killed?"

Again lots of heads shaking but Mike had Roger Knight in the back of his head. He would not say anything at this time but he would see what he could find out about this guy.

There was agreement to stay in contact. This had a huge criminal conspiracy written all over it. This was not a prank by someone, this was pre-meditated murder as far as the men were concerned. Doc had concerns that if it happened once it could happen again.

Doc added, "It seems our Feds should ask the Brazilian authorities to be on the watch for anything concerning birds or migration areas with anything looking out of place. Of course that assumes they'd know what they were even looking for."

Tom Sutherlin had enough contacts both here and with the Brazilian Agricultural Department to ask for this help. He said he'd start on it yet today.

Doc Summers agreed to send this information to Nat Jackson in Indianapolis. Brian had taken notes on his tablet and emailed them to everyone there. Doc sent the letter and the notes to Nat as soon as he returned to his office.

Indianapolis

Nat Jackson shook her head as she read the information she'd received from the Boiler Club. She first gave a small smile they actually signed correspondence as the Boiler Club. She thought it was cool these citizens cared enough to be thinking about all of this. For now, this appeared to be proof the disease in the live-stock herds was intentionally sent this way from the country of Brazil. She had the same questions as the Boiler club, who and why? Nat forwarded the email to Moe Keane and Steve Brad-shaw to give them one more piece which could tie it all together. She agreed there must be a bigger conspiracy happening here. This was a huge economic blow to the farmers and consumers in the United States. What if it was a test run on the livestock? What if the next attack was on our people? This did not seem to be much of a stretch for her to imagine after everything she had seen recently. It gave her a shudder and a reason to work harder to make sure this would not happen.

There had been discussions for years of someone poisoning our water supply. What if this had not been intended to kill the livestock but to infect them so the disease would manifest itself in our consumers? She was on a roll today with thinking terrible thoughts. These thoughts would all go into a report to Steve. Why not get more minds percolating on this?

Fort Meade

All the information coming out of Indiana was incredible. Proof there was a plot to kill livestock using birds from Brazil was huge but the thought of the attack being ramped up to kill humans was chilling. This would be like someone spreading Ebola to the masses in any country. Very scary stuff indeed. He added this new information to his search engines and forwarded to Moe Keane.

Washington

Moe had been taking the situation seriously but the document he received made his skin crawl. These thoughts by Nat Jackson in Indy had to be taken very seriously. His responsibility was to Homeland Security and boy did this look like a deadly threat to fight. A *natural* attack like using birds could come from any-where and all directions. He didn't know how to fight it; you couldn't kill all birds crossing the borders. You couldn't test all birds coming over the borders. This looked impossible.

News of this type of threat would cause a national panic. There'd be good old boys standing in front of their houses with their shotguns shooting at every bird in the sky! He was surely overreacting, but it had worked with livestock. He could not in good conscious let this go without some planning and lots of common sense thinking. Common sense was sometimes hard to find in Washington; he was glad the folks in Indiana were on the case.

Chapter Fourteen

Atlantic Ocean off the coast of Spain

Mulina's voyage had been uneventful, and he was bored stiff. He had great food and plenty to drink, actually too much to drink while traversing the ocean. His strong stomach had served him well. The alcohol kept his mind off things that were weighing on him.

The last week had given Mulina a lot of time to think. He was traveling to his new home with his two most trusted body guards. There had been a lot of faithful watchers left behind, he'd gone from a small army to two in his entourage. He was going to a very nice place that was as secure as you can make it with funds to last a lifetime if used properly. He'd left things on shaky ground with Asis and had demanded an additional five million dollars or else, whatever the hell "else" means. This was now looking to have been a bad decision and he was feeling more like a team player.

There was no way to communicate securely from this vessel, and he was feeling remorse which was something he'd never experienced. He was frightened at what might wait for him on shore. He decided to contact Asis as soon as possible and bury the hatchet. He was immediately sorry for that mental picture.

The voyage was coming to a close. The First Officer had knocked on his door to let him know they would be in the Port of Valencia in about three hours. He could go ashore shortly thereafter and they'd arranged for him to bypass customs. He would enter Spain with a new identity and the ship's crew had not been apprised of that identity. He was now close and his nerves ramped up even more. He knew the sooner he could speak to Asis the better off he'd be, this was priority number one.

When it was time to go his two men accompanied him to a small fishing boat where they left to go back south along the coast. The trip to Cullera was much rougher than the large cargo ship he departed. This short voyage left him ready to step on land and stay there for a while. They entered a small fishing port and stepped out safely on Spanish soil. He was soon to be a citizen of Portugal. The trip from Cullera to Portalegre, Portugal was 850 kilometers and would take about eight hours driving time. They would be there before daybreak tomorrow.

His men used GPS to make the drive across Spain. It made sense to travel at night but each of them wondered what scenery they were missing under the safe cover of darkness. Only one planned stop for fuel and they arrived on time by daybreak. Bags were carried in by tired men who wanted nothing more than to sleep. Mulina was feeling more confident in his future this morning and told the two men to get some rest.

Morning broke to reveal a beautiful vista of a small village changing to green valley below him. His new home or casa here in Portalegre was fantastic. He needed to make sure he would live to enjoy it. He had a small staff of two who would maintain the casa and keep him well fed. A breakfast of local fruit and eggs along with some of the best coffee he'd ever drank, and he was from Brazil! Things were looking good, but the stress of everything had now caught up with him so he laid down for a late morning nap.

He awoke startled, not knowing where he was for a few seconds. What he understood was a man with a knife above him. He managed a slight scream as the knife came down towards his chest. He rolled towards his attacker enough to take the first thrust on the inside of his left bicep. He kicked and caught the man in his right thigh. The attacker pulled the knife up and was lunging again when Mulina heard the gunshot. A fine red mist spread all over Mulina and the bed as his attacker fell on him with the knife still in his hand just missing the left side of Mulina's face. The man was pulled off by Mulina's bodyguard who was holding his Beretta M9 9mm in his other hand.

Mulina knew he was lucky, and he knew who had sent this assassin. No one knew his whereabouts other than Asis. If he had sent a killer, then he would send another one unless he could do something to change his mind. Asis was Mulina's source of money but he'd go to London and kill the asshole himself if it came to that. They had to consider the assassin may not be traveling alone, so assassin number two might be close behind. No one else would try anything yet, they would not know the first man failed until he failed to check back in.

Greenville

Roger Knight had heard there was an employee at one of their bank branches north of Indianapolis who had made some disparaging remarks about him. He could not imagine why this would be, he'd never even been to the Greenville branch or met this peon of a branch officer. He decided to take a drive to Greenville and pop in for a visit. It was a short drive to Greenville from Indianapolis and he decided he'd do it more often so he could admire acres and acres of farm ground that belonged to him. Everyone here believed it was all owned by a holding company out of Illinois which was true but that holding company was good ole Roger Knight and he basically owned the whole damn county.

The crops were all looking good this year, the farmers who worked for him had done a nice job planting his corn and beans. He had never felt so full of himself as he did making the drive on this beautiful morning. He arrived in town and found the branch of his bank. Roger knew no one would know him here, so he decided to have a little fun milling around the lobby to see who might feel compelled to offer good old small-town customer service. He didn't even have to mill, the lady at the desk closest to the door welcomed him and asked how she might help him. This took him off guard and he was impressed. He was ready to have fun belittling someone, instead they made him feel welcome. He thought this is a place where people would want to do business.

Melissa was busy preparing paperwork and ending a phone call when she looked up to see Roger Knight. She knew who he was and immediately felt the knot grow in her stomach. He'd never been here before and a visit from this jerk could not be good news. He was having a conversation with a teller and both of their heads turned her way at the same time. She tried to avert his gaze but was too late. He saw her looking at him. He ended his conversation with the teller and made his way past several customers in the lobby. He walked through the bank as if he owned it.

Roger walked up to her office door and leaned against the door frame.

"Melissa my name is Roger Knight and I'm your boss from Indianapolis."

Melissa said, "Nice to meet you Mr. Knight," using all the fake friendliness she could muster.

"Well maybe not that nice. I've heard you have been saying some terrible things about me."

This took Melissa aback, and she gave him a look of what are you talking about?

"Now nothing to say about me, huh?"

"Mr. Knight, I don't understand what you're talking about?"

Roger raised his voice to make sure the entire lobby could hear, "You sure as hell do and you are on the thinnest ice you can imagine!"

Melissa was absolutely stunned. She lived in Greenville and was embarrassed as anyone could be. She had no defense and no answer because this was so outrageous.

He said, "If I ever hear one more shred of evidence you are making negative remarks about any of your superiors including me then your career in banking is finished!" At that he turned, smoothed out the lapels on his suit and walked out.

The old you could have heard a pin drop thing had just made its way to the lobby of the local bank. It stayed this way for the better part of a minute until Melissa gathered herself and stood, walked to the door of her office and announced to everyone in the lobby and the other officers who were now standing at their doors how sorry she was for what had just transpired.

Melissa needed to get out for a bit so she took an early lunch. She had plenty of sympathy and empathy from everyone there which felt good. The truth was Roger Knight was correct, she had been talking about him. She felt he was pure evil. Maybe she wouldn't be working at this bank when he goes down, but she really didn't care. She knew he had hurt people in her town and in Central Indiana. Melissa could not yet prove it but she knew the Feds would figure him out sooner or later.

Roger decided on a celebratory Starbucks on the way out of town. People would now know who Roger Knight was and be wary of him. The feeling of power was amazing. He spent time driving country roads looking at his crops before getting on Interstate 65 and heading back to Indianapolis. Word of the bank incident got around town quickly, everyone was astounded because Melissa was well liked.

London

News of the failed assassination attempt came from none other than Alberto Mulina. Asis could not believe what he was reading in the encrypted email. Mulina was either the craziest bastard he'd ever met or the toughest. He might be both. Mulina described the attempt in detail and realized Asis would know the layout of the house because he is the one who had purchased it for Mulina. The now dead assassin was one of the two staffers leaving only the cook. They had taken all the knives away from her for the time being.

Mulina apologized for demanding the extra five million dollars and said he wanted to continue their relationship. He thought he could be an asset to Asis going forward. Asis had expected none of this especially him being alive right now. The assassin was a trusted jihadist who had failed but maybe this was a sign to go forward with Mulina. Asis could keep him on a short leash for now and think about how he could prove himself useful to the cause.

Asis wrote him back saying he agreed. Their last confrontation had left Asis feeling this was over for good, but Mulina's remarks had changed his mind. Rest up old friend and we will talk soon. Mulina smiled as he read it. He didn't trust Asis any more than Asis trusted him. He did not see that ever changing

.

Chapter Fifteen

Brazil

Moe Keane was planning to push harder in Brazil to get their hands on Alberto Mulina. He feared Mulina was long gone, but they had to exhaust every lead. One avenue that had not been explored was Mulina's niece. He decided to send two of their Brazilian operatives to see her. The local handler sent a man and a woman to ask the niece some questions plus feed her some information.

The CIA officers arrived at her home and rang the doorbell. Celia Mulina answered the door and asked what she could do for them. They told her they had information about her father and they needed to see her. She invited them in and they sat down. Celia said she missed her father very much, he was a good man. They agreed and then asked about her uncle, Alberto. Her expression darkened, she said he was not a good man, and she hadn't seen him for a while. Feeling she was being very honest they told her that Alberto was being investigated for crimes in Brazil and in the United States, no look of surprise was apparent and she gave nothing away.

The conversation progressed with little reaction from Celia until the point when they revealed her uncle Alberto had arranged for the funds to buy her new home and for her very healthy investment portfolio which was providing her income. She bristled at this and said her uncle Alberto told her the funds were from a life insurance policy her father had taken out for her protection. The funds came from her father not her uncle.

The CIA folks were fishing at this point and said, "We believe your uncle talked your father into taking down the airliner five years ago in the Pacific Ocean for reasons we are still investigating. The money you have and your home came from a terrorist organization."

Celia sat stunned. She had always questioned her uncle's claim about the life insurance money because she was the only one who knew her father had a rare form of cancer which would have prevented him from qualifying for life insurance, and he wouldn't be able to fly much longer. The thought of him agreeing to a plot by a terrorist organization may have been his way to provide for her. This all raced through her mind at once. She needed time to think, and she did not want to talk any more.

The agents could tell they had struck a nerve. They were trained to read people and her face was talking. It was too bad her mouth was not following suit.

"Celia can you help us?"

"No I can't, and I'd like you to leave."

The agents did not want to close this door completely and stood to leave without further requests. They thanked her for her time and said they would be in touch. Her face showed she'd rather they not return, but she was smart enough to know this would not go away easily.

When she closed the door behind them she felt a sadness wash over her. She missed her father every day, and it had been five years. It sounded like he may have made the ultimate sacrifice for her but how would she live with the fact he had taken 277 other lives with him to do it?

She knew Uncle Alberto had left the country. He told her for her protection he wouldn't tell her where he was going, but as a lifeline he left a contact email she could use if needed. He made her promise this would only be as a last resort and she had reluctantly agreed. She knew he was a bad man but all the family she had left.

The agents sat down over coffee and compiled their notes to send to their handler and Moe Keane. They had not brought back any new information but knew there was more here. This report arrived on Moe's computer and he knew they were right. This goes deeper, much deeper. He asked the agents to give her two days and go back. This time they would ask where to find her Uncle Alberto.

Two days later a knock on Celia's door revealed the same two visitors. Celia had been thinking about nothing but their last visit and was trying to decide what to do. The only thing she had to give the agents was her uncle's email address which he told her was very secure.

The agents were prepared with a game plan and an entire list of questions to ask in a certain order. As they started the process, it was not long before they could tell that Celia knew little if anything about any of this, her father and uncle had kept her in the dark for her safety. After about forty-five minutes of questions she gave the only information she had.

"My uncle has left Brazil and I have no idea where he went."

The female agent asked, "Did he leave you any way to contact him?" With all the care and concern he had shown her he must have given her something.

Celia said, "Yes I have an email, but that is all. He told me to only use it if I really needed help."

The agents gave each other a look and pushed forward. This was something they were hoping for and they had come prepared. They came prepared for two reasons. If they left with the email themselves, she would immediately contact her uncle to tip him off and secondly, they wanted to make the contact from her home on whatever technology she had available. A secure phone he had left for voice or text or this email or whatever else it might be.

The carefully worded email sounded like it came from a scared young woman. It asked for her uncle to send someone to help her, someone who knew what was happening so she could be protected. It also asked if her father was in any way responsible for the plane going down, she could not live with herself any longer without knowing the truth. She basically threatened suicide if he did not tell her more. She said I may not like what you tell me but I cannot go on without knowing more. They hit the send button and told her they would wait. Celia protested, but they appealed to her by saying they already had enough information to take her away from all this but if she cooperated that result might be stopped. Cooperation was her only chance to keep her way of life. Taking her away not only meant giving this all up, it meant many years behind bars in Brazil which she knew was not an option she wanted. It was hard for her to take because she felt totally innocent in all of this.

Portugal

Mulina got little email at this point in his life and was surprised to hear from Celia. He wondered if she was under duress or just letting her mind get the best of her. Either way he cared about her very much. He'd made a promise to his brother to watch over her. His brother had traded his life for his daughter's well-being and for Alberto. He would reveal nothing to her but he'd give her some information concerning her father.

Alberto typed the response:

Celia your father loved you more than anything. He would do nothing to put his passenger's lives in danger. He was the most honest, decent man I ever knew and you are just like him.

Love, your Uncle Alberto

Brazil

They all read with different emotional responses. Celia as expected getting information her father was not involved. The agents knew Mulina would not give up much, but this was nothing more than a lie. Should they give this one more shot at a more pointed reply? They had to make it sound like Celia.

They had not left a vehicle close thinking if Mulina sent a henchman over to Celia's they did not want to spook him or her. It was time to sit back and wait. They allowed Celia to lie down in the next room, this gave them time to think about crafting a new message. They desperately wanted more information on the plot to poison the birds, most of all they wanted the London connection. This would prove the most useful. They drafted a message saying Celia appreciated his response and asked if he would come home soon, and if not, could she come to see him and hit send.

Portugal

He smiled as he thought of little Celia. He wrote:

I will not be home soon and I'm sorry but you cannot come see me for your own good. I love you Celia, stay safe.

Brazil

The agents read the response and knew she should see the affectionate response from her dirt bag uncle. He at least loved her. Their instincts both caused them to put their heads down when the gun shot pierced the quiet of the house. They jumped up and ran to the door to see Celia lying on the bed with half of her head splattered on the pillow and wall. She had left a short note in Portuguese saying she could not live with the fact that 277 people died so she could have this life. She did not want to go to jail for something she didn't do.

This was all put into a report as the local authorities cleaned up another mess involving the American CIA agents.

Washington

Moe Keane was not overly shocked as he read the report. Not much new in the way of information. They now had reasonable proof the airliner was downed on purpose. It seemed to Moe that when all of this comes to light someday the families of the 277 people who died on the Brazilian 777 would want restitution from the Mulina family fortune.

For now, they would use all available resources to locate where Mulina was living from tracking his email. He would be a very mad man when he learned of his niece's violent death.

Portugal

News of Celia's death hit Mulina very hard. He had done everything possible to make sure she was set for life and safe as well. News of an apparent suicide did not ring true to Alberto. He knew murders could look like suicides, he knew this first hand. He would get more details and deal with whoever and whatever pushed her over the edge if it was suicide. Whether someone else pulled the trigger, or she did it herself, someone would pay.

He emailed one of his former employees in Brazil and told him to look into it. He'd now wait for information.

Mulina had settled nicely into his new home. As each day passed he felt more comfortable he was safe, but this may be exactly what Asis hoped for. He felt he could never let his guard down again. He had ventured into the small town more than once accompanied with his bodyguards. He had not tried to meet anyone; making new friends did not seem like a good idea yet. He couldn't lie to himself, he had his eyes on the local women. A female companion would be welcome.

Greenville

Mike hit the floor earlier than normal this morning. Sleep came harder than it used to, his dad said this happened as you got older. He always chuckled to himself but damned if Dad was not right again. Sure enough, he had been dealing with enough things in his life the past few years to disrupt sleep patterns. Two days of growth made him go ahead and drag the razor over his face this morning. He got the water good and hot and put on plenty of shaving cream. As he held his razor under the water he seemed to forget time. How long he stood there looking at himself he'd never know, but at that point he realized something he'd never wanted to admit. He had always believed you must take the high ground, always do what is right. Mike had lived his life this way and got kicked in the teeth a lot. He was not so naïve to know life was not fair, but it should be.

He knew he would never give up on the Golden Rule treat others as you want to be treated principle, but he also felt that sometimes you had to fight the fight your enemies didn't expect you to fight. There were many men who came home from a war who only made it home because they did what was necessary to win. Prisoners of war who got to come home came home with stories we could not believe. The bottom line was bad people did not fight fair. We cannot fathom what the terrorists will do. They have no regard for human life. He was not sure he could do it, but might find himself in a situation some day when he might have to do something totally against the way he was taught.

Mike finished shaving, rinsed and toweled off. He did not want to share these thoughts with Sandy or his kids or the Boiler Club. If this constituted pre-meditated anything, then so be it. He wondered if he could do it; it went against everything he had been taught or believed. He then thought of his dad's gun he had hidden in the barn. That gun was not traceable as far as Mike knew.

Indianapolis

Nat Jackson was overwhelmed with everything happening in central Indiana. The thought of trying to solve the mystery was very stimulating to her, but she also wanted to make sure they were doing everything possible to not let any terrorist activity happen again. She knew they could do everything possible but the bottom line was there was no way to keep this from happening. When the terrorist groups could recruit over the internet and get young American students, usually boys who were the outcasts, to do things to their fellow countrymen it was a bleak time.

Nat had gone into the FBI after a short military career. She had enlisted right out of high school with the thought the military would be her only way out of the brutally poor situation in which she had been raised. Alcohol played a part as it often does. Her father was a mean drunk. He would hit her mother and abuse her siblings in any way that came to him on a given day. Only one time had he crossed the line with Nat and her sister. It was the worst night of her life. After sexually assaulting Nat he had turned to her younger sister in the same room. As he started toward her Nat hit him in the head with a softball bat she kept under her bed. The blow to the back of his head was enough to crush his skull, and he slumped off the side of her sister's bed. She had delivered the blow with all the force she could muster which was more than needed to stop this sick man. Her mother came home from work to find the girls sitting in the kitchen crying. When she asked, they told her what had happened. Mrs. Jackson found her husband in their room and called the police.

"Girls I'll tell the police I did this to protect you both. I came in to find him with Elise and hit him!"

Nat said, "No mother you didn't do it!"

"Nat go get the bat."

When Nat came back with the bat, her mother wiped the handle down carefully leaving the blood on the barrel of the bat, she then grabbed the bat as if she were the one taking the swing. Any other finger prints of her girls would not be suspect on a bat they owned.

She would always carry that night with her. She had killed her own father. Yes, the bastard deserved it, but that violent night would never go away. Her military career started off well, but she soon realized she wanted to fight bad guys right here at home. She successfully completed one tour of duty and then it was off to study criminal justice. She applied to the FBI right out of school and was accepted into their training program. Things almost never got off the ground during questioning and completing a polygraph. Her mother made them promise to never speak of her father again. Intense questioning about her father's death at the hand of her mother nearly tripped Nat up. She was well practiced to defeat the polygraph, but it was still quite a challenge. DNA evidence from that night proved her father had assaulted her before turning on her sister. She had wanted to tell the truth from the beginning. She killed him and would do it again.

Investigators were satisfied, and Nat was admitted into the program where she did well. It seemed the vetting she had endured to gain admittance to the program ended with the polygraph. She still worried every day she would be discovered as a murderer, kicked out of the program and go to prison.

These worries carried forward to her career in the FBI after she left Quantico. She had been subjected to rigorous questioning but never a polygraph. Nat always imagined the second time would not go well and her past would finally catch up with her. She always felt her mother should have told the truth. Nat had struck her father to save her sister and herself, it was the truth and should have been enough. Her mother was trying to protect her girls and Nat would always appreciate how her mother had put her life on the line.

A thorough investigation had been completed and her mother had been exonerated from all charges. The District Attorney believed her and never put her through a trial. Her mother had passed from a massive stroke one night and had taken all that guilt to her grave. She was a strong woman and Nat wanted to be like her minus the alcoholic husband. These events with her father made Nat very careful when it came to letting a man get close to her.

Brazil

Mulina's contact had already been gathering information before the email hit his in box. He was not surprised to see it and knew Mulina would be incensed. Mulina had read the obituary online so there was no need to share any of this information. He only shared what he felt was pertinent. The biggest part of the information was that he'd learned Celia had been visited by two people who were not locals. They had been to see her one day and then came back two days later. They were there when she committed suicide. The local authorities quickly ruled it was a suicide, and the visitors had left town. He knew Mulina would think there was nothing fishy about any of this story. He was very glad he would not be in the same room when Mulina read it. The same country for that matter. He was certain Mulina had already left Brazil.

Portugal

Mulina was about to explode before he finished reading. Celia was innocent in all of this, yet had been so frightened or worried she ended her life or was killed by United States agents. They probably had not pulled the trigger, but it didn't matter to Mulina. They would have wanted to keep her alive to extract whatever information they could get. She ended her life because of it. She was getting the big squeeze by these trained professionals and she knew she had nothing to tell them, she felt totally trapped. Celia took the way out that saved her from their torture. He must make them pay for this.

Chapter Seventeen

Fort Meade

Steve Bradshaw had been so focused on the new information he'd received from Keane that he'd nearly missed a couple emails out of Brazil. These emails involved the death of Celia Mulina and had originated from Portugal. Mulina in Portugal would not be a stretch for a man fleeing Brazil. The email from the Brazilian end was not as secure as in the past, so with some work he would be able to get close to Mulina. The United States had friends in Portugal to help. Portugal was not a place that wanted trouble, they kept their head down.

Steve kept working his magic and got the Portugal email location down to a small enough area to ask for help. He called Moe Keane and gave him his thoughts.

Moe said, "Send over a map showing your best guess and we'll see how much help we have near that area."

Moe forwarded the map to his CIA contact to learn there was enough manpower to ask questions of the locals. They'd report back as soon as they knew more. Hopefully Mulina was not as protected in his new surroundings.

Portugal

The CIA operatives had moved to the area and began putting out feelers for a new resident. There would be four small towns and one slightly larger one to work. Day one yielded nothing, day two the same but day three gave them a lead. There was a nice home in the upper hills just outside of Portalegre that had some new residents. Locals thought them to be a little mysterious and told the agents they wanted no trouble. The agents assured them this information would not get back to the residents. They questioned shop owners if they had seen them and if there was a pattern to their shopping for groceries. Shop owners had seen three different men and one woman. They were never all together but if they saw the older man the two younger men were always with him.

When they asked shop owners about security cameras they were met with laughs, it seems they do not need them in this part of the world. Thus, no pictures of the men. The agents spread a little money around to certain shop owners so they would keep their eyes open plus the agents would do surveillance themselves. They assumed Mulina would have already recruited informants to watch for people just like the agents. They may have already been spotted and Mulina may know they were there. For this reason, they could not wait too long to make their move. They'd report their findings to Langley and await further orders.

The information from the CIA found its way to Keane. He called his contact, and it was agreed they could not wait long. They would send more agents before making their move.

Reinforcements arrived in the area in the form of eight Navy Seals and a briefing was scheduled. They had the best diagram of the house they could find from the local title company. This process worked differently than it did in the States but there was still documentation which had to be recorded publicly to show ownership of real estate. They had to assume it was well fortified with armed guards. They didn't believe the home had lots of manpower when they estimated the amount of food they were buying on a weekly basis. There couldn't be an army to feed with the small amount of provisions.

Orders were specific to take as many of them alive as possible. They wanted to interrogate them, especially Mulina. It was decided to take the house tonight, each hour they waited made the chance greater a local on Mulina's payroll would tip him off. The Seals had night vision goggles and weapons that were silenced as much as assault rifles could be silenced. Each Seal had his job and point of entry. There was a rear entrance on the second floor along with an entrance leading to a basement. These would be the two areas to breach. This plan was relayed back to Langley, and it was vetoed in the late evening.

The people in Portugal felt certain there were only four people inside and Langley felt they had a large enough group to take the house at first light in the morning as a show of force. The Seals did not like this change, they liked to work under cover of darkness but it was an order. Overnight everyone carefully moved into position with the Seals leading the way.

At first light they sent a man dressed in the local utility company's coveralls to the front door. He'd pulled up with a service truck. One of Mulina's bodyguards answered the door and was taken down with a taser. Troops quickly entered and moved upstairs to surprise the other bodyguard and overtake him with a taser. Two of the Seals went towards the kitchen and then down to the basement and were fired upon by the female housekeeper who had heard the commotion at the front door. She shot one Seal in his left arm and was killed by the other Seal at the same time she fired.

The last two Seals found Mulina sound asleep in his king size bed and were happy to bring him out of his slumber with two gun barrels with laser sights pointed at his chest. They hauled him out of bed as he protested, he was trying to figure out what the hell was going on. He has hoping this was a bad dream, but he knew quickly it was the day he always thought would happen. They put his robe on, checked it for weapons and led him downstairs to join his two men. He glared at them as they sat in plastic cuffs watching him come down the stairs. He yelled an obscenity in Portuguese as he was roughly put into a chair.

One of the Seals was relaying information back to their check point and asking for trucks to be sent. They would make the hour drive to the airport and be on their way out of Portugal. The Portugal authorities knew what was happening and the United States had their blessing to get this man out of their country. As far as they knew he had committed no crime on their soil and they wanted to keep it this way.

The Portuguese Army trucks took the entourage to the airport and they boarded a United States Air Force C-130. The three Portuguese Nationals who were CIA operatives had left Portalegre before the trucks had arrived. It was important to keep their identities safe from the local authorities. Portugal knew they were in country, but did not know their identities.

The C-130 received clearance to take off shortly and lifted off with no incident. They were on their way to a base in Germany for processing and initial questioning. In cases like this the contents of his small office including laptops, external hard drives and some files may be the bigger catch for intelligence but it was also good to have the real flesh and blood in custody. He could be prosecuted and punished and his files might allow the capture of others to save lives.

Washington, Fort Meade and Indianapolis

Word of the capture made its way to Moe Keane, and he immediately notified Steve Bradshaw and Natalie Jackson. Everyone was thrilled to know he was in custody and Steve was especially thrilled they retrieved his technology. Moe said news of his capture may break in the next few days and they decided to let the Boiler Club know he was in custody, no other details except he is in custody. It was assumed the person(s) in London would learn of Mulina's capture quickly, if there was any advantage they had currently they'd have to move quickly. Moe confirmed all Mulina's computers were coming to Steve Bradshaw on a flight that had already left Lisbon.

London

Asis received word later that same afternoon that Mulina was in custody by the United States military. This was bad but not the end of his plans. He had lost someone he had basically already lost for his usefulness. Hopefully Mulina was smart enough to have destroyed any information about his London connections. Asis had to assume they would have taken all technology they could find; thus he would have to change his contact and email accounts. This caused a setback but there was no choice.

He hoped the U.S. would use their normal rally point in Germany for detainees. They were very consistent where they took people like Mulina. If that were the case the intelligence assets he had in place would give him confirmation of Mulina's arrival at the medical center next to Ramstein Air Base shortly.

Greenville

After Mike's bus route, he headed home to make coffee. He always wanted it before the route but he'd learned the hard way you cannot have coffee before the route. One morning he had nearly burst all his internal organs not just his bladder from a big cup of coffee before his route. He thought he surely must have damaged things that morning including the bus steering wheel he had gripped so tightly. He vowed he wouldn't make this mistake again. The water was boiling, and the kettle was getting ready to whistle when Mike realized he was getting low on Chemex coffee filters. He put this on the shopping list. If he ran out, he could just run the boiling water through a dish rag or old pair of under-wear like the restaurant he frequented!

He checked his phone and saw he had a text message from Nat Jackson asking him to call.

He called after making the first pour in his Chemex, "Morn-ing Nat," Mike said.

"Good morning Mike, how you doing?"

Mike responded things were going fine and hoped the same for her.

Nat said, "We have information to share with your friends."

"That's sounds good, go ahead and I'll pass it along."

Nat told him that Mulina had been captured in Portugal and was being interrogated by United States officials.

"I am not at liberty to give you any details, but wanted you to know we have him. The story will probably break soon in the media, he's not well known yet and the story might get buried. We believe when it becomes public he will be considered a very nefarious man and people will want justice and vengeance."

Mike listened intently and said, "Ok, wow. Glad you have him. Thanks for letting me know Nat and let us know if there is anything we can do."

Nat thanked him, and said she would before she ended the call.

Mike made his second, third and fourth pours into the coffee in the Chemex filter and waited for it to run through. In about four minutes he was having a cup of coffee that tasted extra good this morning. He knew Mulina was a bad man who had killed a friend of Dr. Sutherlin, and would have probably killed his friend Brian along with Dr. Sutherlin. They knew Mulina was mixed up in some wild plot to poison birds and transfer a disease to live-stock in the United States. Mike hoped they were squeezing this guy hard for any other deadly plans he may be working on.

Mike sat down and drafted an email to the Boiler Club members with the information Natalie had given him along with his own thoughts. He knew they would be very pleased this man was in custody. Brian had responded in less than an hour, he hoped Mulina was getting some of his own medicine, his description involved the words squeezing and testicles. Dr. Sutherlin and Doc Summers responded late that afternoon they were proud of our military and government to have this man in custody. They all agreed when more information came in it would be time for another meeting of the Boiler Club.

Chapter Eighteen

London

Asis was notified within 90 minutes of the Mulina capture. He put all sources on alert to keep eyes open to track where he was taken. It was no surprise that stop number one was the U.S. Air Base in Germany, the normal stopping point for injured soldiers coming out of the Middle East. It would be a perfect place to evaluate the health of the prisoner and begin interrogation. Asis had assets who could tell him when and if the prisoner was moved. All the while they had no information on Mulina's health. No idea if he had been wounded in the capture.

Several days later Asis was notified their Brazilian friend was going somewhere late that evening. They would watch departures to identify planes coming and going. It seemed at this point the Americans had no idea anyone was watching and monitoring this process.

Members of the Baltimore cell would monitor Washington D.C. airfields for incoming flights. They knew there was a private section of the Montgomery County Airport used for flights that needed to be kept quiet and secure for whatever reason. This was the closest airport to the Bethesda Army Hospital. Sure enough, there was a landing during the time window they had calculated for a flight that would have been coming from Germany and it was verified this was the same plane.

Mulina was quiet and very solemn for the hours he was awake, he slept as much as possible. He was resigned his new home would not be a pleasant one.

"Where are you taking me?" Mulina asked the CIA men sitting near his bed. He was answered with the most blank, empty stares he had ever seen. No sense of humor with these guys.

A military helicopter landed four minutes after the plane had taxied to the block building at the end of the distant runway. Powerful binoculars let Baltimore cell members see someone being taken off the plane on a stretcher and loaded on the helicopter. The helicopter lifted off within seconds and was headed southwest over the countryside.

Rural Virginia

Members of the Baltimore cell had been buying drones from different manufacturers along with cameras and other equipment to use with the drones. They were experimenting with disguising a drone to make it look like a large bird, maybe a hawk or barn owl or something like that. The owl disguise was pretty damn good from a distance, which was their goal.

They made several trips to the Shenandoah National Park in Virginia. This offered them a lot of space to test the drones with as much privacy as possible. This was a two and a half to three-hour drive from Baltimore. They varied their route to make sure there would be no pattern from traffic cameras. The final flight scheduled for this drone would carry enough explosives to leave nothing for government investigators to piece together or trace back to them.

There was another reason for varying their routes. Recruiting and surveillance. When you get into areas off the beaten path you get to know an area. You lose your ability to blend in but you gain the ability to meet people who may be of service. The Baltimore cell members that Asis had recruited were not all people of Middle Eastern descent. He had locals, and they had some local friends across the countryside. The locals they recruited were people who thought the government knew too much and were easily swayed towards conspiracy thinking. The notion of the CIA having *safe houses* sprinkled around the Virginia countryside was accurate. Heavily wooded areas controlled by the government were bordered by other areas with families who had worked the area for a few generations. These folks noticed things out of the ordinary and people out of the ordinary and were suspect of both. Keeping their eyes open to alert other people of like mind when an Army helicopter was landing in the area was possible. Forty-eight minutes after the helicopter took off it landed in the Virginia countryside and a call was made to the Baltimore number that had offered cash for information on a helicopter landing.

Asis had given them the go ahead to act quickly when they had the location for Mulina. The sooner he was dead the better. Asis knew he would not be afraid to talk to save his own skin and cut a deal. Asis always made sure Mulina didn't know where to find him, but he also knew enough to cause problems.

The drones were prepared and ready to move into the area. They would have at least a two-hour drive, maybe closer to three with morning traffic. As always, they traveled according to the posted speed limits and were careful not to bring any attention to themselves. Getting stopped would be very messy for all involved.

Cell members were working off GPS coordinates which had been called in and were not 100% accurate. Spotters had given a very close idea of the landing point. This would be good enough for Waqas and Saad. They were now very experienced pilots and had a camera that would allow them a range of five miles out. Five miles was pushing it, four would be better if the safe house perimeter would allow penetration that close. Waqas was driving and Saad was using his laptop to dial into the GPS coordinates.

"Take the next exit and turn left," Saad told his partner without looking up from the screen.

"We are less than 15 minutes away. I found a back road that looks very secluded and has plenty of cover."

Waqas nodded and was looking for the exit. A few turns and about 15 minutes later they pulled on a side road undetected. This was one of those roads that had grass growing in the middle of it within 100 yards. More of a lane than a road. One of those roads you traveled only if you belonged there, for this reason they'd make sure they were gone as soon as possible.

They pulled off to the side, jumped out and pulled the drones out to make final preparations. They checked the internal batteries that powered the drone and the onboard camera. Engines were tested, and all hummed to life. The explosives had been checked and triple checked before leaving but were checked once again to make sure the wiring was secure. They were set to explode upon impact. With all the trees in this wooded area there would be an explosion one way or another, they had to make sure it was into the correct house and not a tree.

Each man carried his drone out to the road and set it in motion. They were flying about 50 yards apart to make sure they did not get into each other on the trip. The GPS coordinates had been programmed into each drone but they were still using the camera to make sure they were identifying the correct house. Flying at 20 miles per hour they should make the trip in approximately 13 minutes from their location. The height of the forest was uniform allowing them to fly along without a lot of changes in altitude, they were keeping a close eye on any natural or manmade structure out of the ordinary. They were both a little shocked when the house suddenly appeared and they stopped forward progress to hover for a few seconds. They could see technology in the way of antennas that would not have been on a house of this age in this part of the country. This had to be correct.

Saad said, "Hit the side closest to your current location and I'll hit the other."

Seconds later both cameras went blank, and they heard the explosions in the distance. One had hit about two seconds before the other but both had detonated. They hoped Allah had granted them a successful mission. No sooner had they heard the explosions they were heading for the van and Waqas was making his way back to the interstate.

Dan Brackett was on his six-hour security detail today and things were quiet as usual on the block of monitors in front of him. Thank God they rotated shifts and duties. Sitting in front of the monitors was easy but as boring as you could imagine. It took some creative thinking sometimes to not let anyone see your eyes glazing over. He much preferred the outdoor shifts. These carried a higher danger, but he had grown up walking the woods with a rifle in his hands or sitting in a tree stand with a Barnett cross bow.

About all he got out was a "What the hell," when he saw the two flying whatevers. They looked like two big birds with large wing spans, something was not right. He saw them stop in mid-air as if hovering and then racing directly towards the house. The next thing he would ever see was a bright flash with a white-hot blast. There had been no time for Agent Brackett to issue any warning to everyone else in the house.

The three agents outside all survived the blasts. The closest man being 50 yards from the south side of the house. He too had noticed something that looked like two owls flying into their perimeter and then after hovering for seconds flying into the east and west sides of the house. The explosions were seconds apart and the entire house was in flames or still in the process of coming back to earth in pieces. He raced towards the house with his gun out of the holster wondering if there would be more to this attack. He was looking from side to side and then signaled his two fellow agents as he saw them doing the same thing. They quickly assessed the area and saw no threats on foot. They moved towards the house and were pushed back by the flaming debris. All three circled looking for a way in but found it all destroyed.

Chad Pope couldn't believe what he was seeing. He pulled out his secure phone and called his superior.

"Lawson," was all Chad heard.

"Sir we have been attacked, the house is in flames!"

A short pause followed before Lawson said, "Have you engaged the attackers? Any prisoners?"

Pope replied, "Sir we saw no one, it appears the attack came from the air."

"Plane, helicopter?"

"No sir, it appeared to be a drone that had been disguised to look like a large bird."

"No shit, where the hell did that come from?"

"We have no idea sir, they appeared over the trees."

"They?"

"Yes, we saw two of them fly into the east and west side of the house."

Agent Lawson again hesitated before saying, "Do everything you can to save anyone possible, help is on the way."

"Yessir," then he clicked off.

Pope yelled to the other agents that help was on the way and instructed them to circle the house to look inside for survivors. The blaze was still raging as they followed his lead.

Pope was doing a mental checklist of people who were in the house. Dan Brackett was on monitor shift, Jeff Stanger and Bill Newman were working the interrogation running audio and video equipment. Moe Keane from Homeland Security was the lead on questioning and the prisoner was named Mulina. Five men in the house, four good guys and one bad. Three had just left in the last hour, one FBI agent, one NSA analyst and another FBI agent driving them back to DC. Fallout here will not be good. How in the hell did they find this place he muttered to himself?

First responders came by way of helicopter with firefighters following in the next few minutes. The flames were extinguished and what was left was not much to see.

Pope heard one firefighter say, "No one will have survived this, what the hell happened?"

First responders from the helicopter were Marines trained to rescue in all conditions. They searched the rubble as soon as the hot spots allowed them in.

The officer in charge of the Marines asked Pope, "Can you advise where we should center our search?"

Pope said, "There was only one agent on the main floor, three agents and one prisoner were in the lower basement level."

He got a nod from the officer and he was off to tell his guys to find a way into the lower level.

Pope moved closer to point to the area he knew led downstairs and could tell there was nothing left. They made their way to this point and began digging. They found what appeared to be stairs leading down and pulled back enough debris to see they were at the right place. The first glimmer of hope was felt as they could see there were some stairs remaining. Evidently the basement seemed to be more fortified than the ground and upper floors of the house.

Headlamps were switched on and Marines headed into the basement area. The first body found was a young man wearing headphones. He was lying under a beam that crushed him from knees to naval. No pulse. The next man was older and not breathing, he was twisted in a grotesque fashion. He was under debris but had been protected by a short block wall that had stopped the same beam that killed his partner but still no pulse. They could see into the next room where the prisoner was in dark coveralls and slumped over a table, he was cuffed to the table by his wrists.

Moe Keane was on the floor with his head and shoulders under the table; he had sustained a head injury that didn't look life threatening. When the first Marine medic checked his pulse, he found it very weak. His breathing was shallow. The medic could see a large bruise along the right side of his neck and then realized the prisoner had put his sandaled foot on his neck hard enough to cause the contusion. Keane's injuries were worse because of the prisoner. He next turned his attention to the prisoner who still had a pulse. This is when a man looks inside himself knowing he must do the right thing but wanting to end this bastard's life right now. Saving him may lead to information that could save many more. All five men were loaded into three ambulances and taken to the nearest clearing to board helicopters. The flight to the hospital took twelve minutes for Keane and Mulina. The other three agents had not survived the blast.

Washington

Nat Jackson and Steve Bradshaw were sharing a ride back to the city after leaving Moe Keane with Mulina. Steve had his first taste of being in the field versus working in an office and he liked it. He was not trained in ways of prisoner interrogation but had watched enough movies and read enough reports to make him want to take a run at a piece of shit like Mulina. He knew the current stance on how prisoners were to be treated and only imagined how Mulina and his men would have handled guys like

Keane and himself if the roles were reversed. Steve did not want to imagine what it would have been for Nat Jackson.

In the short time he had known Agent Jackson he knew he'd like to spend more time with her. He could tell she was professional and very smart. She cared deeply about her country and shared his dislike for anyone wanting to harm citizens. He was secretly hoping they hit worse than normal traffic in the Washington beltway to make this trip last a little longer.

Steve's cell phone rang first with Nat's buzzing seconds later. Both answered with their last names and sat listening in silence. They looked at each other in disbelief. Both were being recalled to their base of operations. They clicked off and again looked at each other. It was one of those times where emotions are indescribable going from outrage to fright. They had both just spent time in that house. Not that they needed more conviction, but this gave them more than enough to take this fight all the way. They were not given information on casualties but were told the situation was dire for all in the house.

Mulina and Keane were taken to adjoining rooms for initial treatment. Mulina had lost a lot of blood from an injury to his right shoulder from debris. He was in shock and not expected to survive. They began the process of giving him blood as soon as they knew his type. He was taken to surgery to repair his shoulder wounds.

Moe Keane had fared better because of the steel table where they had been seated. He was bruised and beaten up but would survive. The most serious threat came from the pressure which had been applied to his neck by Mulina. A couple more minutes may have done serious damage to his brain from the lack of blood flow. Moe was now conscious and wanting to know the details of what the hell happened. Doctors were trying to calm him and the sedative they ordered was not well received by Keane. He only backed off after a short debriefing from one of his staffers. It was incredulous they were attacked by drones out in the Virginia countryside. He felt he hadn't underestimated his enemies but then this happened. A safe house attacked by drones, how the hell?

Moe leaned back and closed his eyes. He very much wanted Mulina to survive, he wanted another crack at him. Whoever had gone to these lengths to kill Alberto Mulina wanted to make sure he would not talk. He must be very important.

Chapter Nineteen

Greenville

Sandy Baker and Pam Miller met for coffee and began the discussion of Roger Knight. They both knew the name. Mike and Sandy had heard about him from Melissa and Mike had seen him at the meeting for the farm employment after Melissa had identified who he was. Melissa told them he lived twenty minutes away in Elm Grove, in a very nice home. This got Sandy and Pam thinking about a plan.

They were in a local organization that made money each year by sponsoring a tour of local homes in Hampton County. Homeowners with nice and interesting homes would be approached to be on the tour and the revenue from the tickets would help local philanthropies. This happened each year around Labor Day.

Roger Knight was someone who would be classified as narcissistic in every way possible including his home. They would appeal to him to have his home on the tour and hopefully be able to do some investigating while he was gone during the tour.

The Bakers and the Millers met for dinner that night and after dinner Pam started the discussion.

"Guys, Sandy and I have a plan we'd like to share. As you know the annual home tour is coming up."

Brian looked at Mike and mouthed the words, "Oh no," while making a pained face.

"No, we're not asking you knuckleheads for help. We're going to submit Roger Knight's name for his home to be on the tour. We have few homes in the Elm Grove area."

This brought a puzzled look to Mike's face.

Sandy said, "It would be a great way to get into his home and have a look around. Who knows what we might see to give us a clue."

"You think it's crazy?" Pam asked.

Mike said, "Crazy good! Why not give it a shot?"

Brian said, "The FBI would love more info on this jerk."

It was then a plan and when it came time for the group to submit ideas of which homes to include on the tour this year Sandy and Pam lobbied for his home. It was added to the list, and he was approached to have his beautiful home on the tour. Roger was first not interested but a little thinking made him have a change of heart. It would look good for a local businessman to be included. He agreed.

Virginia

News of an explosion in the Virginia countryside made the National news with little information available. Theories flew when news teams realized it was not a personal residence. Access to the property was cordoned off and warnings were given by local law enforcement to heed this warning.

No information was released concerning Moe Keane and Alberto Mulina. The families of Dan Brackett, Jeff Stanger and Bill

Newman were notified and their deaths were made public. No other explanation was given other than an explosion of unknown cause. The investigation was under way and details would be released in time.

Indianapolis

Mike Baker made the call to Nat Jackson.

"Good morning Nat, can I stop at your office for a quick meeting?"

"When can you be here?"

"Forty minutes."

"Sure, but I don't have a lot of time in my schedule."

"I won't keep you long"

"Ok." They both clicked off.

Mike checked in and Agent Jackson was called down to meet her guest.

"Hi Mike, follow me."

Once behind her closed office door and a quick exchange of pleasantries Mike got to business.

"Okay, listen to this story."

Mike laid out the plan Sandy and Pam had cooked up to get Knight's home on the tour with Jackson listening while shaking her head from side to side.

"They approached him and he agreed. We all decided we had to tell you."

Mike knew full well she may say they couldn't take any liberties to look around, but she didn't, instead she said, "We'll run this past the higher ups and see if we might take advantage."

"Please do not move forward on this until you hear from me."

Mike nodded his understanding and rose to leave. Nat held out her hand, and they shook with her giving him a look that thankfully included a small smile.

Later that morning Nat sent Keane an email. Reading from his hospital bed he was amazed at the moxie of these women and replied he'd do some work on his end.

Keane thought about it the rest of the day. Bradshaw had sent him a report with findings from Mulina's laptop and external hard drive, the yield was small and gave them no firm leads. They also found a small address book full of names from Brazil. Names that should be helpful for local authorities. A few Anglo names showed up with one being Roger Knight in Indiana, U.S.

Moe felt they had enough intelligence on Roger Knight to warrant this action and he agreed only if Nat Jackson was the one to look around. Their main target would be his computer and they knew they'd have to be lucky, but it was worth a shot. Anything they found would be inadmissible in any court but they needed leads more than convictions.

Missouri

Janet Knight was wondering more and more what brother Roger was involved in. As time passed, she decided he was getting more dangerous, not yet reckless but his bigger than life thoughts of himself could get quickly out of hand. Problems with him could cost her financially which she didn't like for selfish reasons, but if he brought problems on himself, then so be it. She knew little about him and decided that was exactly how she wanted to keep it. He was a loose cannon. Roger had called to tell her how he publicly dressed down one of his people in a branch in Greenville, and did it in front of other employees and customers. He was very happy with himself and she could tell he very much enjoyed sharing it with her. Janet thought this wasn't the kind of publicity he should want in a community where he'd purchased all the locals' farm ground.

A smart and ruthless man with an ego to match could be dangerous and that ego was growing. Janet also had ownership in the holding company, it would not look good for her if this all came down around Roger. She needed to have a face to face with him which she normally avoided but this time he needed to hear it from her.

Janet sent Roger an email saying it had been a while since they'd talked, and she'd like to get together soon. It was not at all harsh or threatening, just a request to talk sometime soon.

Elm Grove, Indiana

Roger opened the email from his sister that evening and found it curious. This request didn't happen often and was usually due to business. Theirs was not a touchy-feely brother-sister relationship. He decided late that evening to invite her to Indiana for a few days. He could take her out to the country to see their farm ground plus she'd be around to help him with the home tour.

Roger sent an email explaining the upcoming home tour. Janet was surprised at the offer and decided why not? She figured she'd probably regret it, but she'd try. A few days away would not hurt, even though she should go spend those days in some exotic location instead of Indiana. She answered she would come, and told him when she'd arrive. The home tour was two weeks away; she'd get there on Thursday before the tour on Saturday.

Indianapolis

Nat Jackson worked with Sandy and Pam on preparations for the home tour. The sponsoring group would have ladies stationed in each home to answer questions and watch over things. Nat would be free to roam the house as soon as Roger left. This would give her at least two hours to look around, maybe three. Sandy and Pam received information on the house when Roger gave the ladies a tour, they were not starting from square one. Nat would be on her own to get as much covered as possible.

Elm Grove

Janet arrived at Roger's home as he was getting home from the bank.

"Would you like to go to dinner?" He asked.

Janet said, "Yes but nothing fancy, let's get a quick bite and come back to rest and talk for the evening. Do you have any Jack Daniels?"

"Of course."

They went to a small local hangout and got a booth in a darker corner. Janet ordered an Amaretto Sour and Roger ordered a Long Island, it had been a long day and week. Janet decided she wanted a burger well done with mayo and seasoned fries. Pickles on the side. Roger wanted a blackened salmon with asparagus on the side and water with lemon. They made small talk and nursed their drinks until their food arrived. They both ate and enjoyed their dinners. They were not close, not close at all but when you got down to it they were all they each had and they knew it. It was more awkward than anything but they had learned to deal with this relationship.

They finished dinner, Roger paid the check, and they got up to leave. They made the ten-minute drive to Roger's home and settled in for the night. Roger broke out the Jack Daniels and two highball glasses and poured each of them two fingers over ice.

"Ok I'm ready," Roger said.

"Ready for what?" Janet asked.

"We both know you're here for more than just some quality time with your bro," Roger said half-smiling.

Janet smiled and said, "You're partially right. I am worried about you and worried for me."

Roger raised an eyebrow.

"You have done what you needed to do to get over 12,000 acres of prime Indiana farm land purchased. What now?"

"What do you mean, Janet?"

"I am worried you're getting over confident and losing your edge."

He dismissed this and waved the comment off.

Janet mimicked what he had just done and said, "Just like that, you're too confident."

They both took a long drink of their JD and let the words and the bourbon soak in.

"Remember telling me about the incident of you dressing down a branch employee in public? You're making enemies whether you think it or not, it's true Roger; and doing this in small towns where you have bought up their way of life is not wise."

He didn't want to hear it but she had spoken her piece. He stood and told her he was heading for bed and asked if she had everything she needed, she shook her head yes.

Janet just sat for a while before going to her room. Maybe this visit had been a mistake, she knew she'd have that feeling while here and here it was. She always had that feeling when visiting Roger. She also had the feeling she was always being watched only because he had more mirrors in his house than anyone. Roger never met a mirror he didn't like, "Vain" should have been his middle name.

Chapter Twenty

Elm Grove

Saturday arrived, and it was time for Roger and Janet to leave the house. The ladies were arriving who would be hosting the home tour, they all looked like nice women. The house was clean from top to bottom as it always was, Roger had a cleaning service that kept it top notch.

Overnight surveillance had revealed a female in the house, the FBI determined this was Roger's sister. She was in the investment business and lived near St. Louis. Her car was in the garage, they had video showing the Missouri plate. The Missouri BMV confirmed owner's information.

When Roger and Janet left, Nat came into the house along with Sandy and Pam. They had been given information before hand and Nat knew where she wanted to focus. Other members of the group had been kept in the dark for obvious reasons. If this got out, there would be a lot of talk feeding a pipeline they did not want. The other ladies found it odd they were told where they would be stationed. They usually got their way and some feathers were ruffled.

There was one room upstairs off the master bedroom that was locked and they had been told this was not a part of the tour and would be off limits with no questions asked. The organizers agreed. This room was target number one for Nat. There was an entrance to this room from the upstairs hallway and another from the master bedroom. Nat would attempt to get in through the master bedroom. Sandy and Pam were stationed in the sitting area next to the bedroom to keep watch. They had twenty minutes before the tour officially started, time to get to work.

Nat brought everything available to get past a lock except for a cordless drill and it was a good thing. This was no ordinary room to room lock, it was a more secure design but not one she couldn't defeat. She was given specialized instruction on picking locks the last few days and had video capabilities with her phone to another agent who was waiting if needed. She was able to open the lock after about five minutes. Nat entered with caution and slower than she would have preferred but she had to check for all forms of security including alarms.

Finding none, she used her own light instead of turning on the one in the room. She didn't want to risk any more than she had to. This room was basically an office and a small museum. There was an antique curio cabinet that held books and small items like a military medal and old toys. The desk drawers were also locked, but she found these easy to open. The gloves the FBI provided for this work were perfect, she felt her fingers were more agile than normal wearing these. As she checked drawers there was a surprising lack of files, even in file drawers. She searched further and found nothing of interest until she arrived at a drawer containing two flash drives.

She had not yet tried to turn on the laptop; she had been warned this would be fraught with danger. His laptop could be set to notify his smartphone with any activity, for this reason they sent her with a device that once activated would block any signal leaving the room or coming in. This would hamper her in trying to derive information from the laptop but also protect her from possible detection. She turned on the laptop after making sure her device was working. The flash drive she inserted to download information from the hard drive would work even if not logged on and that is how they were working today, no need to work through finding his password, they didn't have that kind of time, anyway. She was surprised how quickly this told her it was complete, there was little stored on the C Drive. She shut the laptop down and turned her attention to the flash drives.

Roger and Janet made their way to a local Starbucks when Roger had an idea.

"Did you meet any of the women who were hosting?"

"Two or three as we were leaving. Just a quick introduction."

Roger said, "I would like you to go back to my house and go through yourself as if you were taking the tour."

Janet gave him a puzzled look but agreed and they gathered up their coffee and headed back to his car. Five minutes later he was dropping her around the corner from his home. Janet made her way to the front door. The tour was just getting ready to start and several others were waiting to enter.

Nat put the first flash drive into her device which was itself an external hard drive on steroids with its own USB port. It was small enough to fit in her purse and more powerful than many business computers. The transfer of data started immediately and took a little longer than she wanted, number one finished and she inserted the second drive. This one took longer yet. Hopefully this would be the information to help them, for all she knew it would be full of porn.

Janet entered the front door with the other guests and declined signing the guest book. She started her slow surveillance around the first floor. She listened to comments from the others and gave them all a good look including the hostesses. The first few people were making their way to the second floor, and she followed.

Sandy was watching guests and interacting with people when she saw Roger's sister start up the stairway. She quickly walked into the master bedroom to alert Pam.

Pam whispered, "Shall I get Nat?"

At that moment Janet entered the master bedroom. She had already checked Roger's office door from the hallway entrance and it was locked as it should be.

Nat was working as quickly as possible and being as silent as she could. She was startled by the noise on the other door handle. Someone had given it a try even though they knew better. She finished copying the second flash drive, removed it and put it back in the drawer as she had found it. She locked the drawer and was ready to leave his office.

Janet said hello to Pam and Sandy and asked about an old clock in the master bedroom. They told her this piece was a family antique and heirloom from Mr. Knight's grandfather. Janet continued walking around the room and came to the door of his office.

As she reached to check the knob Pam touched her shoulder to say, "This is Mr. Knight's private office and is not part of the tour."

Janet smiled at her and continued on. She gave a look at the base of the door to make sure there was no light coming from his office and was satisfied to see none. She thanked Sandy and Pam and wandered on to the other upstairs rooms.

When Janet was safely out of the room Pam gave a light triple knock on the door which was the agreed upon signal for Nat to safely come out. They knew Nat would wait for the signal because they were already past time for her to be out of the office. Nat came out slowly and then locked the door behind her, she removed the gloves she had been wearing and put them into her purse. Nat had heard the discussion with the guest but would not know until later that afternoon who it was and how close she came to opening the office door.

Nat told them, "Thanks, we'll talk later."

She then left the room to leave the house.

If Sandy and Pam would have taken the time to let her know the guest who almost turned the knob was Roger's sister Janet, then Nat would have made sure she was gone before attempting to leave the house but that did not happen. Nat came around a corner at the bottom of the stairs and practically bumped noses with Janet. Janet was just as startled and knew instantly this was not someone she had seen enter the house in the twenty minutes it had been since the tour began. Janet's powers of observation were keen and she was using them to their fullest this afternoon. She kept count of visitors until now along with hostesses, she stepped over to the guest book and counted. The person she ran into was one extra, she did not know the names of the other guests but the count was one off. She'd make sure Roger knew about this little tidbit.

Indianapolis

Nat arrived back at her office as quickly as possible to get information to Moe Keane and Steve Bradshaw. It was Saturday but their work didn't know normal hours or normal days. Normal for most people. She put the first flash drive in her laptop, pulled up Keane's secure email and hit send with the flash drive contents as an attachment. She repeated the same process for the second flash drive and sat back in her seat to take a breath. She hoped there was something worthwhile here.

Nat opened the second flash drive while she still had it in her laptop, opened the first document and smiled to herself.

Washington

Keane headed to his office when he got word he was receiving information from Nat Jackson. He apologized to his wife and the friends who were visiting and was on his way. His driver had him to the office twenty-six minutes later, and he was on his way up past security. He was still not feeling up to par from the explosion with Mulina but was mentally ready to work. He downloaded the attachments from her emails and opened the first one.

It was apparent this was valuable intelligence. He initially was skeptical and had to read more because this information was not something you would want to come into anyone else's hands. It was apparent Roger Knight wanted to make sure he left his legacy, he was very proud of his accomplishments. It was one of those types of things you see on television when someone says, "If you are reading this I'm dead, and I want you to know the whole story." They knew he was a vain person, and this proved it. He would be a narcissist in death as well as life.

Documents laid out plans he had made with a contact in London. This was the person Homeland Security wanted to find. There was mention of Alberto Mulina and poisoned birds. There was mention of a downed airline and a US submarine. There was information on buying farmland at depressed prices due to changes in weather and livestock diseases. It seemed everything flowed through the contact in London. Unfortunately, the contact in London was never referred to by name.

Indianapolis

Nat Jackson was enthralled; she couldn't quit reading. She knew the way this was obtained would be a huge problem with future prosecution but that just didn't seem to matter right now. She called Steve Bradshaw, knowing it was all in front of him.

"Son of a bitch", is all he could say.

"Will you copy me on your thoughts back to Keane?"

"Will do Nat." He clicked off.

Steve's jaw hit his keyboard as he opened documents. He quickly called his wife to say to have dinner without him and that he loved her. Keane called Steve and asked him to think how they should play this information with further searching on the NSA computers.

Greenville

The Bakers and the Millers bought rib eyes and beer and big Idaho potatoes and fired up the grill. What a day! It seems Sandy and Pam were so full of adrenalin the men could not get a word in. They felt like they were in a scene out of a spy novel or a thriller movie or "The Sting". Whether Nat Jackson could glean any information out of whatever she found or not, they were involved in something today they would never forget. They admitted to each other and their husbands it was a little disappointing they could never share this escapade with anyone, it was not only scary but exhilarating.

"A toast to our hot wives!" Brian said.

"Cheers" was repeated all around and glasses clinked.

Chapter Twenty-One

Elm Grove

When Janet met back up with Roger, she related the story of running into a certain woman who she had not accounted for, he was less than worried.

"You didn't see her come in," he said with an unconcerned shrug.

"That is exactly right, and I had that uneasy feeling in my stomach about her."

Roger again shrugged it off but filed it away in his mind. No man wants to think women have some sort of intuition they don't have but he'd seen a few examples over his lifetime where this was true along with every other man.

"I appreciate your help, it makes me feel better knowing you had a look around."

She frowned and shook her head.

Roger said, "Let's go have dinner and we can plan tomorrow."

"I'd like that but I leave in the morning." Janet said.

Roger was surprised but just shook his head ok, he was secretly happy for her to be heading back.

The next morning after a quick breakfast he carried her bags down to the garage and she gave him a half-hearted hug and backed onto the street. There was no I love you or anything like that between them. He waved goodbye and she was gone.

Missouri

Two days later Janet had settled in for the evening and was online looking at news stories. One story led her to the Indianapolis Star. As she read further, she came to a picture. She looked at the picture and did a double take. The person on the left was the woman she bumped into at Roger's house on the day of the tour. It was the women she felt funny about and had not seen until the moment they were nose to nose. The paper identified this woman as Natalie Jackson, she was an FBI Special Agent in the Indianapolis field office. This was very interesting. On one hand, she could very well be in the sorority that was hosting the home tour, on the other hand Janet felt she startled a woman who seemed to be out of place.

She opened her email and wrote a short note to Roger along with a link to the website. She'd told him about this woman and she could now show him her picture. He had dismissed it pretty quickly, now he might squirm a little knowing he had a visitor from the FBI in his home. He could have been compromised that day. She hit send.

Elm Grove

Roger read her email that evening and opened the link. He remembered Janet telling him the story, and he agreed it was an interesting coincidence. He could see no reason someone from the FBI would have enough information to come to his home and they hadn't produced a warrant. He guessed it would not be breaking and entering since she could walk right in my home. Saying yes to the home tour might not have been such a good idea.

Roger knew a lady down the block he could call to verify if Natalie Jackson was a member of the sorority. He found her number and called her. He asked if there was a Natalie Jackson in her sorority and she said she'd never heard of the name. Roger thanked her and ended the call. Well the only legitimate reason Natalie Jackson was in his home would be if she were on the tour herself. What's the chance of that he wondered? If he attempted to call Ms. Jackson himself, that wouldn't look good. He would have to just leave this alone for now.

A fitful night of sleep followed and on the drive to work the next morning he came up with a plan. He called his neighbor friend later in the morning.

"Sorry to bother you again Michelle, but could I trouble you to send me the names and addresses of your friends who helped host at my home, I would like to send them thank you notes."

Michelle said, "That would be no problem at all, could I email them to you?"

Roger told her that would be great and gave her his home email. When he arrived home that evening he had an email from Michelle with seven names and addresses in it.

Five of the women were from Elm Grove and the other two were from Greenville. He looked at the names and addresses and knew there was something interesting about those two names from Greenville. First, Sandy Baker's address seemed familiar. She lived out in the country in an area that would be farm ground he now owned. The address looked familiar and after some thought he checked his list of farms and employees. There was a man by the name of Mike Baker with the same address on the list and yes, this was a farm he had purchased. They had been forced out by Roger's bank. Mike Baker was the man who drove the busload of explosives away from the school. He was a local hero.

The other name was Pam Miller. He did a little searching online to find she was married to Brian Miller. Brian Miller was the man who was held captive in Brazil with the Purdue professor named Sutherlin. Miller was a birder, and he was poking his nose around in Mulina's territory which is what got him abducted. For what Roger knew, Miller was lucky to be alive after being snatched up by Mulina's men. He must have some powerful friends to get rescued like he did.

Finding this information made him feel he was right to look further, this was too coincidental. Add to this the FBI agent and he did not know what to think.

After a few days Roger realized the notion of having an FBI agent snooping around his house was eating at him. No search warrant, just an FBI agent coming into his home during a home show tour he agreed to do to be a good guy. "Bullshit!"

He felt confident she would have found nothing, but that nagging feeling came again. He was searching his brain for any way he could find out more. Maybe he should get Janet involved in this. He didn't want to involve her any more than he had to, but it was Janet who noticed this person and had the intuition to follow up on it. His sister was very astute and he admired her and was also jealous of her. I must think this through carefully he thought to himself.

Roger decided to reach out to Asis. He carefully composed an email asking if there was a way to communicate safely and hit send. Roger felt the government was investigating him and had no idea what or how much they knew. He suddenly felt very vulnerable and alone. With Asis as his only real friend and ally he realized this only ally may be his biggest enemy.

It then came to him that the thought of losing everything he had worked to achieve would be the worst outcome of all. He now had an empire of farm ground. His plan of revenge was nearly complete but all could be teetering. This was too much to consider.

London

Asis read the email with great interest. Knight was possibly losing it which he saw as a threat. Technology was the fastest way to do things but fraught with danger. It was now time to use his people in the U.S. to help with communication and surveillance. Since communication by way of email with Knight was likely compromised, he would use the Chicago cell to set up a system of passing information using dead drops like you see in the old spy movies. It was old school, but it worked if your surveillance was up to par.

Asis devised a system that would work for Knight plus it would get his cell a presence in the Indianapolis area. This presence would allow them to keep eyes on Knight and find ways to deal with him if needed. Knight's spy craft was nonexistent for changing up his schedule and travel habits. He was bullet proof in his own mind but also not wise in the ways of the devious.

A well encrypted thumb drive was prepared as to the updated plans and was on its way to the Chicago cell two days later. Asis had cultivated several businesses he could use to send parcels to the States which included thumb drives, sim cards and digital camera memory cards. You could send reams of information safely. He never sent reams and never sent everything in one parcel. If it were intercepted, they would only get pieces of a mission.

Asis laid the groundwork for a drop plan to the cell members and would rely on them to pick remote locations to make it all happen.

Elm Grove

Days went by with no answer from Asis. Roger found himself checking email hourly as the days passed. He arrived home one evening to find an envelope in his mailbox with only his first name. He pitched the rest of the mail on the counter in the kitchen and opened it. Inside he found a typed message that was very interesting and gave him a damn good chill down the full length of his spine. Asis had people in the area and they had been to his house.

It looked like he'd be taking some new routes home from work starting tomorrow. The letter detailed several drop points he and *they* could use to pass information securely. No more email. This would be slower and harder but he felt like a spy suddenly. He felt a huge sense of relief. If Asis were going to the trouble to create this arrangement, it had to mean Roger was important to Asis and now safe.

The letter detailed continued caution in not using names or sensitive information about locations, but they could be more open in what was asked and answered. There was a schedule of which days to check each location. Roger decided he would now begin the process of planning how he might cause problems for Nat Jackson.

London

Asis loved living in London. His parents had moved to London for business when he was a child. He initially hated leaving his friends and their home in Saudi Arabia where it was hot and dry. London was always damp and chilly. He quickly learned there was a lot more to do in London versus his birthplace. There were lots of very interesting people to meet with many varied backgrounds. Behind closed doors his parents would chastise the Londoners as unruly and unholy people. His parents tolerated the people because they needed them for business. Asis secretly liked the Londoners better than the people they left behind.

Asis had no desire to ever return to the Middle East. He hated the United States and the infidels but he had no desire to have much to do with the Middle East. He may have been the man without a country but he had London. His parents were now deceased, and he was left to run the family business. He was very comfortable in that role, also very comfortable financially.

He planned to travel to the United States soon to see things for himself. His business would allow that to happen. He would then be free to put other plans in place and recruit more jihadists. That seemed to get easier and easier as young Americans were unhappy with their country. They spent a lot of their time online and that was a place to recruit. Other terrorists' factions were using it successfully. National news sources in the U.S. were reporting weekly about how one or two American students were detained for trying to fly to Syria to join the jihad. What they did not realize, was the number who were making it through to do the same. Asis liked recruiting young people but didn't want the extra headaches of trying to get them out of the United States. This opened him up to possible discovery by agencies on guard for this plan. He liked the idea of getting them needed training right in the U.S. They would not have to travel to a foreign training base to learn how to wreak havoc in their own country and then travel back. He could encourage his recruits to play selected video games to get much of the training they needed. Asis knew they were safer and better off living in the United States but they didn't seem to realize that. He could use that for his own gains.

"Stupid infidels!" he said to himself.

"They have everything but think they have nothing."

Chapter Twenty-Two

Chicago

Bisma opened the package and smiled to herself when she found the carefully packed thumb drive.

"Can I give this a look Hazaq?"

Hazaq was eager to have a new assignment and was hoping for any word from Asis.

"Yes Bisma, take a look and don't tell me if it's more bullshit or busy work."

Bisma put the thumb drive into her laptop and read with great interest. Her eyes widened with the news and Hazaq could tell this was better than the norm.

"What is it?" he snapped.

Bisma outlined a plan where three of their team would move to Indianapolis to begin surveillance on a person or persons. They both knew there would be further details to follow.

"This means we will search for a place to rent in Indianapolis."

Hazaq followed up with, "Bisma search for anything you can find on the internet about Indianapolis. Look for neighborhoods where we can blend in, places where the crowd is younger and more open to an international presence."

"Will do," Bisma replied.

Bisma spent much of the next three days learning everything there is to know about the largest city in Indiana. There were neighborhoods like Hazaq mentioned plus two medium-sized colleges and one larger university downtown. These were the best places for them to blend in.

During this time, another package had arrived detailing more plans of looking for drop zones for passing information. Hazaq was more than a little irritated at this old school shit when we had the latest technology available to pass information. He was more interested in plans to attack crowded places. He wanted action, and this did not sound like action. He was tired of just being a foot soldier, he wanted responsibility and he knew he could organize and recruit others. Maybe he could do this away from the eyes of Asis and the others. He would travel to Indianapolis with Bisma to look around and get things set up. For now, he would follow orders.

Bisma on the other hand had grown to appreciate more about the United States than she had ever thought possible. Her father had been killed by Russian forces in Afghanistan when she was four years old. Her mother and older sister had been helped by United Nations relief forces and taken to a camp in Turkey. They were offered passage to England and a chance to start a new life. The new life did not turn out to be a glamorous one but it was certainly better than what they would have experienced in their home country. Bisma could attend a nice school and get an education. Her mother encouraged her to take advantage of every opportunity and made sure she realized how lucky she was to be in this situation. Bisma understood but also understood she was in this situation because of how her father was slaughtered by opposing forces. Not a day passed she did not think of her father fighting for what he believed and she decided she'd take this fight further. Even though it was the Russians who killed him, the Americans were now fighting in Afghanistan and she would be content to fight them.

"Tomorrow we will leave for Indianapolis Bisma, have you completed our agenda?"

"Yes Hazaq, I have three places for us to consider and have booked rooms for three nights."

Hazaq nodded but showed no smile. Inwardly he knew Bisma was the best of all in his group for logistics and doing this research.

As Hazaq packed for the three-day trip, he made sure he was taking firepower with him. He lived with the realization they could always be captured or detained and he would never go without a fight. He would not hesitate one second to take out as many infidels as possible if this were going to happen. The secret compartment built into the car's dashboard was fitted with two Glock handguns plus some carefully packed military grade C4 explosive. The removal of the passenger airbag was a small price to pay for this space. The lining of this compartment had been designed to make sure the bomb sniffing dogs would be none the wiser to alert their handlers if it came to that.

The next morning Hazaq and Bisma left Chicago for the three-hour trip south to Indianapolis. Traffic was heavy as usual but soon they were motoring down Interstate 65 through the farm fields of northern Indiana. Neither hardly spoke as Hazaq drove.

There was mutual respect but no friendship between these two. Hazaq carried the basic *look down upon women* shared by his fellow jihadists. Bisma knew it. She didn't know he respected her abilities more than most of the young male jihadists under his command.

"Where did you pick for our lunch?" Hazaq asked.

Bisma told him about a restaurant frequented by both students and faculty of the IUPUI campus in downtown Indianapolis.

"This place should allow us to blend in and watch the locals," Bisma told him.

"Direct me to parking Bisma and let's walk around the area before we eat."

Bisma had been waiting to ask the next question and was ready to be a little bold. "Hazaq have you given thought to looking for possible college recruits in Indianapolis?"

He shot her a sideways look that showed he did not like her thinking operationally like this. "That's for me to decide and not your place."

Bisma gave him an icy stare and decided she would say no more, she would act as she saw fit. She would never be an equal. She would end up being superior.

The next three days proved to be very productive for them. They rented an apartment in a busy area including the university and several hospitals and gained valuable information on the area. They each walked the area and made notes of places for personal meetings and places for dropping off and picking up information. Asis had a high-profile contact in the area to go to this trouble. They both made careful notes of all traffic cameras, business cameras and campus security cameras they found. It seemed

Indianapolis had done a fine job with setting up local security, but as in every city of this size there were areas left uncovered or sparsely covered. They would take advantage of this.

Indianapolis

After much persuasion Bisma convinced Hazaq to allow her to move to Indianapolis to live in the apartment with two others from the cell. She purposefully nagged him to a point he was happy to have her gone. He would have liked to have shown his displeasure with the back of his hand.

The move date was selected as soon as Bisma and her two compatriots signed the lease for their new home. They had credentials in order including a credit rating that qualified them for the apartment and any needed furniture. After one night in a hotel the furniture was delivered, and the apartment was ready to serve as their base in Indy. All this information was relayed to Asis. He could now send his new Indianapolis cell directions for missions. He could now compartmentalize his plans between the two cell locations protecting both cells. Asis made sure Hazaq had picked a competent assassin as one of the three new Indianapolis cell members and he made sure he had the necessary weaponry available.

Bisma was thrilled to get away from Hazaq. She respected him operationally, but hated him as a man. She thought back to when she was granted the right to continue her studies in the United States, and jumped at the chance. Her mother was not convinced but Bisma had grown into a strong young woman. She bid her mother farewell for now and promised to return making her proud. Bisma was on her way to a foreign city in a foreign land.

Her plan came to her in pieces. Never one to take chances the plan stayed grounded firmly in her subconscious and never on paper or media of any type. She never shared with any of the other members of her cell in Chicago. They were mostly hot-headed jihadists who wanted to cause explosions and kill people as soon as possible. This would most likely include killing themselves. Bisma's plan was far more detailed. She would live the good life of an American and work her way into places to cause real damage to the infidels.

Roger Knight had thought about his options for three days. He had cultivated relationships over the years with people who would get their hands dirty if needed. He'd helped them financially with his influence as a bank officer, and they owed him favors he'd never cashed in and hoped he never would. If he were to have someone killed, who would it be? The FBI Agent would not be a good idea for obvious reasons, they'd hunt him down. If he had one or both sorority women killed they'd put him on a suspect list for sure. As much as he'd like to teach these people a lesson it would do him more harm than good unless he could do it another way. Maybe he'd ask Asis to target them someway. Before that would happen, he had fences to mend with Asis.

Washington

Moe decided it was worth the travel to bring Nat Jackson and Steve Bradshaw together for a meeting to discuss what they had found. He composed an email and sent it to both. Within fifteen minutes he was reading responses from them saying they would be in Washington tomorrow late morning.

Chapter Twenty-Three

Washington

Nat Jackson and Steve Bradshaw took seats at the small conference table in Moe Keane's office.

"Thank you both for coming on short notice, I felt the need to talk this through in person." This got two nods.

"I'll start by saying this will never be allowed in court, but this is an issue of national security and we must proceed." Again two nods.

"This brother and sister are in this up to their necks. Honestly, it looks like the damage has already been done."

"What concerns me is who they were working with," Nat said.

"Agreed," Keane said.

"Can we agree with 100% certainty that Alberto Mulina is involved?" Steve said.

Keane said, "At least 99%."

"It's a shame we can't question Mulina on all of this. That piece of shit knows exactly what he was trying to do," Nat said.

The small smile on Keane's face made Nat and Steve look at each other. They'd never seen him smile.

"As you know Mulina suffered life-threatening injuries in the explosion and died. That is what we wanted the world to know. He was moved to a secured facility and we have nursed him back to health. He is alive and well and has been cooperating on a limited basis. He thinks his cooperation will get him back to a minimum-security prison in Brazil. A prison where he would walk out shortly after he arrived with his connections. He of course will never leave this country alive."

"This information will never leave this room unless there comes a time we can use it to our advantage. As I kept considering the measures some group took to kill him, I knew he was worth a lot to us."

Lunch was brought in and they spent the rest of the afternoon debating ways to use everything they had. Keane brought them up to date on intel from Mulina. They learned there were inconsistencies between Mulina and information on the flash drives from Knight's house.

Keane asked, "If you could have either of the Knights in an interrogation room, which one would you pick?"

Nat answered immediately, "Janet, but my gut tells me Roger is the one I'd like to lock up."

Steve said Janet as well.

"Okay let's each develop a list of questions we would like to ask Janet. Keep in mind to develop these questions using what we have learned from Knight and Mulina. When we pick her up, she will ask to have an attorney present, in which case I have a thought. If your gut is correct Nat, her brother is our focus and she may cut his balls off when she learns what we know. We won't tell her where this information came from. She won't know what to think at first. I want her head swimming. I want her on an FBI jet in St. Louis headed directly to Washington."

Nat said, "She'll know we are dead serious."

"We will hold her as a terrorist, let her know her due process rights go out the window as a threat to national security. Are you both good to stay in Washington tonight to work on the questions?"

They both nodded yes and Keane said, "Good, I have your rooms booked."

On the ride to their hotel Nat and Steve made small talk. Their driver from Homeland Security was no doubt listening as best he could. As he dropped them at the front Steve asked, "Can we meet for dinner?"

"Sure, how about one hour as she looked at her watch?"

"See you in an hour."

Check-in was quick, Mr. Keane had connections. Nat grabbed her carry-on and Steve had brought little in a backpack.

Fifty-five minutes later Steve was in the lobby followed by Nat in two minutes. He admonished himself for admiring her as she came through the lobby. He arose and awkwardly stuck out his hand as if to shake. The look she gave made him forget his name for a few seconds. Damn.

Dinner was enjoyable and not about business. They each needed a break. Nat asked about Steve's wife and other things about his personal life. He found it very interesting he wasn't wanting to discuss his wife with her. He told her about his days at UNC and being recruited by the National Security Agency.

She was less forthcoming about her past but he determined she was three years older than him and not married nor ever had been. The waiter told them the check was already taken care of and to have a nice evening. With that they headed for the elevator. Steve noticed Nat pushed floor fourteen, he pushed floor eleven. As the door opened for his floor, he looked at her to say goodnight. He looked into her eyes and realized he wanted to go to the four-teenth in the worst way.

"Good luck on your questions tonight," Nat said.

Steve looked back and could only get out, "Oh yeah."

Nat pushed the open-door button as the door began to close and gave him a smile he'd not soon forget.

"Good night."

"Good night," she said.

The next morning Steve was up early for breakfast when he saw Nat enter the dining room. He caught her eye, and she came over to join him.

"Good morning," she said.

"Good morning Nat, how'd you sleep?"

"As good as I ever do in a hotel, you?"

"Not great, too much on my mind. I worked on my list of questions and every time I thought I was done I'd come up with something else."

"That's normal for an interrogation, you keep wanting to drill down further," Nat said.

"I'm always thinking of how to word a computer search, you know looking for angles, but I rarely get to ask a direct question."

"That speaks to your line of intelligence gathering, you may like this."

"I wanted to ask your opinion, what do you think of us asking Keane if we can watch the interrogation when it happens?"

Nat said, "I wondered the same thing. I'm assuming as you probably are that Keane will conduct the questioning."

They were again informed by the waiter the check was already paid. Nat had received a text ten minutes earlier saying there would be a car waiting for them at 7:30. They walked out at 7:35 and headed for the Division of Homeland Security.

They were ushered into Keane's office and the door closed. Keane pointed to the coffee pot, they both said yes. Moe poured three cups of strong coffee and asked, "How did you do on questions?"

Both sent documents to a printer in his office and he made three copies of each.

"Let's start with Steve's thoughts."

They all perused his sheet and Moe said, "Let's read Nat's to see how we line up."

At least one *Hmmm*, happened as both sheets were surprisingly similar.

"You guys spend the night together?" Keane smirked.

This brought a small amount of crimson to Steve's face that didn't go unnoticed by Nat or Moe. His awkward chortle didn't help.

"No, but we had an intimate candlelight dinner, and I had to fend off her advances," Steve said smiling.

"Let's get to work," Keane said as Nat gave him a look that said, *you wish.*

This process took less time that Keane thought it might since they were pretty well focused on the same line of questioning.

Keane said, "Let's get you both back to your desks and talk in 24 to 48 hours, I'll call you both. Questions for me?"

Nat spoke up first, "We're assuming you'll do the questioning of Janet Knight, is that correct?"

"As of now that's yes."

"We would like to observe."

Keane had not given this much thought but replied, "Sounds like a good idea. You are both up to speed and could offer additional thoughts between sessions."

Nat was looking at a whiteboard on the wall to the left of Keane's desk. "Mr. Keane can I ask you a question?"

"Just call me Moe and I'll say yes."

"May I see the picture of the woman you have on the board?" as she pointed.

"Yes, that is Janet Knight."

It took Nat about two seconds to realize it was the woman she had seen in Knight's house.

"She was in Knight's house the day of the home show. We practically ran into each other."

"Well then she will recognize you Nat. We will make sure she sees neither of you when we question her."

With that they all rose to leave.

"See you soon Special Agent Jackson," Steve said as she headed for her ride to the airport and he headed for his own car.

Nat smiled at him.

Chapter Twenty-Four

London

Asis was very skeptical when he read the request from Roger Knight. The drop points were working as planned and communication was clear and direct. No need to word things in a clever way, just get to it.

Roger told Asis about the bus driver/farmer who had stopped the attack on the school. Asis knew the name having read all about it on the internet. There had been no mention he was one of the Hampton County farmers who had lost his farm due to all the weather and economic stresses the last few years.

This man's farm was now owned by Knight as part of his land grab that had worked so well. Roger also told him the full story about the home tour and the FBI agent being in his home. This was a concern for Asis to a lesser extent but to Knight in a big way. Another tie to this man was that his wife Sandy was one of the women in the sorority who was in Knight's home. Asis had to agree this seemed to be too much of a coincidence. Bottom line: Roger Knight wanted Asis' people to kidnap Sandy Baker. He did not share what he wanted done with Sandy Baker, but he wanted to hurt Mike Baker. Asis liked the idea much more than Roger Knight would ever know and for no other reason than to get back at the man who had stopped the attack on the school. The big hero of the little town will be sorry he ever got involved.

When Knight finds out that I'm granting this request, he'll be very indebted. When Knight finds out she's dead, he'll be terrified. Both were good as far as Asis was concerned. He will grant Knight's request to have her kidnapped. This will keep Knight in check for as long as needed.

Indianapolis

Bisma was visibly shocked when she read the mission from Asis in the latest package. Instructions were to kidnap and kill a woman from Greenville, north of Indianapolis. No reason was given and there would be no way Bisma would know any of the connections. She knew about the attack on the school that failed in Hampton County, but knew none of the connections.

Things like this were not a negotiation, when Asis gave them a mission it was to be carried out. There were several things he had the cell planning and researching along with the necessary surveillance. This was an assassination. She shook her head thinking the law enforcement capabilities in the States were very advanced. How would they get away with murder?

Bisma received little information on Sandy Baker from Greenville. There was a picture and a short bio so there would be no mistake on getting the right person. It appeared she would have to do the groundwork to figure out the best place and the best time to make this happen. She had a chill go up her spine.

Bisma got online to find any information about Sandy Baker. She was not surprised when the news article came up about Mike

Baker. She read the Indianapolis newspaper article about Mike Baker saving the school from the terrorist attack and his wife, Sandy Baker, staying by his side the entire time. It was all clear now, this was only revenge or vengeance or whatever you wanted to call it. Hurt the American by killing the mother of his children. The jihad seemed sick to her at the realization of all this.

Further research led her to the name of Nat Jackson. Jackson was a Special Agent with the FBI and had worked closely with Mike and Sandy Baker. Bisma knew Nat Jackson would work endlessly to solve the kidnapping and killing of Sandy Baker. This mission looked more dismal all the time.

In the time Bisma had been in Indianapolis she was getting very comfortable with the area. She liked the people she met. She spent time on each of the local college campuses and made conversation with students in the common areas. Bisma felt like she could fit in here just fine, become a student and get an education. This was not the Middle East, here it could happen. Her cell members had no idea she would entertain thoughts such as these. The other cell members were almost all men. There were two other females in Chicago. Her two male apartment dwellers here in Indianapolis were hard core jihadists. Most evening conversation was about wanting all infidels dead. The hatred these men had in their hearts was frightening. It was all learned from the jihadists' brothers. You were not born this way, at least Bisma hoped no one could be born this way, it was all taught. She too had been indoctrinated in the hatred and there were many things easy to hate about the United States and its people. You could see there were many Americans who hated things about their own country. They said it out loud on television and on social media.

Bisma planned to travel to Hampton County to see where Sandy Baker lived and worked. She did not want to be seen enough to be remembered. She'd look for security cameras and she needed to know the daily schedule of Mike Baker. She wanted no part of this kidnapping/murder plot, but she had no choice.

As the next few days passed Bisma grew more agitated about how to achieve this mission. Her two roommates could tell she was struggling. They were not so much worried about her; they were worried about how inaction would reflect on them if she didn't get going on this assignment.

One night Bisma said, "This is just suicide for us to murder her!"

That night Abbas lay thinking until late. He put together a plan in his mind that would solve the problem for Bisma, more importantly it would make him the martyr he longed to be. It was all keyed from her comment that this mission was suicide.

Abbas thought about it most of the next day. As usual he was out all day doing research and surveillance, making mental notes for security reasons. They had a nightly meeting to share what they learned. The verbal reports that led to questions from the other two would either bring more light on what they witnessed or help to clarify what they still needed to do. At the end of the night's meeting Abbas told Bisma and Haris he had an idea and needed their help in planning. He could do the deed but needed their brains to make the plan.

Abbas began, "Bisma you mentioned the Baker woman works at a restaurant in Greenville?"

"That is correct."

"Then I will kill her as she works with many others."

Bisma stared at Abbas and said, "What do you mean?"

"I will either wear explosives myself or take in explosives during a busy time."

There was silence at the table, Bisma and Haris could tell he was very serious and had given this some thought. She did not like the idea but it would certainly achieve the mission. It would also draw the wrath of a state and a nation. This is why they were here.

No mention was made of the attack the next evening but it was the main topic the following day. They had little in the way of weaponry in their Indianapolis apartment, but the Chicago cell had or could get what they needed. It was agreed Abbas and Bisma would drive to Chicago to meet with Hazaq and get his blessing and help.

"Bisma, do you think Hazaq will approve?"

"This is exactly what Hazaq wants, he will help you make this happen."

Chicago

Upon arriving in Chicago Abbas and Bisma sat down with Hazaq to discuss the plan, he didn't try to hide his excitement. He couldn't believe his good fortune. Jihadists under his command would carry out an attack in the heartland to truly cause terror. This same community had stopped his cell before, one man had stopped them.

"Now Mike Baker will feel the crushing grief he stopped last time! Now we will show them we will keep coming!"

Hazaq told them, "I will begin preparations immediately to get what you need."

Hazaq was off early the next morning to bring together what they needed. They had supplies for explosives hidden away at multiple locations for safe keeping. He would not bring everything back at one time for obvious reasons. He would make sure this was ready within 48 hours. The look in the eyes of Abbas showed Hazaq this would be a suicide mission. There would be no backpack or parcel left behind to possibly be compromised leading to a failed attempt. No, Abbas would wear this into the restaurant with him. Any attempt to stop him would still result in a major explosion in a crowded restaurant. The thought of someone giving their life for the jihad also sent the most chilling result to the infidels. This is what creating terror was all about. Hit your target anytime and anywhere.

The next day Hazaq called a meeting for late in the afternoon. He wanted to prepare Abbas and get he and Bisma on their way back to Indianapolis while traffic was light. He also wanted this to happen as soon as possible to make sure Abbas had no lingering second thoughts.

"Abbas you are preparing your way to Allah!"

Hazaq began this final meeting with his best jihadist inspired pep talk. A few minutes later Abbas was ready for anything, Bisma on the other hand was again wondering how it ever got this crazy. Her lack of fervor was noticed by Hazaq and had always been a worry for him. She lacked what was needed for expanding the cause. He would always have that thought in the back of his mind.

When Hazaq produced the vest that had been made for Abbas he carefully watched his eyes for any emotion and saw none. This was more good than bad but not unexpected. If he had shown fright or terror imagining himself wearing the bomb versus carrying it and then leaving it behind would have been cause for concern. That was not evident, he was resigned that this was his time to be a martyr and get his reward. He had initially thought of the plan and would see it through to the end. Hazaq was pleased.

"Let's sit down and celebrate our good fortune," Hazaq said to Abbas and Bisma.

Dinner was brought out and several others from the Chicago cell joined in the meal. It was meant as a celebration and felt like one. Everything they did chilled Bisma to the bone. She ate and was ready to leave as soon as possible. Careful packing of Abbas' vest would give them as much protection as possible if they had the misfortune of being stopped by authorities on the three-hour trip back to Indianapolis. Their worst fear could come from one of the canine units that were being used to combat the drug trade. It was well known the Interstate 65 corridor was used to move drugs between the two cities and points further, thus the chance of being stopped and searched by dogs was possible. They could hit on explosives even though these dogs were trained to detect drugs.

Chapter Twenty-Five

Greenville

It was another Saturday and Sandy had agreed to work again at the only BBQ restaurant in town, the most popular restaurant in town. The addition of several big screen TVs a couple years ago brought men to town. On Saturdays, they brought wives, girl-friends and kids if they had them. Sandy was a team player and knew this was the hardest day to get help. People liked their weekends off. For Sandy and Mike, it was different. They had a life during the week. With Mike farming and driving a school bus they had time together during the weekdays and week evenings. It may be working together on the farm but it was together, nevertheless. Sandy could make more in tips on a long Saturday afternoon into evening than she could working five nights in a week. Mike encouraged her and it worked well.

This would be a busy Saturday with several games going on with local interest. These games began at noon with the last one kicking off at 9:00 PM. Her shift would end before the last games started which was fine with her, more alcohol consumed during those late evening hours led to an unrulier bunch. She'd take the packed house afternoon into early evening. She kissed Mike goodbye and headed to town at 10:45 AM.

Sandy's friend Holly was busy wrapping silverware in paper napkins to set at tables and booths when Sandy arrived.

Holly said, "You ready for this girl?" and gave a big smile she was known for.

Sandy smiled back with a nod and a thumb up and jumped in to help. Opening was at 11:30 AM and cars were soon pulling into the lot. The day started as expected with lots of people coming and going all afternoon. At 5:15 they were full, and the entrance was filling up with people waiting. The bar area filled up fast with people waiting for tables. Sandy glanced every so often to the front. She was half expecting Mike to show up for dinner. She also knew he hated to come in while she was working and it was busy. He knew she didn't have time to sit with him. She still looked anyway.

Abbas quietly entered the restaurant at 5 minutes to 6:00 PM and asked for a table for one. He was told there would be at least a 40-minute wait, he nodded, gave the name Alex and said he'd wait by the bar. This was both good and bad for Abbas. Good so he could survey the scene and watch for Sandy Baker. Bad in that waiting was hard on the nerves. His religion did not condone the consumption of alcohol, but Abbas had an occasional beer and truth be told he liked it. Tonight he ordered a beer, a little nerve calming was in order.

He picked a spot to stand where he could see a TV, fit into the crowd and watch the comings and goings of Sandy Baker. At the 15-minute mark he ordered beer number two and decided he had a good feel for the tables Sandy was serving. The restaurant was open with few walls. The bar area was standing room only; the front entrance area was the same. Abbas downed the rest of his beer and walked up behind Sandy Baker. The family at the table gave him a look causing Sandy to turn and look at him. He put his hand in his right coat pocket and in a loud voice screamed, "Allah Akbar!!"

The detonation was instantaneous as was the searing heat. Hazaq had made sure there was enough explosives in his vest to do the job intended.

Bisma was parked about a quarter mile away in a secluded lot with no security cameras. They had just perpetrated mass murder, she was ready to carefully leave Greenville. As she pulled onto the highway to head south she was met by law enforcement, fire-trucks and responders of every kind. She waited along the side of the road as they passed with lights flashing and sirens blaring. She then made her way through town and merged on the inter-state to return to the apartment. She was supposed to be filled with excitement from a battle won, instead she was filled with remorse and a dark dread.

Sheer devastation was the only way to describe it. The inside was a charred carnage of bodies. Part of the front of the building had been blown out along with all windows on the front and sides. Responders did all they could to get to bodies as soon as possible, even though it was evident there would be no one to save. As the next 90 minutes passed, they found six people who had survived. Two were in a back corner, a mother and daughter. The mother was badly burned and her daughter was alive because her mother was sitting close enough in the booth to shield her. One person was found alive in the men's bathroom and the other three were all working in the kitchen at the time of the blast. It seemed they would survive with varying degrees of recovery time. The mother could tell the paramedics of the scream she heard, "Allah Akbar". The three men just looked at each other, they had heard of this before. This immediately went from a tragic gas leak explosion to a terrorist attack.

The same agencies who had been called after the school attack were called and on their way to Greenville along with every news team from Indianapolis. Preliminary information was being scrolled along the bottom of the screens of all local stations promising more to follow. Mention of an explosion in Greenville was all that was currently being reported.

Mike Baker was filling his evening by heating leftover pizza and opening a beer to wash it down. He had two games of interest this evening that he'd flip between. He was more interested in reading a new book. Mike reminded himself Sandy always reheated the pizza in the oven because it came out better than the microwave. He agreed she was right; he didn't like it limp. He chuckled to himself as he said out loud, "That's what she said." Mike busied himself with doing a little cleaning in the kitchen, he wanted it to look tidy when Sandy got home. He felt she deserved this plus he liked it that way as well.

With hot pizza on his plate and cold beer in hand he moved to the family room to see something on the TV that was not the game. They were doing a live *Breaking News* feed from somewhere. He listened for a second then read what was scrolling under the reporter. It said at 6:12 PM there had been an explosion at Barny's BBQ restaurant in Greenville, Indiana.

Mike knocked the TV tray over as he stood to head out the door. He grabbed his keys and headed out the front door for his truck. Mike checked his pocket for his cell phone, pulled it out and hit Sandy's number. The *phone is not in service* message did nothing to ease his worry. His foot pushed harder on the accelerator. The fifteen-minute drive to town took eleven long minutes tonight. As he approached the edge of town, he could only see flashing lights and mass confusion at the location where the restaurant had once occupied. He had to park the truck and walk. As he came near he was stopped by a yellow police tape perimeter he ducked to go under.

He was met by a deputy, "Sir you cannot come any closer."

Mike yanked his arm away and stood to face him, "My wife is working tonight and I'm…"

The deputy said, "Sir I cannot let you go further, please let me get you help."

The deputy recognized the man as Mike Baker. The incident at the school had made him a local hero which was not what Mike wanted, but he accepted it reluctantly.

Mike's cell phone was buzzing in his shirt pocket. He wanted to see Sandy's picture when he grabbed for it but instead saw the name of his best friend Brian Miller.

Mike clicked him on and answered, "Hey Brian."

Brian asked if Mike had seen the reports on TV and Mike said, "Yes I'm here now and it looks terrible."

Brian said, "Is Sandy working tonight?"

Mike said, "Yes."

There was silence and Brian said, "Can I come wait with you?"

"Okay, I'm across the highway in the parking lot."

"Be right there."

It took Brian 40 minutes to get to Mike with traffic blocked and the area in a gridlock. He might as well have walked from home two miles away. He offered his hand to Mike and Mike grabbed him for a hug. Mike may have needed someone to hold him up. The last 40 minutes had not given them any news and for sure no good news. It was just wait and watch. It would be a long night. The only hope came from seeing a few ambulances leave the scene in a hurry.

Indianapolis

Bisma arrived at the apartment and entered to find Haris watching TV. The stations were broadcasting live from Greenville and giving sketchy details of what they thought might have happened. There were already theories being tossed around with the main idea being a gas explosion in the kitchen of the restaurant. It would be very interesting to see if an *act of terrorism* theory may surface. The thought of a terrorist attack was not foreign to this Indiana town. Bisma knew Hazaq would monitor the internet for news and keep up to date. There was no need for her to make any form of contact at this time. It was their way to take credit for any death they may or may not have caused. It would be interesting to see how Asis would handle this part.

Asis was always watching for any world problem. He had ordered the death of Sandy Baker at the request of Roger Knight. The search engine had just given him a link to a major explosion in the town of Greenville, Indiana. He could not wait to see more. As he watched and read all he could he knew this was perpetrated by his cell. This was not just a murder for hire, this was a major attack on the same community where they'd failed a few months ago. This was more than he hoped. His people were well trained and prepared to further the jihadist cause. He would get confirmation as soon as possible and make sure the world knew who plunged this dagger into the heart of the Midwest.

Hazaq received the short email from Asis that told him to send more information. He laid out the plans for the attack and the confirmation and packaged the encrypted flash drive to send first thing tomorrow morning. He could not imagine how this successful attack would elevate him is Asis's eyes. He could imagine more and more power to lead the cause right here in the United States. Hazaq still wouldn't trust Bisma with too much information or responsibility, but she'd helped in a big way to make this happen. He would have to decide if he needed to send another young recruit to Indianapolis. The apartment that had three now had two. This could be explained that one had moved back home. Abbas's DNA was now mixed with the DNA from several dozen other infidels.

In the next hour Mike received a call from his son and made a call to his daughter. They were on their way back to Greenville. Mike needed them both to be with him now. He had no idea what to say to them. They were close and thus needed few words, just being together was enough.

Bisma slid between the sheets but found sleep would not come easy. Her chest felt as if there were a thousand-pound weight sitting on it. She was glad she took Abbas's cell phone before he left the car. There should be nothing left to connect him to her. She was now personally in deep. This was the first time she was involved in an attack. There was no evidence she had any part in the making of the bomb, but she had previous knowledge of the intent and that would never leave her.

What would the Americans do with someone like her? She had information about the Chicago cell and a connection in London. She had never seen the London person or spoken with him but she knew he existed. Could she trade information like that for freedom here in the United States? She shuddered to think what even having these thoughts would cost her with Hazaq. He would kill her and it would not be quick. She would take her own life before she let him get his hands on her. She would not hesitate to kill him or give him to the authorities for her freedom.

Chapter Twenty-Six

Greenville

Mike's kids arrived by sunrise. There were a lot of tears and not a lot of words.

"Dad is there any way she's okay?"

"They are telling me she is not one of the six they found alive. It was a terrible blast and people inside would have known nothing."

Mike's head dropped to his chest, and he sobbed. His kids put their arms around him and just held him.

After several minutes of letting this out Mike said, "Let's talk."

Sarah filled the tea kettle and turned on the burner. Dave got the coffee out and put it in the filter and sat with his dad. Mike had so many thoughts running through his mind. This could not be real. He imagined Sandy coming through the kitchen door and asking if there were enough water in the kettle for a cup of tea.

Mike and his kids spent the day together. They told stories all day long, they decided this was the thing Sandy would want them to do. They were sure of it. One story led to another and then another. Tears came from each one of them at different times.

Some were tears of happiness from the stories and others were of great sadness. A day full of emotion, one of many to come.

London

Asis decided to get this information out to the world as soon as possible. He used his usual channels to get the information to Syria. They were thrilled to do this. They were good at it. The black hoods went on and the filming began. Asis had given the pertinent information so the statement would be accurate and believable. He had them include a small statement about *not missing this time*. They finished the recording, did a little editing and began the process of sending it out.

Asis saw it quickly and was pleased. This was big. It would be the new one to be talked about. This was the first big attack by a suicide bomber in the States and it was in the heartland, not New York City, not Los Angeles but a small town north of Indianapolis. He would have to think about the two cell members still in Indianapolis. He felt they should keep getting established there, keep building information and maybe do some recruiting.

Asis now had a trump card on Roger Knight and he was thinking about playing it soon. He had the email Knight wrote him about having Sandy Baker kidnapped to get back at her for bringing an FBI agent to his house. He needed to make sure Knight knew he would use this if things were not going well. Keep the screws on Knight. Asis also thought he could get this information to Mike Baker and let Baker take care of Knight. This would take care of both of them for all practical purposes. Knight would be dead and Baker would be in jail or dead himself.

Greenville

It was Nat Jackson who called Mike after learning a terrorist group had taken credit for the attack. The *not missing this time* was not lost on her or the people at the FBI and Homeland Security.

"Mike this is Nat Jackson."

"Agent Jackson I was expecting to hear from you."

Nat began by giving her condolences to Mike and asked him to share them with his children. He thanked her and knew she would be thinking of them.

"Mike, I wanted you to hear this from me, a group in Syria has taken credit for the attack."

The words hit like a 2x4 on his chest. Yes, it had crossed his mind briefly, but not enough to think this could have been more than a terrible accident.

"They included a few details that made Homeland Security feel it is probably true."

There was prolonged silence at the other end. She knew this had to sink in.

"Mike would you be up to a visit from me tomorrow morning? Are your kids with you?"

"Yes, Nat please come to the house. I'll see you in the morning."

Mike clicked off and turned to face the kids. "I'm sure you heard that was Nat Jackson, she told me a terrorist group has taken responsibility for this explosion, it was a planned attack."

Stunned silence followed with more tears following this news.

"Those bastards came back and killed Mom," Dave said.

Sarah was just shaking her head in disbelief.

"Why the hell would they want to do something like that in Greenville, Indiana?" Dave said. "What have we done to them?"

None of them had the answer. It was just unbelievable. They had asked each other this same question when they heard stories of school shootings at different places in the country or any random violence where multiple deaths occurred. Why?

It was personal before as Mike was laying in the hospital bed after the attack on the school. He felt so happy he could help that day. It did not cost him his life, and he had helped. Now he couldn't feel more helpless. Someone had walked into a crowded restaurant intending to kill women and children and families. He knew rage was coming, he didn't want his kids to see it. Mike was not sure what to do, but he wanted to hurt them back. He was a Christian man, but he wanted to hurt them.

There was some sleep in the house that night. They were all spent emotionally which takes its toll. Mike was up first to make a big Chemex full of strong coffee. He fried a package of bacon, he needed something to do and knew they'd all eat bacon and scrambled eggs. He figured Nat would eat some too. Before long they saw Nat coming up the drive. Mike met her at the door where she gave him a hug. She got one back in return. She saw an extra plate at the table and pointed at herself. Mike pulled a chair out for her to sit. They passed around the bacon and eggs and ate. Coffee all around washed it down. Little talking happened while they were eating.

As they finished Sarah and Dave gathered up plates and put them in the sink and sat back down at the table.

"I am so sorry," Nat said as she looked at all of them. "It is our job to stop this kind of thing from happening and I want you to know we had nothing that gave us any sign an attack was being planned."

Mike said, "I've always heard you can stop 999 out of 1,000 attempts but if they get that one success, you feel you have failed."

Nat nodded.

"I know you are very dedicated Nat, you can't control all of the evil that goes on. How in the hell can we expect the good guys to always be a step ahead of the bad guys? We can't! But the good thing is, you usually are."

Nat said, "That one in a thousand is so devastating." All heads shook in acknowledgement.

"Mike there is not much to tell you yet, you know it was a powerful explosion."

He said, "Someone mentioned those inside would not have known what was happening."

At this Sarah began to cry.

"There is a little comfort in that, just a little." said Mike.

Nat agreed, "That is what they think."

There was not much more to say and after a few minutes, Nat told them she'd be on her way. Nat got hugs from all three Bakers and headed for the door. Mike saw her out.

"If there is anything I can do?" Mike asked.

She looked at him with sad eyes and said, "Just be with your children."

Mike shook his head and closed the door behind her.

As she drove back to Indianapolis her heart was broken for Mike and his children. She was a special agent for the FBI and expected to be strong but her heart was broken. She decided that however long it would take she would make the terrorists pay for this murderous attack.

For years Mike had been doing something he'd never kept a secret. When he would think of a memory from his past, he would scribble a note to remember it later and put it in a cigar box from his father. He had notes of his childhood, his college days and his years as a family man with Sandy and the kids. From time to time he had taken some of these notes and typed out a story. He had a lot of fun doing this. With Sandy now gone he would do more of this to honor her. He knew she would like that, and he would have his children help him. Mike found notes she had made from time to time. They weren't diaries more like journal entries from a Sunday school class or things the kids or her parents did. These things now were treasures to keep for the kids.

Mike also decided he wanted to buy a handgun. This was something Sandy never wanted in their home. He would now have one and learn to use it. He would do research on hand guns and decide what to buy. Mike had a Remington 870 pump shotgun and a Ruger 10-22 rifle. He had owned these guns since his teenage years when he talked his parents into letting him buy them. He hadn't shot anything but a target and he and Dave would shoot clay pigeons occasionally. They had a hand thrower, and both were decent at it for no more than they practiced.

It was funny why he was deciding this now, but he felt the need to have protection. Terrorists had just taken away his best friend, and he wanted to have a handgun. He was in the middle on the gun control issue which was burning hot in the States right now. Mike believed in the Second Amendment but also felt there should be good guidelines in place about who could buy one. That all sounded good except he also knew if a bad guy wanted a gun he would find a way to get it. He wanted to carry this firearm and would investigate what he needed to do to have it with him.

Their church family came together to support Mike and the kids. There was probably not a church in Greenville that didn't lose a member from the attack, some more than others. Churches helped their members and came together to support the community. Mike felt more strength from this support and the love their church showed.

It was no surprise there was news media from all over the United States that had arrived at the scene within hours of the attack. Residents were being questioned about things they knew nothing about and giving answers that were as far-fetched as you could imagine. Mike couldn't turn on the television; it was too painful to see the images and hear the reports.

Mike and the kids decided to have more of a memorial service than a traditional funeral. They gathered family pictures for a slide show and chose music to go with it. Church friends brought food for after the service. There were local friends and friends from their college days. Stories were told and retold. Sandy would have shared in some tears and appreciated lots of laughs. This lasted for hours and hours. Mike was exhausted and so were

Sarah and Dave. Lots of hugs were given and people promised to keep in touch.

Sarah and Dave stayed a few extra days and then had to head back to school. This was the time Mike had dreaded. He paced in the house. He opened closets and drawers and saw Sandy everywhere. It was still sinking in. How could it still be sinking in after spending time at the memorial and talking to people, but this time in their home without her was hitting hard. He spent time outside working on equipment and just sitting and watching the sky.

Mike went out late one evening for a walk. He was watching the sky and thinking of his dad. When he was a boy, they would work together doing evening chores. At that time Dad was raising hogs and feeding out a few steers each year. They would be out pumping water for the livestock and watching jets in the sky. As cold weather moved in during the fall, the sky looked different. Many evenings had beautiful sunsets. He'd heard the colors came from a lot of dust and other small particulates in the air, the sun coming through this dust and the wispy clouds gave beautiful colors. The two of them would see who could find the most jets in the sky. Mike thought his dad had once found fourteen jets in the sky at one time. Funny how you could remember small things such as this. Looking up at the sky brought this all back.

Mike hoped he had passed on something like this to his kids. It seemed like the legacy one would hope for.

He busied himself in the evening researching the best handgun to buy. This took a while, there were as many opinions as Google searches. He decided he would buy a Glock 21 45 caliber handgun and learn to use it. He picked out two stores and would go talk to them and decide. He was also trying to decide if he wanted to carry this gun with him, this required an extra permit, but why shouldn't he carry it? All this bad shit had not happened in his kitchen, but it had happened right in his home county. The Glock he chose was a little bigger than other choices but he wanted a gun that would knock down a bad guy. It would be easier to conceal in colder weather under a farm jacket or vest, otherwise he might leave it in his truck while he was out and about.

Mike headed out the next morning to buy a gun. He took himself out for a big breakfast so he could think. He decided he wouldn't tell his children or friends about this, and make the purchase outside of Greenville. He'd go to the south side of Indianapolis and do his practicing there as well. He shopped both of his chosen stores and found little difference in price but could get shooting range time with one for free. This made his choice easy, and he made his purchase. The paperwork would take time in Indiana and he would pick up his gun after that.

Mike spoke to a trusted friend about classes and how to use the gun. He was offered a choice of classes but also encouraged to do some practicing on the farm afterwards.

When he asked why, he was told, "You want to feel comfortable with it in the place you might need to use it."

This made perfect sense to Mike, and he filed that info away for the future. This all seemed weird to Mike as he thought about Thanksgiving coming up next week. Nothing seemed right.

The morning of Thanksgiving arrived and Mike decided they'd all stay busy. Mike was glad to have the kids back home with him. They needed each other to lean on. He wanted to give the prayer for their meal but he was choking up just thinking about it. His strength came from knowing Sandy would want them together and to be thankful for all their blessings as a family. They all had their jobs in the kitchen and were working to keep from falling over each other. They had decided on a schedule of who put what in the oven at what time and temperature. Amazing but it all made sense.

Mike had gotten persimmon pulp from a good friend. He and Sandy used to go pick up persimmons at his uncle's house and then run them through the colander together. It was messy but great fun. He always had the end result in mind, he loved persimmon pudding. He had Sandy's recipe and was following it closely. As he was stirring everything together in the big glass mixing bowl, the smell hit him. This smell of persimmons was not overly strong and the pudding baking was not an overpowering smell but it was a smell that took him back.

"Your grandmother made her pudding a different way," he said out loud to Sarah and Dave. They both looked and nodded but did not say a thing, they had both heard this story many times and were happy to let him tell it again.

"Grandma Baker put hers in the oven and about every twenty minutes she would open the oven door, pull it to the front and stir it. It was actually a pudding and we would put it on our plates with a spoon and smother it with whipped cream, real whipped cream mind you and eat it like there was nothing better on earth!"

"When did you start baking it like it we do now?" Sarah asked knowing the answer to the question.

"Your mom brought her recipe to our union from her mother and I've had it this way ever since."

"Which is best?" David asked.

"Both!"

David knew that answer was coming.

"Did you buy heavy cream to whip?"

"Nope, bought the stuff in the can," Mike answered. "That'll work."

Mike thought about his mother and grandmother. They would make a big traditional Thanksgiving dinner and always have the persimmon pudding along with pumpkin pie, sugar cream pie and pecan pie. Any other meal this big you would decline dessert but not at Thanksgiving. He had been known to have some of every dessert on the dessert table. Today Sarah was making a sugar cream pie recipe passed from Sandy's mother to Sandy to Sarah. Mike loved that pie!

The Macy's parade was on in the background as it was every year and they all worked together. Mike saw Sandy in both of his children and that made him glad and sad.

David seemed more talkative than Sarah. Their mother's death was devastating for both kids but Mike often wondered how it was for a daughter?

Chapter Twenty-Seven

Elm Grove

Roger was heading out for a Thanksgiving morning run to clear his head. The news of the explosion in Greenville had hit him hard. He had asked Asis to kidnap Sandy Baker instead they killed her along with seventy other Greenville residents. If he were ever linked to any of this his life was not worth living.

Asis would have the flash drive where he made this request, thus it was now being held over his head. Asis had him by the ass for sure now. He never considered that when he made the request.

On the other hand Roger Knight could not believe his good fortune. The holding company now owned thousands of acres of prime Indiana farmland. His grandfather would be so proud. Roger had grown up hearing the story of what might have been. How his family might have been rich and noteworthy and then how it was all taken away. They were ruined by the banks and greedy businessmen who took it all away. Roger's father had lived through this nightmare as a boy and young man. He had not done well in life himself. This was blamed on the circumstances of his childhood.

Roger loved his parents and his younger sister Janet even though they were poor and living week to week. His father had turned to alcohol as an escape and there were all those resulting problems. It all ended when his father had killed his mother one night and then took his own life with a shotgun. Roger's grandfather made the gruesome discovery when he was bringing Roger and Janet back from a weekend with the grandparents. Roger and Janet were old enough to realize what had happened, but couldn't understand why. Janet seemed to deal with it worse than Roger which indicated things to come. Janet still had feelings and cared about her parents, Roger not so much. The time spent at their calling and funeral was terrible for the children, knowing their parents were in those closed caskets because of something their father did to their mother and himself. Then it was over for Roger and he did his best to put this in a deep dark corner of his mind.

This terrible end to that generation only added to the Knight family story. Roger had decided back then he would be rich, and he didn't give a flip about who he had to hurt to get the job done. He had the "I am entitled because of what everyone has done to me attitude" and would stop at nothing. All he'd been involved in for the last few years proved he meant it. He was now the owner of thousands of acres of land and he wished his grandfather could see what he'd done. The Knights now owned more farm ground than anyone else in the state of Indiana including the same few acres his grandfather had lost in the 1930s. Interestingly enough, he had done it as a banker which was the profession his grandfather hated so much. Thus, he'd taken it away from others the way his family perceived it had happened to them. This irony was not lost on Roger but he didn't give a damn. To have done this fair and square would never have worked any-way. Knowing he had helped make this happen made him feel very proud and empowered.

Janet was terrified after the death of their parents and went off on her own tangent to be self-sufficient. She had never worried about relationships, all she needed was herself. Seeing how her father had taken out his family was enough for her concerning men. She felt the same way about her brother Roger. She didn't trust him at all, but he was all she had in the way of family. She had helped him achieve his goals of owning land by funneling money into his holding company but it was just a way of diversifying her holdings, not really to help Roger. Janet respected him as a ruthless business man but did not want to see him very much. She moved to Missouri after finishing college and remained there since.

They were about as dysfunctional as a brother and sister could be but doing well for themselves financially. Janet didn't know about Roger's dealings with anyone in London although she knew he had acquaintances there. She thought the possible fringe area they were dealing in was buying the ground from auctions of families which Roger's bank held the notes and mortgages. She felt there was nothing illegal about it but in her gut, it felt dirty. It felt even dirtier because she thought Roger was enjoying it immensely. She knew all about Grandpa Knight losing his farm to the bank but she knew it happened to a lot of others and they were not being singled out. Roger was on a personal vendetta against Indiana farmers and getting revenge as a banker. It felt wrong to her, she tried not to think about it much. She was making money due to the problems with agriculture but she had nothing to do with causing those problems. She wanted to be left alone and she'd work with Roger for now, but she wouldn't allow herself to get into any trouble for him. He wasn't worth it.

Greenville

Sleep was fitful for Mike in the days after Sandy's death. He had always dreamed, but his dreams were never too vivid or much to remember. It seemed this had changed. The thought of her life ending so abruptly and for such a reason as a terrorist attack had left him shaken to the core. He had always felt safe living in the Midwest and the southern part of the United States. Terrorism had done its job on Mike, he was now not as much scared for himself but scared for every other person he loved. His children were both in college and college campuses were places that seemed to be ripe with possible danger. The country had instances of shootings in places you would have never imagined a few years earlier.

His dreams were taking him to these bad places where his kids were hurt at college or his friends were killed in an explosion at the grocery. He never had shit like this going around in his mind before, now he wondered if it would ever end. His dreams now woke him up at night in a sweat.

One night he dreamt he came face to face with the leader of the terrorist group who had taken responsibility for the restaurant bombing. He wasn't sure what he would do, he felt the Glock he purchased in his coat pocket and aimed the handgun at the man's chest. It seemed the man had no fear and offered no resistance, Mike wasn't sure what to do until he saw the man smile. The man knew Mike was not like him, life meant something to Mike. As he started toward Mike, the gun erupted and the jihadist felt the burn in his thigh. He turned and spun to the ground. As he reached for his weapon another 45-caliber bullet hit him in his left shoulder. This pain was much worse.

Mike approached the man and kicked him hard in the back which rolled him forward. As Mike held the gun on him hoping he would make any move to give him cause for the third fatal shot he pulled out his cell phone and called Nat Jackson to tell her he needed help and with luck they would have a prisoner to interrogate.

Mike was now awake and out of bed. It seemed so damn real he was looking around for the wounded man. His gun was safely in the drawer where he left it. He sat in his recliner and replayed it over and over in his mind. He thought it might be troubling to him but honestly, he very much enjoyed shooting the man, that was the troubling part. His mind was going 100 miles per hour. He thought maybe he needed to get mentally prepared if this ever happened. He remembered perfectly how he shot the man in the leg and shoulder when he was good enough to have put a round in the middle of his chest. He wanted him alive but he more so wanted him to suffer.

Brian decided he would talk to Mike about going on a man vacation. Do man shit and eat man food. Something to get him away for a while. Brian was worried about him. Mike had grown more distant from everyone in the time since the death of Sandy.

He spent time away from Greenville and was not forthcoming on what he was doing with himself. Their best conversations happened over biscuits and gravy and his text message to Mike asked him to meet tomorrow morning. Mike saw the text and decided it would be good to see him.

The next morning, they met and ordered their normal crappy coffee and good breakfast.

Brian asked, "How you doin' old buddy?"

Mike looked at him and his expression said it all, but he answered, "Not bad."

That not bad was plenty for Brian. Not bad was plenty bad, and they both knew it. Brian had never held much back on Mike and dove in.

"Ok listen to this idea. How about the two of us head out for some man adventure? A trip south or west or east."

"Brian, I wouldn't be much fun as a travel partner right now."

"That's why we need to do it, I'm not looking for you to entertain me; I'm looking to just spend time together. I don't care if we drive for five hours and don't say a damn word, just take in this beautiful country. Let's go visit somewhere we've never been and eat good food and drink a cold beer."

"Because it's you I will say I'll think about it. I'm not going to say yes yet but I'll think about it."

"Fair enough," Brian said.

They finished breakfast and made small talk about local sports. Mike could not believe how bad the coffee was in a breakfast type of restaurant. He drank three cups to make sure it would leave him remembering how good his own Chemex coffee was compared to this stuff.

"How do you get this coffee to taste so bad?" he asked the manager as he was paying. "I love this place and will always come here but your coffee is the worst" he said in a low voice so no one else would hear.

The manager was a little stunned.

Mike said, "Do you drink your own coffee?"

The manager shook his head no and Mike smiled, "You should."

Brian told Pam of their conversation that evening and she was not surprised but optimistic that Mike might say yes.

"I will not push him, if we don't do it now then hopefully soon."

Pam shook her head in agreement.

"When are we heading out for another adventure?"

Brian smiled and said we need to plan one. They did not need to say to each other how the explosion had rocked them into thinking life and time together was precious and could be ripped away in a heartbeat. Pam missed Sandy every day.

Mike sat down that evening and brewed a hot cup of tea like his dad used to do. He turned on the television and found a ballgame. Twenty minutes later after not remembering anything he saw he was about to decide. He always teased his dad about saying no to everything and he found himself going this direction. It wasn't really what he wanted but Sandy would have gotten after him for declining Brian's offer.

"I might as well say yes," Mike said out loud to himself.

Asheville, North Carolina

Two weeks later Mike and Brian found themselves at a craft brewery on the north side of Asheville, North Carolina. The brewery was two blocks from their hotel and Mike was enjoying the distraction of being away and hearing people talk southern. He liked to say "y'all" and missed living in Georgia. He and Brian each made their choices for a flight of six local beers and critiqued as they moved from ales to porters. A young woman sat close to them and was enjoying listening to the men talk.

Thirty minutes later they headed back to the hotel and hit the hot tub to let the alcohol burn off and get ready for a good night's sleep. Mike had not had many of these since Sandy's death. They walked back and met up again after changing into swim trunks that should have been retired a decade ago. Thinking they'd have the hot tub to themselves on this chilly late fall evening, they were surprised to find the very attractive young woman they'd noticed at the brewery sitting in their hot tub.

Conversation came easily with her, maybe too easy. The conversation went down a path that surprised both of them. The woman told them how she'd always wanted to write a murder mystery. She looked to be in her early forties and neither noticed a wedding ring. She not only wanted to write it, she was downright giddy about wanting to kill someone. Both men clutched their manhood as she talked with glee. Glee is the only way to describe it. It was the middle of December and she was getting jacked up to start writing (killing) on January 1st.

She got out of the hot tub and said, "You guys wait here I've got something for you!" again in a gleeful giddy wildass tone.

What made them stay for the seven minutes it took for her to return they will never know, she returned with a bottle of wine. She stepped back into the hot tub at 2 AM and pulled the already loosened cork with her teeth and spit it over the side. She took a big swig and handed the bottle to Mike.

He accepted it with a, "What the hell," and was hoping it was not poisoned while he took a big swig himself. He liked books but did not want to be in hers. Brian followed suit and handed it back to Sue Grafton or whatever her name was. This process took three rounds to finish the bottle. They all looked at each other and laughed. Looks like glee is catching.

Mike enjoyed the best night of sleep he had in a long time. He and Brian returned home the next day full of good food and good stories.

Greenville

Mike could not get Roger Knight out of his mind. With the information Melissa gave him and learning how he'd treated Melissa in the bank lobby that one day this guy was a number one prick. Mike was not sure what to do about him. Roger was wealthy and had power in the banking industry, a person you wouldn't want to have as an enemy. It seemed he was already an enemy and Mike had done nothing to bring on his disdain.

Asis also had Roger Knight on his mind. Knight had changed since his younger days. He was now full of himself and had achieved a level of wealth and power that had gone to his head. He had alienated enough people that his mysterious death would not cause long lines of mourners. They'd probably throw a party.

Asis would not hesitate one second to make this happen if he ever thought Knight would cause him problems with the security of his cells on United States soil.

Roger Knight did not believe in much outside of himself. He was sure of himself and his accomplishments but something had crept into his mind. It was the worry of what would happen if he lost it all? His grandfather had lost everything and he didn't want that to happen to him. He also realized that having accumulated so much was amazing, but he had no one to leave it to. He had allowed no one in his life, he had taken being selfish to a new level. He was pissed these thoughts were gaining a foothold in his mind, he'd never let that happen before.

He then began thinking about who he'd call if he had a problem, his only answer was Janet. It seemed their relationship was more of a business nature than a brother and sister. He should probably work on this but it didn't seem like a good use of time. Janet didn't cultivate it either which told him something. Either it wasn't important to her or she just didn't like him. She may not like any man, she hadn't developed any relationships either. He was puzzled when he thought about that. They were so focused on building their own empires there wasn't room for anyone else. It's probably for the best, spouses would have slowed them down, gotten in the way and wanted to take half of everything anyway.

Indianapolis

Nat was in a funky mood, she had a place for this mood. This place was in the basement of her office building. The FBI had a state of the art firing range underground. Besides the normal range time everyone was expected to log each month, she usually logged more time. In times like this she had another place she liked to go. This gun range offered reduced rate memberships for law enforcement and she loved this place. She would see everyone from business people learning or trying to learn with their first weapon to parents bringing a child of varying ages to her favorite, rednecks. These guys were fun to watch.

Nat checked in with the front desk, showed her weapon and was given a lane number and targets. This day she'd forgotten to bring her own targets. She walked over and prepared to shoot. Nat owned her own ear protectors. She thought to herself, I do not own a decent frying pan but I have a pair of kick-ass ear protectors. Guess that sums up my life to this point. These thoughts did nothing to ease her foul mood, it seemed to get deeper. The shooting also did not ease this mood as it normally did. Knowing central Indiana had been attacked twice by terrorists was unimaginable to her. The times had changed and not for the better. The good guys would have to get better at stopping the bad guys. Sounded simple, but it wasn't.

She took a break to look over today's crowd. Seemed like the usual mix. She took a walk to look at a new section of the building that had recently been updated and expanded. Looking through the door she was surprised to see several people practicing with lethal looking bows and arrows. This bunch looked the redneck hunter type. She noticed one female in the bunch. This woman was very focused on using a crossbow. She appeared to be very accomplished. Funny the sight of this young woman amid all the camo seemed to lift her spirits. Maybe she would consider getting herself a crossbow. It was unlikely the Bureau would like the idea.

"Stodgy bastards!"

"What?" a fellow in full camo mode asked as he came up behind her to enter the archery room.

"Nothing," an amused Nat said as she gave him a slight smile.

She shook her head and headed back for more time on the line. She was more focused now and was rewarded with the accuracy she usually enjoyed. This was not wasted on the gentleman two rows away especially because she put nine shots from each clip into a hole the size of a half dollar. That first hole was in the target's forehead, second in the heart. She sometimes put one or two shots between the legs for good measure.

She packed up and walked out without a word to anyone.

While doing endless research on Roger Knight, Nat had stumbled onto information about Janet. She learned that Janet Knight was most proficient with a cross bow. This was back in her college days and seemingly ended after that. It may have just been an outlet from rigorous classes in Finance. The recreational class with the cross bow led to her being invited to take part on a team. She quickly rose to the top of the team and was the anchor. Her success might have been nothing more than her success at anything she did. She also liked the thought of besting the men (boys) on the team. This was revealed in an interview she had given for the school paper.

Chapter Twenty-Eight

Russell County, Indiana

Hazaq decided to hit them while they're down. He liked wielding his power and liked setting plans into motion and then letting Bisma know about it. Kept her in her place. Hazaq moved another team into place near Indianapolis and then planned for an even bigger attack. He had gained recruits in the last few months and they were all United States citizens who could blend in easily. This would make everything so much easier. Hazaq had been doing research on recreational vehicles and decided on a pull-type travel trailer. It was amazing what you could buy. These trailers were better equipped than the apartments they rented in Chicago. It would be pulled with a pickup truck and could move around freely. This would be much easier than trying to rent a house or an apartment like they had done in the past. There were RV parks everywhere, but he had his mind on another type of base for them.

Hazaq sent Chris and Joel on a Monday morning to complete the purchase of the travel trailer. They arrived at 10:15 AM at the home of the retired gentleman who had advertised his used trailer. A short period of negotiation to make things look good was followed by a handshake and a trip into town to the license branch. Nearly an hour later they walked out to make the trip back to the seller's house. He helped them with the hitch and got all lights plugged in and they were on their way after another handshake.

"I'll be damned." The seller said as he again counted out the 95 one hundred-dollar bills he had been given.

They drove away and headed directly for the RV park where they had booked seven nights in a spot at the back of the campground. They were greeted by waves from fellow campers as they pulled in to find their spot. After one wrong turn, they found their pull through spot and had no trouble getting settled. Hazaq had trained them well in addition to watching videos on the internet they learned what they needed to know. They were a little taken aback by the friendliness of other campers. This bunch of people were friendlier than Chris and Joel needed.

"I guess this is better than making us feel like outcasts."

Joel agreed, but they were still wary. They were used to keeping everyone at a distance. They unhitched the trailer and after getting the electric hooked up they were off to look around.

They found their way to the county seat which was the biggest town for several miles. They got a bite to eat and made plans. They knew what they were looking for but didn't know how long it would take. Fall was coming to a close and winter was approaching. Many older farmers would head south soon and this should make it much easier.

Five days later they found what they'd been looking for. The old abandoned barn looked like what you might see in a painting. It was off a dirt road down a long lane. Whatever house that would have accompanied this old barn was long gone. There was farm ground close but the wooly woods with some rolling hills kept the barn obscure. They knew the locals would know the barn was there and had been standing for decades. That was fine, it was better that way. The barn had been rented and was theirs until next spring. The owner was away for the winter and was happy to have extra income for Florida. The old farmer was surprised his old barn would be an artist's studio for the winter. The artists wanted their privacy and they would have it. They might also have to snowshoe their way out of the woods if they didn't keep their eye on the weather.

Chris and Joel picked a cloudy afternoon and hitched up the trailer. They pulled out of the campground on Tuesday of the following week after extending their stay a few more days. Two weeks was the maximum stay, and they made it work. They were pulling down the lane by late afternoon. Sunset was coming sooner each day. Chris pulled around and backed the trailer up to the barn doors. Joel got out and pulled the doors open. These doors were on overhead tracks and both had to be opened to get the trailer in the barn. Chris backed it in while Joel watched.

"A few feet more."

He was waving him back as he watched in the side mirror.

"Stop," he said.

The electric wires that stretched back to this barn from the road were a little worrisome, but the farmer told them there was electricity. They hooked up the trailer and everything seemed to work fine. They had also purchased a generator for back-up. They unloaded it and set it behind the trailer. Joel got in and powered up three different computers. They wanted to check the satellite dish, if it didn't work, there would be problems. All worked fine, looked like the speed was a little slow but it worked.

They unhitched the trailer, got it secured and set in place. The trailer would sleep up to eight members of the cell and cots could be set up for others as needed. There were few barn windows to deal with and they went about putting up black cloth for privacy. They did not plan on letting anyone get close to the barn while they were there but if they did, they wanted the windows secure. They locked the back door of the barn from the inside with a padlock and did the same with the front door. When the others arrived, they would always post a sentry in the woods to insure they were alone.

They settled in for the night and decided to make their way into town tomorrow to buy supplies. Chris would make purchases at multiple locations to not raise suspicions. They would buy several large containers of LP gas for their stove. Before turning in they sent Hazaq an email to let him know their day had gone as planned.

Greenville

Mike just returned home after another morning at the practice range with his Glock. He had made progress and was feeling much more comfortable carrying the weapon. He wasn't sure how he'd react in a crisis but he was doing his best to be prepared. His Remington pump shotgun sat by his side of the bed with a 12-gauge shell ready to rack into the chamber.

Mike thought about the good guys and bad guys when he was a kid. In the movies, the good guys wore white hats and the bad guys wore black with black hats. The violence was someone getting shot and falling while clutching their chest. Now you can't tell the bad guys from the good guys. They walk into a friendly restaurant wearing their suicide vest and kill innocent people. Mike had found local classes for handguns, but decided he'd keep traveling to the south side of Indianapolis to practice.

He was also getting very good with his father's Colt 45. This was the gun that would get him in trouble if he got caught. It had no providence. This gun was under the radar for Mike. As far as the government knew he was the owner of a Glock handgun. He had learned how to sight in this gun and was now aware of what he could hit and at what range. He never wanted to use it for anything other than a target, but he was prepared to do otherwise.

Mike was glad to get the text from his son David late one afternoon, it said *Dad I'd like to come home to talk to you about my future.* He texted back *It will be great to see you* and David said he'd be home next Saturday morning. Mike bought a couple rib eyes for Saturday evening along with a six pack of beer. David got home about 10:30 Saturday morning and Mike met him in the driveway. David brought home laundry and threw the first load in the washing machine. Mike poured some coffee and handed him a cup.

"How you doin' dad?"

"Doing okay son, day by day."

They drank their coffee and smeared strawberry jam on an English muffin.

"What did you want to talk about son?"

"Well I'll just put it out there. I want to join the Marines, Dad. I want to do it as soon as I finish college next May."

Mike just listened, he was not surprised. He was mainly thinking about how this would have worried Sandy and wondering if he wanted to do this because of what happened to Sandy.

"Have you already talked to a recruiter?"

David shook his head and said, "Yes I've spent time with a recruiter on campus and talked to some of the ROTC guys."

"Why Marines?"

"I want the possibility of flying or taking Seal training."

Mike finally said it, "Is this because of your mother?"

David looked at him with a hard gaze that made him look older suddenly.

"That's partially it Dad, I won't lie. I'd like the chance to take the fight to them."

Mike nodded with a look of resignation. He secretly wanted to take that new gun and put some hurt on the guys who had planned the attacks here in his home county.

"What do you want to do today son?"

David said, "Let's watch football this afternoon and just hang out together." Mike smiled and couldn't think of anything he'd rather do.

They spent the afternoon talking about things David was doing and studying at school. Funny stories with friends and a girl or two he'd met and liked. Mike talked about farming and they shed a few tears over missing Mom. The house was not the same and never would be.

Chicago

Hazaq was pleased to get the email, the first phase was complete. Their base of operations was set up and he would soon send the other three men to give them enough manpower for security details and to share guard duty. The next morning, he gathered the cell and filled them in on more of the plan. He was still withholding many details, only giving them what they needed to know. If anyone was captured, they couldn't tell what they didn't know. He picked his three to send, and they were given directions and GPS coordinates. They would take supplies with them. He sent them on their way the next morning and sat down to report to Asis.

The men left in a silver sedan with explosives hidden in the secret compartment behind the passenger air bag. This had worked well before and still seemed their best bet. They were model citizens as they left Chicago and headed south into Indiana. All traffic laws were obeyed, and they monitored traffic with their smart phones. Any sign of traffic problems would have them exiting the interstate and traveling state highways and back roads.

They made the three hour fifty-minute trip without incident and found their two cell members at the barn. They called to let them know when they were a few minutes out and arrived as planned. The vehicle was unloaded and everything stowed away. They would assemble suicide vests but did not know who would wear them yet. Hazaq had not told them how and when they would become the next martyrs.

Russell County

That night they set up a plan for guard duty and posting of a sentry. They felt confident they would not be bothered. Hazaq had asked Chris to go to Indianapolis tomorrow to meet with Bisma. He was to update her on the plan and make sure she could get them anything that might be needed over and above what they brought. She had been in Indianapolis for a few months and knew her way around better than anyone. Chris knew Hazaq did not fully trust her, but she had proven herself to the rest of the cell with her planning of the restaurant attack. He had seen her picture but they had never met.

Chris left after a sparse breakfast to make the trip into the city. Bisma met him at a Starbucks on the southeast side and they blended in with the crowd. Chris liked going to Starbucks and being with people. Since he joined the group in Chicago, there was no time to enjoy the comforts he was raised to enjoy. He believed in the jihad and their way of life but let himself enjoy his favorite hot beverage, coffee. Bisma ordered hot tea, and they sat in a corner with their backs to the wall. Seemed cliché, but it was good spy craft.

Chris filled her in on the base that was in place in the abandoned barn. She had no idea Hazaq was moving people back into the area for another mission. That seemed like they were hammering central Indiana hard when they had done nothing in the Chicago area. Guess Hazaq didn't want to shit in his own bed.

"We had three more arrive and final plans are being made." said Chris.

Bisma showed more surprise, "Sounds like five total, that's a big operation!"

Chris nodded and shrugged "We have no idea, Hazaq has us on a need to know basis."

Bisma smiled and asked, "Would you like to see around Indianapolis?"

"Sure would, I grew up in Northern Iowa and have never been here."

They walked out to Bisma's car and got in.

"Let me show you the Indianapolis Motor Speedway!"

They spent the rest of the morning driving around and talking. There was a little bit of a spark between them. Bisma liked Chris and even though she knew he was very dedicated to the cause, he was still born and raised an American and was letting it show a little. They picked a lunch spot and enjoyed their time together. Chris thanked her and said he should get back. She drove him back to Starbucks and he left. She was sorry to see him go but felt she had a new friend for the time-being. He had shared the GPS coordinates of the barn in case Bisma needed to get there to help with anything. Bisma had given him a number to safely reach her if he needed another contact. She hoped that might happen.

Over the next few days the men assembled bombs. They were making suicide vests and preparing ammunition that could be carried in backpacks and gym bags. The men were ready for jihad and their talk was basic and about death. Sometimes they talked about the death of infidels and sometimes they talked about their own. They were very calm to talk about both and each wondered if the others were as cool about all of this as they seemed. Part of their training was to not question each other about whether they could and would go through with it. This was not to be asked, rather they would discuss paradise. Inwardly they still wondered if they could push the button to detonate. Hazaq had picked Chris to inspect the vests after they were each finished. Part of his job was to add the last piece to the vest which was the remote detonator. No one knew about the remote detonator but Chris. This would cause a stir if discovered. Chris had control to detonate any vest on any man if that man failed to do so on his own. It would show a lack of trust that wouldn't go well, a lack of honor would be perceived. They would first be offended, second pissed and lastly, they'd question things Hazaq did not want them to question.

Chicago

Hazaq was wrestling with a list of potential targets suggested by Asis. Asis had done his research and always had a reason for each idea. Reasons ranged from largest number of potential victims to an area where an attack would cause the most fear and terror, the best was both. They were looking for both. Cooler weather was here which offered better concealment for their explosive vests under winter coats.

Chapter Twenty-Nine

Washington

Moe Keane decided it was time to question Janet Knight. He emailed his thoughts to Jackson and Bradshaw laying out his plan to pick her up in St. Louis and bring her to Washington by government jet. He told them he planned to pick her up in two days and would do it early that morning. Moe asked if each of them could be there that morning. Each responded in the affirmative within minutes.

Keane made the arrangements and logistics were confirmed. The timeline was to his liking and gave her no time to object. Her request for an attorney would come immediately. That request would be denied. Keane thought about allowing her to pack clothes but then decided she might be more cooperative sitting in an orange jumpsuit in white socks and sandals.

Missouri

Thursday morning came and four FBI agents out of the St. Louis office pulled into Janet's neighborhood. They stopped down the street and watched the house for a few minutes. A few days of reconnaissance told them she was very precise in pulling out of her garage at 7:10 AM. Lights always came on in the house by 6:00 AM. They had decided a 6:50 knock on her door would have her dressed and ready for her day. This day would be like no other she had ever experienced.

Two female agents knocked on her door at 6:50 AM. They made sure they were visible in her security camera. A few seconds later Janet asked through her front door speaker, "May I help you?"

"FBI, please open your door."

Janet asked to see identification, and they both held up badges. She opened the door and they stepped in.

"Ms. Knight you will accompany us for questioning regarding your brother Roger Knight."

Janet was astonished.

"Am I under arrest?"

"Not at this time."

"Then I will be going nowhere with you until I talk to my attorney."

"That is not an option, this is a matter of national security."

With that each agent took an arm and headed out the front door to further protests all the way to the waiting SUV. Another agent told her the front door was locked and secure. Janet knew that was probably a lie. This was incredible, she wasn't sure if she was in deeper than anyone could imagine or would be that much richer after she won the lawsuit for this violation of her rights.

Washington

The jet landed on schedule at 9:03 AM Eastern Time. Janet Knight had been told little. She was in denial she could be treated this way. The four FBI agents had said virtually nothing and showed no emotion at all. They wanted her to know this was serious business.

She was put into the stereotypical dark-windowed black SUV with three different agents and they were on their way.

"Where are we and where are we going?"

"You'll know soon enough Ms. Knight."

Further questions yielded no response from the agents. Twenty minutes later they pulled through the gates at the Division of Homeland Security. They made sure Janet saw this, they were waved in and after driving around the building, entered through an overhead door that shut behind them.

Forty-five minutes later Janet sat in a room like you see on TV. She was wearing an orange suit like a criminal and could not imagine how much the lawsuit would be.

Moe Keane, Nat Jackson and Steve Bradshaw were sitting in the adjoining room. They knew it would be cold in the room Knight was in. This was all part of the planning. Moe looked at his watch.

"It's time."

He picked up his yellow pad and list of questions.

"Make notes of anything you hear that needs further questioning or anything new we need to ask."

As he entered the room Janet let loose a barrage of expletives, threats, and anything else she could think of that lasted about two minutes. With that Moe stood and left the room without saying one word.

Nat and Steve smiled as he came into their room.

"Let's go have a nice long lunch."

Ninety minutes later Moe Keane came back into the room with Janet. She seemed a little more relaxed but was still ready to be mouthy.

"Ms. Knight I would suggest you be quiet. You will answer my questions and talk when you are asked a question."

Her glare was as hateful as she could make it while inwardly she knew she must be in deep shit.

Keane began by feeding her some basic information they had gleaned from her brother's laptop. Information that should get her into the right frame of mind to cooperate. Keane was trained at reading the non-verbal cues as was Nat Jackson. Janet Knight was wearing her growing discomfort plainly.

"You have questions at this point?" Keane asked.

Janet shook her head from side to side.

"Ok let's begin by you filling in some of these holes. Remember Ms. Knight your cooperation can only help you in the long run."

Janet asked, "Will you tell me why I'm not allowed representation?"

"You are being questioned as someone who poses a threat to national security."

"I for the life of me cannot fathom what you think I have done to threaten our country."

Keane said, "Let's get started."

The next two and a half days were very enlightening. A reluctant Janet Knight became more talkative when she learned what her brother had been up to over the last four years. It seemed he might very well be a threat to national security. Janet's plans to make money any way she could and invest it in Midwestern farmland with her brother was full of greed but nothing more as far as she knew. She was not part of a conspiracy.

Keane felt he had learned little in the way of new information. It seemed the real villain here was Roger Knight. He had done an admirable job of keeping his plans to himself. Janet's cooperation grew when she learned her brother was implicating her in matters that could have caused major loss of life. She claimed she didn't know a man named Alberto Mulina from Brazil and Keane was inclined to believe her on this one.

Jackson, Bradshaw and Keane had based their questioning largely on assumptions of what they thought may be the truth. Intelligence gathered from Roger Knight's computer was mostly family history. This gave them a very good idea of motive. They knew he was a narcissist son of a bitch who craved wealth and power, but the family history angle zeroed them in. They had the right guy.

Keane's ultimate goal was to get Janet Knight to a point where she would work for them. He was not to this point. Moe debriefed with Jackson and Bradshaw after each session. He had another gentleman sit in with them to watch all the interrogation.

"There's only one reason she wouldn't throw her brother under the bus," Moe said.

They all looked at him with varying amounts of emotion.

"Any guesses?"

Nat said, "She does not want to lose her fortune. If Roger goes down, she loses it all."

"My thought exactly." Moe said.

"For that reason, I will make her some promises I have no reason to honor or the authority to do so."

"So, don't be 'what the hell is he doing?' when you hear me."

"Don't over promise, she'll see through that," Steve said.

Moe nodded.

"Let's get her a decent dinner, give me some time to think and reconvene at 7:30 this evening."

"I want to get this thought in her mind tonight and let her sleep on it."

At that Moe stood and went in to tell Janet they would talk again after dinner. He sent in someone from their dining room to give her some dinner choices. They watched her interaction, and she seemed to be a more mellow person than the one they brought in two days ago.

Moe excused himself to his office leaving Steve and Nat to go to dinner. As with other government facilities this one fed its people well. Food and surroundings not over the top but good enough. They found a booth and placed their order.

Natalie could tell Steve was interested in her. She also knew he had a wife. This wife would be growing uncomfortable with a husband who was gone much more than he was home. This type of work was not at all good for a marriage, even if your spouse was also in this line of work. For this reason, Nat didn't see a full-time relationship in her future. She had desires she was trying to keep in check for several reasons.

After a nice meal it seemed they were running out of things to talk about. Moe asked they not discuss details of their detainee outside of the confines of his office or the interrogation rooms. They complied even though they felt safe here.

"You ready to head back to the room?" Nat asked.

"I'm ready to get out of here. How does a beach somewhere sound?"

"Beach? What's a beach? Is that a place where ocean meets land and people go there to relax?"

Steve smiled and gave her his best *I want to be there with you* look he could muster.

"Wait, I felt the cool water on my toes!" he said.

That made Nat smile.

"After a long walk on the beach I'll get us two drinks with little umbrellas," he said.

"You better get three," she said.

Steve looked puzzled.

"One for Mrs. Bradshaw."

Steve rested his elbows on the table and his chin on his hands and just stared at her.

Nat slid out of the booth after several quiet seconds and Steve followed her to the door. She'd be interested to see how he'd handle things going forward.

Everyone arrived back at the interrogation room and they took their seats on the observation side of the glass.

"I'll go as slow or as fast as she allows," Moe said.

With that he headed for the room.

"How was your dinner?" Moe asked Janet.

"Good enough, it would have been better with some Char-
donnay."

Moe smiled and gave her a slight nod.

Moe then launched into a carefully thought out presentation.
It was disturbing at her most basic level. He wanted her to see
everything she'd ever worked for was at risk. He did this in a
matter-of-fact, non-threatening way. She did a very nice job of
not showing her discomfort.

He gave her time to respond, but she seemed to have nothing
to say or ask.

After a few seconds for him to shuffle papers he said,
"Thoughts?"

She shook her head no.

Janet was not in her element. Her element was being the one
in control. She'd also watched enough movies in her time to
know what was happening. She was not in control, but she'd keep
as much of it as possible. Janet had always heard in any negotiation the first one to talk usually loses. For this reason, she planned
to just listen. Moe Keane had to be at the point to dump the whole
load on her and see what happened. She'd not give him anything
back, at least not yet. She was ready to get the hell out of here,
but she'd willed herself to keep the damage as small as possible.

Moe was ready to give her some rope. She was proving
tougher than he imagined, but he wasn't surprised. He began to
lay out a plan of how they might work together. The plan at the
core was for Janet Knight to become an informant for the Department of Homeland Security. It was not without risk for her, but

the risk came from her brother. Keane felt she wouldn't see becoming an informant as much risk. She listened, again without speaking, but Keane did detect some non-verbal cues at this point. It is very hard for someone to hide all their non-verbals. They can refrain from smiling and frowning but the subtler things done with the eyes and mouth and the rest of the face can speak volumes to a trained person. Now he was getting somewhere. The three people behind the glass were seeing things. One camera was focused on her face. Nat was making notes of what Moe said and what she saw on Knight's face.

"You have done a fine job of using the *he who talks lasts loses,* strategy Ms. Knight. I appreciate your tenacity, but it's now time for the equally important, 'shit or get off the pot'. Either you or your brother or both of you are involved in some deadly serious shit. If it's him and not you, I would recommend you give this plan your utmost consideration. Your answer tomorrow morning should tell me where you stand."

With that he stood and turned for the door. Janet was led to her room which was slightly more than a cell. Her toilet did have a seat. The room was also monitored by a female agent. Janet Knight would not be ending her life on their watch.

The days of wearing a wire were not gone, but technology had advanced. Everything was now wireless and much smaller and easier to conceal. Moe was looking through choices appropriate for women and found two he would consider for Ms. Knight. He would most like to have her wearing the device and not know it, but he could not guarantee she'd have it with her when she saw her brother. For this reason, he'd have to convince her to work with him.

The next morning Janet awoke from the best night's sleep she'd experienced since her arrival, not because she was more comfortable, because she was exhausted. She was told to change into a new orange jumpsuit and be ready for breakfast in ten minutes.

Keane was now ready to set the hook. The questioning up to now was not threatening or shocking, today would be different. Janet Knight was ushered into the room and sat down across from Keane.

"Good morning Ms. Knight."

"I'm not seeing the good Mr. Keane."

"Maybe not, but we'll see if we can make progress today to get you back home."

This seemed to make her eyes brighten a little, but she gave no verbal response.

"You've not been very helpful up to this point," Keane said.

"I am inclined to believe part of this may be due to the fact your brother is more complicit in things we've been discussing than you are."

Again, she gave no response.

Keane said, "We believe your brother is connected to both of the terrorist attacks that have happened in Hampton County causing serious loss of life."

"You cannot be serious!" Janet said.

"Very serious Ms. Knight."

"One of you is involved with a jihadist from England who has perpetrated attacks on American soil and caused death to American citizens. This involvement is considered an act of terrorism."

"Surely you don't think I'm involved in terrorism. I am a business person, I have no reason to harm innocent Americans."

"We're not sure you are or are not."

Janet was stunned, she had played many scenarios out in her mind but nothing like this was even close. She needed to think but Keane pressed on.

"We know of your involvement and ownership of White Oak Holdings. We know this company has purchased a large amount of farmland in the same area as the terrorist attacks. We know you were involved with a group from London with ties to the attacks."

Janet was shaking her head no at this point.

"The first two statements are correct, but ties to a group in London is absolutely false. I have no idea what you're talking about."

"Information has come our way to say otherwise."

"Then your intelligence is wrong."

"We also know your brother is involved with all of this."

"We are joint owners of White Oak Holdings and I have no reason to think he would be involved with terrorists!"

"Then you will help us find out."

"How…"

"You will pay a visit on your brother. You will be wearing a device that will let us listen to your conversation and you'll do everything I tell you. If you follow my instructions, you won't have to see your entire damn empire come crashing down around you and your brother and you might not spend the rest of your life in a Federal prison or on a table with a needle in your arm."

"You do not---"

"Don't tell me what I can and can't do Ms. Knight. You are in deep shit. If you help us, you might just help yourself."

"Need a little time to think?" Keane said.

She slowly nodded. Moe got up and left the room. A minute later they took Janet a glass of water and a package of peanut butter crackers. She tore into the crackers like she'd not eaten for days.

Keane joined Jackson and Bradshaw in the observation room.

"Well," Keane said.

Nat said, "She's ready, show her the device and tell her what to do."

"We'll follow her at all times to make sure she doesn't run, but she has too much to lose. Her life is her wealth."

"Do you think she'd give up her only brother, her only family member to save it all?"

Both Nat and Steve nodded in the affirmative.

Keane turned and headed for the door. He opened the door by almost taking it off the hinges. Janet's reaction was exactly what he hoped for. She jumped. She was rattled. Keane sat down.

"You had enough time to think?"

Before she could answer he said, "Let's move forward then."

He reached into his pocket and pulled out a necklace. It was pretty but unassuming. Something you might find at any nice department store. He laid it on the table in front of Janet.

"This is what you will wear. It provides both audio and video transmissions and everything will be recorded."

She slid her hand towards the necklace as Keane watched and waited. After several long seconds she raised her eyes to meet his.

"What do you want me to do?"

Keane outlined a plan that was not as bad as she was expecting. Janet thought to herself she could do this, and if they learned Roger was involved in terrorist activities she wanted nothing to do with him. She knew he was a narcissistic jerk, but never imagined this.

"I'll do it."

"What assurances do I have I will go free if I help you?"

Keane had expected this. She had regained some composure.

"If you help us find information that leads us further down the path of protecting this country from future attacks we'll make sure you walk away with no indictment."

"I'd like that in writing."

"That will never happen, and if you think about it, you will understand why."

"I want---"

"No shit, you want Ms. Knight, I want dozens of dead Hampton County residents alive again with their families. Not happening is it?"

She knew she had no real bargaining power here.

"Let's get on with it," she said.

Chapter Thirty

Indianapolis

Bisma kept up her day-to-day work gathering intelligence and the nightly meeting with Haris. Another member of the Chicago cell had joined them to take Abbas' place. His name was Mohid, and he was smart and probably not as reckless as Abbas. He was adapting to Indianapolis well and seemed eager to do damage to the infidels but not as much to himself. Bisma kind of liked this one but knew not to trust anyone but herself with her thoughts.

She had decided to test the water with Special Agent Natalie Jackson to cut a deal for herself. This seemed like the only way to get her away from the organization that would ultimately lead to her own death. Research on Nat Jackson led her to the decision this was not a good idea. Jackson might talk to her but her superiors might not. This led her to a farfetched idea that might work. This idea involved Mike Baker. He might listen to a woman who could help him get to the bottom of the death of his wife. Bisma could explain she was not a willing participant in the plan to blow up the restaurant. If she could get through to Baker, he might help with the FBI. It seemed he had the ear of Jackson and this might be a better route to take than trying to contact Jackson directly.

Bisma had to keep all of this in her head for the time being. She could commit nothing to paper that the others might find, that would be the end of her. She took her time and decided on a course to take. She typed her notes and got the letter printed the same day. Nothing was saved even though she knew it was never totally erased. She handled the paper and envelope while wearing gloves and put the letter in the mail.

Mike brought in the mail and besides the usual stuff had a letter with no return address that didn't look like another marketing piece to buy hearing aids. He opened the letter and read lines that left him shaking his head. After the third time through the letter he laid it down and got up to get some cold water. What the hell was he going to do about this? Mike was given no details on how he was to proceed which made no sense. His only assumption was he would hear from this person again, he hoped it would be sooner rather than later because there was enough shit in here to worry him until he did. He could sure use advice from the Boiler Club.

Bisma had done research on Mike Baker's children. Things were pretty much an open book in this country especially with Facebook and social media. She knew enough about them to worry Mike with what she wrote. Bisma had no intention of hurting his children, but she had to pose enough of a threat to keep him working with her. She also knew she was dealing with a man who just had his wife brutally murdered along with other innocent people from his hometown. He might do something desperate if given the chance. This would be multiplied if he ever learned his wife was the actual target.

Bisma knew she was playing with fire, so she moved this along. She came up with a plan to communicate safely with Baker and typed her next letter.

A few days later the afternoon mail found another strange letter in the box. Mike opened it and sat down to read. This was incredible. He was not sure if he could believe what he was reading. The letter detailed things Nat Jackson would sure love to know. It tied together loose ends that the authorities probably could never figure out. Mike's common-sense meter was going haywire, why in hell would anyone tell him all of this? What's their motive? This would be easier to believe if he knew the motive. Again the mention of his kids infuriated him, he was being extorted with the threat of harm to his children. Hadn't the family paid enough?

The letter told him to reply with his willingness to take part. Take part in what for crying out loud? There was a detailed explanation of where to leave his letter seven days from today by 3:00 PM that afternoon. This gave him a little time to think.

Mike went to church on Sunday morning and took himself out to lunch in Indianapolis. He picked a coffee shop he used to frequent with Sandy. This seemed appropriate. He unpacked his laptop and wrote. He was careful not to implicate himself in anything that would hurt him later. Hell, he was communicating with a murdering terrorist, that was implication enough. He said he would be interested in knowing more and would do nothing to endanger his children. Even though he knew it wouldn't mean shit to the person he was dealing with he asked to please only deal with him and leave his children alone. He had told no one and wouldn't share anything about the letters he received.

He saved the letter and headed home. At home he printed the letter and put it in an envelope. Tuesday he would go to the drop point in Indianapolis.

Tuesday Mike left home to have lunch at his favorite BBQ restaurant on the northwest side of Indianapolis. He and Sandy had gone there for years. It felt like home even after a couple of remodeling jobs over the years. He drank more sweet tea than he should have and got a to-go cup. He drove to the used bookstore and parked his truck. Mike was at least an hour early and wanted to just sit for a while. He wasn't sure what this would gain him, but wanted to test scenarios in his mind. He saw no one who stood out or gave him any notice. At 2:30 he entered the store and browsed the stacks. He found the photography section at the front and the shelf mentioned in the letter. He slipped the letter at the end of the stack behind the books. Satisfied it was not showing from where he stood he moved along and after browsing a few more minutes to not arouse suspicion, left after buying a book on Alexander Hamilton he'd always wanted to read.

As much as he wanted to just sit and watch everyone for the next hour he started the truck, pulled out and turned west for home. He would risk nothing that could be construed as an attempt to gain information. Mike was afraid for his children; he was not afraid for himself.

At 3:20 a young lady made her way to the front section of the store and found the photography section. She went to the third shelf from the top and pulled out a book on digital cameras. She could see the envelope, she reached in and brought it out. She carried that book and then picked out a couple more in different parts of the store. She pulled out a white sheet of paper as she moved about the store and referred to it often. When she folded it to put back in her messenger bag, the envelope went with it. This should arouse no one watching a security camera or reviewing video later. She paid for her purchases and headed for her car. The young lady drove to the parking lot of a nearby strip mall and waited.

Bisma had been watching everything that afternoon from a small restaurant near the bookstore. She saw Mike Baker come and go and her contact do the same.

She pulled up next to the young lady and put down her window, "Did you get it?"

She nodded yes. Bisma opened her door and got out, she handed the young lady an envelope and was handed another envelope in return. The young lady looked in the envelope Bisma gave her and smiled.

Bisma said, "I may need your help again."

"You know where to find me." said the young lady.

Bisma looked at her and got back in her car and left the same way she came.

David was feeling good about this plan. He'd watched his father go into the bookstore and then leave. He then waited for the call. His friend Jerry was monitoring the security cameras and had easily identified the young lady who retrieved the letter Mike Baker left. He had to admit she was good, her sleight of hand with manipulating a purse, some paper and her purchases would have led no one to see her retrieve the letter. He could give David a perfect description of her and her car. David followed her at a distance. It was a few minutes until she pulled into a strip mall. He found a spot as he saw her come to a stop. He snapped off three pictures with his smartphone before shooting video. The other car pulled alongside and things happened quickly. A woman got out of the second car and they exchanged materials. They departed and he followed the new woman. His photos will show the tags of the first woman, he needed to get the number on the new female's car.

As quick as they came they were pulling away and he would do his best to follow. At the next stoplight he got the plate of her car, it was from Illinois. He got a picture and kept following. Due to traffic, he kept getting farther behind and did not want to get aggressive enough to be noticed trying to catch up. The woman turned off Meridian Street, and it appeared she was heading into an area of apartments close to downtown. This was an area mostly inhabited by students. Two blocks later she turned left and pulled into the lot of a three-story apartment building. He pulled ahead and stopped to watch her go into a door on the northwest corner of the building.

He took a quick picture of the building and called his dad.

Mike answered on the first ring and said, "You ok?"

"Fine dad, I may have a future in this line of work! It's much like in the movies. I can see a hundred ways this could have gone wrong, but I took my time and stayed back and found where she went. I guess we have no idea if she lives here, but it's an apartment building where she stopped."

"Son I'll head that way, give me the address."

"I'm not sure of the address." David told him the streets.

"I'll be there in twenty minutes."

Twenty-four minutes later Mike pulled up alongside David, "I'll go park and come to you."

Mike found a place and got in David's car.

"Now what?"

"At this point we're making it up as we go. I'm struggling with this now, David. I feel I should probably call Nat Jackson."

David just looked at him.

"She will not believe what we've done which I feel confident is legal up to now."

"I can't see we've done anything illegal," David said. "Not yet anyway."

Over two hours later Mike said, "I've got to take a leak."

He got out of David's car and looked around. Ten minutes later he came back looking better.

"Anything?"

"Nothing. What do you think Dad?"

"Let's go get something to eat and talk."

David agreed and took Mike to his car. They drove to a restaurant just north of where they'd been sitting and had a good meal.

"I need to think, David. I do not want to play this wrong. I cannot stand the thought of getting you or your sister hurt."

David said, "We'll be fine."

Mike dismissed him saying, "I've got to be sure, I can't take any more loss."

David could understand and knew it was time to be quiet. They finished dinner and headed back to Greenville and home.

Bisma was pleased with the letter she received from Mike Baker. He promised he would cooperate. The ball was back in her court to get what she wanted from him. She'd been thinking of her options and knew he was worried for his family. Because of her Baker knew there was a terrorist cell located in central Indiana. The FBI and Homeland Security would find that information invaluable. She also knew she might not have much time to use this information. She was given no timeline from Chris on when Hazaq would want to launch an attack, for this reason she needed to keep this moving forward quickly.

Chapter Thirty-One

Indianapolis

Mike and David Baker decided there was nothing glamorous about a stakeout. Honestly, it never looked glamorous on TV anyway and it wasn't. Anything but. They arrived at 6:30 the next morning amidst the traffic of morning commuters. Everyone was going somewhere. The car David followed here yesterday was parked in the same place. They settled in to watch. Overnight they decided they would attempt to follow this woman and confront her on their terms. It might not be the wisest plan but they'd been through a lot and wanted answers. She knew what Mike looked like and they assumed David as well, but they had the element of surprise on their side. She sure as hell wasn't expecting them to be on her trail.

At 11:20 she came out the side door and headed for her car. Mike was behind the wheel of David's car instead of his truck. He started the car as she moved away. They gave her plenty of time and blended in with light traffic. It appeared she was headed back to the north side of town which was better for them; they were more familiar there. Straight north on Meridian and then right on 86th street until she turned left into a major shopping area. They followed and parked close enough to watch her car.

"This would not be good for us, you agree?"

David agreed, "To many people."

Forty minutes later she came out with a bag in her hand and fired up her car.

"Keep your fingers crossed son, I want to get this done."

Mike followed her out of the lot, she turned west. She drove a short time and turned into another strip mall and parked to enter a restaurant. This area was not as busy and they parked close this time.

"What if someone sees us go up to her Dad? Won't this look bad?"

"It could. I'll tell her we need to talk, I'll tell her we found her apartment and we'll turn her in to the FBI."

"What if she has a gun?"

"I have a gun!"

This got stunned silence from David.

"I certainly don't want to pull a gun in a parking lot, but I will if she does. She'll be damned surprised to see my face. I think she'll listen."

No sooner had he finished when she came out the door and headed to her car. They both got out and Mike headed to her car. Bisma was checking her phone and almost ran into Mike. When she looked up, her face showed her surprise.

"You wanted to talk to me lady, here I am."

Bisma pushed past and Mike grabbed her jacket.

"I don't know you, if you don't let go. I'll scream!"

"Go ahead but I know FBI Agent Jackson would like to ask you some questions."

She pulled again and Mike said, "We found your apartment downtown, we followed your contact from the bookstore and followed you yesterday with my letter."

At this Bisma knew she was blown. She could fight to get away but things had changed, she would need to think how to handle things to her advantage.

"I will talk to you but not Jackson."

Mike shook his head and said, "Come with us."

They put Bisma in the front passenger seat and David got in back. They checked her purse and did a half-hearted pat down for a weapon not knowing anything but what they'd seen on television. They found no gun.

Mike started the car and pulled out of the lot.

"Where are you taking me?"

"We need to talk in private," Mike said.

"Where?"

"You sit back and think how you can help me. You do that and we'll work something out, if not you're going straight to the FBI. Honestly, I don't give a shit about you lady. If I were like your kind I'd just kill you like you killed my wife! So like I said, sit back and think about how you can help me."

With this Bisma was quiet. She was not seeing a lot of choices for herself. She had let herself get caught. She did not know how many others besides Baker and his son knew about her. If it were only these two and she could somehow kill them, then she might get away without Hazaq finding out. This might be her only time to cut a deal, but she needed to make a deal with someone more important than Mike Baker.

Bisma got a little nervous as they left the commercial area they were in and moved into a sparsely populated residential area. Not much she could do. Baker pulled into a park, drove for a minute and pulled off into a secluded area.

"Let's get started," said Mike. "I'm sure you don't want to be around me any longer than I want to be around you. You contacted me so you start."

Bisma gave him a long stare and decided how she would play this.

"I want to first tell you I am very sorry for the loss of your wife."

"Are you shitting me? Spare me."

"No wait," Bisma said, "When you hear what I will tell you, you will understand my feelings."

Mike looked at her with an expression of disgust. "Go ahead."

Bisma then told a story of how she had been brought into the organization. She was all alone after losing her parents. Bisma did not give enough details so Mike or his son could corroborate her story. She did not know what she was getting into until it was too late and she always felt threatened after that.

"It's like how gangs work in this country. You're forever a part of the group."

"So talking to us is dangerous for you?"

She nodded in the affirmative. Mike was not sure if this was good or bad, he may put his son and himself in more danger. He could get out of his league quickly.

"Okay, so again you contacted me, what are you wanting?"

Here goes she thought.

"I want out of this, I want to stay in this country and go to school."

"You're wanting asylum or to be in the witness protection program or something like that?"

"Yes exactly. I have valuable information that should be worth giving me protection. They wouldn't hesitate for one minute to kill me so I need assurances."

Mike said, "Then why in the hell did you come to me, I have no power to get you any of these things."

"I knew that, but I think you have enough influence and are liked well enough to negotiate for me."

"What if I can, how can we trust each other? How do I know you will not be gone forever by tomorrow morning?"

"You don't Mr. Baker, but I think you can see my sincerity."

"Well I can believe someone in your situation would want out. Everything seems like a one-way street to a premature death for a terrorist."

Her eyes said he was right.

Bisma said, "I will give you the location of a cell that has moved into central Indiana and is planning another attack."

"That would be dangerous for you?"

She shook her head yes.

"I would like you to explore options for my safety. I am not willing to give myself up to your law enforcement without assurances. You find out what they will guarantee and I'll give you further information."

Mike had to think. If they take her back to her car and let her go, there would be a chance he'd never see her again. Nat Jackson would never forgive him if she found out. Nat had been on the side of the Boiler Club from the beginning and he knew she cared about them. Keeping her out of the loop seemed like the wrong thing to do but if he went to her what could she do? He had always heard the U.S. doesn't bargain with terrorists; he was not sure if this meant we would not offer them safety for information.

Mike had done his best to think this through ahead of time but there was so much he hadn't anticipated. He saw no way to move forward without trusting her. Mike and David were not enough manpower by themselves to keep watch over Bisma. Even if they could, she might contact someone from the cell to kill them. He had to trust her, but they'd take precautions to protect themselves. David would be with him for a few more days, they'd have to make as much progress as possible in short time.

"Before we let you go we need to decide on how to communicate."

Bisma looked at Mike, "Any communication going forward is very dangerous for me, not so much for you."

"Okay, you people do this shit, what works for you?"

She was surprised, this made her smile at him. Americans were straight forward with their talk.

"Well I guess I'm not as good as I thought I was or we wouldn't be sitting here right now Mr. Baker."

Mike nodded.

Bisma said, "Let's meet at this public park, no cameras. If you need to see me call this number."

She wrote a number on a piece of paper including GPS coordinates and handed it to him. Mike looked skeptical.

"It's a burner like drug dealers use. I'll check it daily. That is coordinates where the cell is located. Please try to get my safety!"

He folded the paper and put it in his front pants pocket.

"Let's get you back to your car."

David watched her get back into his car. She seemed to be five feet three inches of spunk. In any other situation he would be figuring a way to ask her to coffee. Her dark complexion and dark eyes cast a spell.

With that they got back in and headed back to 86th street. It was a short drive back east, and they dropped her off with no one talking.

Mike's plans and thoughts would be very dangerous. He in no way wanted David to be involved in any of this fight. He'd shared nothing with David when it came to any violence he was considering perpetrating on this terrorist cell. For all he knew he would back out at the last moment and turn it all over to Nat Jackson anyway. This was the only correct way to do it, but Mike was not feeling like being correct. He wasn't in a state of mind where he couldn't tell right from wrong, he was perfectly lucid in his thinking. Mike wanted to hurt these bastards like they'd hurt his family. It seemed they could do whatever they pleased to whomever they wanted. They knew they could go down in a hail of bullets or with a suicide vest on their own terms. Mike wanted them to feel fear, he wanted them to feel threatened they might be hunted down and blown to hell while having their dinner or saying their afternoon prayers.

Mike knew what happened to the two deputies when they approached the first cell on the old Hinkle farm. They were killed without a second thought and then the cell left behind explosives to kill more law enforcement when they came to investigate. For that reason, he had to plan carefully. David and Sarah had already lost their uncle, grandfather and mother to these assholes. Mike didn't want to add to their grief. He also knew what he was thinking was illegal in the United States, it was cold blooded-murder.

Greenville

As Mike continued to think about his plan over the next 48 hours he was struck with the thought he had no time to wait for the perfect plan. If he waited, and the cell made an attack, he would never forgive himself for not acting and/or alerting Nat Jackson. He'd probably be indicted. Turning it over to Nat seemed the most logical and safe choice for him and everyone else. On the other side, there is no way the FBI would put the same hurt on this basket of turds that he might do. He had no way of knowing what they may have in place for security. Funny how you think you know more than you do, but after years of watching movies and seeing things like night vision goggles, trip wires leading to claymore mines, booby traps found in the jungles of Vietnam and guard dogs you think twice about your actual capabilities.

All of this led him to the idea he would just have to walk in like he owned the place to do reconnaissance. He decided to do this in a personal vehicle wouldn't be as safe as coming in with a company vehicle. The terrorists would surely be wary of hurting someone in a company vehicle. This would take some thinking.

Bisma had told him little, but she had shared that part of the cell was Caucasian Americans from the Midwest who wanted to be part of the jihad. They blended in which gave the cell several advantages. It was easier to move around and shop and fuel vehicles, etc. This could work to his advantage. It would be easier for Mike to talk to these guys. This cell was about a 75-minute drive from Greenville and he was counting on them not knowing him. He'd do a bit of disguising himself to help including having about five days of growth already going on his face.

Mike had a man in mind over the past few days he thought might be an interesting resource. This gentleman had fought in World War II and then came home to farm for the last six decades. This man had three children, one of them a Vietnam veteran and his son was stationed somewhere in the Middle East currently. Roy was about as Mom and apple pie as an American could be. He was also *old school*, and Mike knew he did not like how things were going in the country especially the terrorist attacks in Central Indiana the last couple years.

Mike gave Roy a call to see if he might stop by for a chat. This was not a conversation he wanted to have in the local diner, this was better suited for the privacy of the outdoors.

"Roy, this is Mike Baker, how you doin'?"

Roy gave a little chuckle, "Mike I'm doing fine and I know you are troubled about a lot of things."

"That's for sure."

"What can I do for you son?"

"I'd like to come over for a visit, I'd like your opinion on some things."

"Not sure that's worth much but you're welcome anytime."

"How about tomorrow morning about 8:00?"

"See you then Mike."

"Thanks Roy."

Mike spent the evening deciding how much he wanted to tell and ask Roy. He felt confident he could trust him and wanted to make sure not to put Roy in any danger. He sat down to make notes that would end up being burned before tomorrow was over.

Mike left the next morning with two cups of coffee from his Chemex warming him up and building his nerve. It was a fifteen-minute drive to Roy's farm. Mike pulled in and headed back the lane to the barn. Sure enough Roy was in the barn and still feeding calves.

"Morning Mike, you want coffee up at the house?"

"No thanks Roy, had plenty already. May head behind the barn to get rid of some."

"Make yourself at home."

"Roy, you know what has been going on with me I guess?"

"Sure do and I'm so sorry for all of it."

"I'm sorry for my kids, me, you and our whole country."

"Me too Mike, I don't like what I'm seeing in a lot of areas."

"That's why I'm here. I always like to visit with you Roy, but today I need advice."

"Sounds serious, I'll do my best, fire away."

Mike went into a fifteen-minute story to bring Roy up to date. Roy listened, nodded and shook his head a few times. This was all unbelievable.

"I'm not sure what to say Mike."

"I understand. I feel I need to act pretty quickly either way."

"I can see why. What you are doing tomorrow morning?"

"Coming back to see you I think."

"Sounds good, come back the same time tomorrow morning."

With that Mike pointed around behind the barn and Roy smiled. "Make yourself at home, see you in the morning."

Mike headed for his truck after taking care of business and turned right to go home.

Indianapolis

Bisma was doing her best to keep it all together. She didn't want to show any signs of worry or anything out of the ordinary to her roommates. Her new relationship with Mike Baker had more chances of going wrong than right, but she did not have many choices at this point. He and his son knew where she lived and she had given him information on the cell and its location. She needed something to get her mind off everything. Her best day in a long time was showing Chris around Indianapolis. This was Chris who was an American homegrown terrorist who wanted to kill as many innocent people as he could and go out in a blaze of glory. She wondered what it would be like to have a normal friend?

She went to the Student Union and mingled with students having lunch and coffee and hanging out. This was as close to normal as she could get. It was a short walk and a brisk day. Bisma felt boxed in as to what she could do next. She was not in control and she didn't like it. She very much wanted to see Chris again. Bisma felt comfortable with him and somehow safe.

Greenville

At 7:58 the next morning Mike came pulling into Roy's lane and then drove back to the barn. Roy was feeding as he had been yesterday and waved Mike into the barn.

"Mike I've had time to think and I have an idea or two."

"Morning Roy!"

Roy smiled, "Yes Good Morning! Guess I have things on my mind."

"I understand and hope I didn't ruin your day and yesterday evening."

"Not at all. I want to do bad things to these people and a man of my age does not have a lot to offer you in the way of muscle."

"I hope I'm half the man you are when I get to be your age."

Roy smiled again.

"Mike, my son works for a co-op selling fertilizer and herbicides. You know him?"

"Yeah I know who he is. He was enough younger than me that we never got close, and then I was off to Purdue and then Georgia."

"I think I'll have my son leave one of his company pickup trucks here for a day or two and you can use it to approach the barn we discussed."

"It will give you cause to be there. They are all equipped with radios and have nice big antennas showing."

"Ok I like that idea. It gets me there with due cause. I could tell them I am looking for the owner to discuss applying lime before planting time."

"Tell them there are several of you out working the county."

"I like that."

"Ok Mike, what do you plan to do?"

"I want to get close and get a feel for the layout. I'm not sure if I'll make a move soon or call the authorities. With the truck I'll just do surveillance."

Roy nodded. "I'll call you when the truck is available."

"Ok, thanks Roy"

They shook hands and Mike turned for his truck.

At 8:10 PM Mike phone buzzed. It was Roy.

"Hey Roy."

"Your truck is ready and sitting at my farm."

"Thanks Roy. Give me a day and I'll call you when I am coming to get it."

"Fair enough, I'll wait to hear from you. Good night."

"Night Roy." They both ended the call.

Mike's plan wasn't very detailed. He would drive up to the barn and get out to see who came out to meet him. He planned to go in the morning to get the truck and then make the drive to the farm. If he left Roy's place around 9:00 AM, he could be at the farm by 10:30. He'd not included Nat in any of this and he knew she would not be pleased.

Morning arrived, and he had breakfast and coffee. He called Roy and said he was on his way. "Keys are on the seat and the fuel tank is full."

"Thanks Roy."

Mike clicked off. A few minutes later he was firing up the newer model Ford and heading out to begin the trip. The morning was clear, and the drive was uneventful. As he neared the area to the farm, he exited the interstate and found a fast food place to use the rest room and clear his head. He got a cup of coffee and sat down to go over his plan. Ten minutes later he was as ready as he would be and headed out. It was a pretty drive through this part of the county with farmland more rolling than Hampton County. He found the lane and turned in to drive back to the barn. It was back off the road and Mike could see why they picked this place. He was still over a quarter mile from the barn when he saw two men come out the side door. He would have greeters.

Mike was a little surprised to see two young men who looked like farmers approach his truck. He had done some racial profiling in his head and was expecting to see men of Middle Eastern descent even though Bisma told him otherwise. These guys were regular guys from rural Indiana. He felt bad about this for three or four different reasons that he didn't have time to dwell on now.

"Good morning." One farmer said in a raised voice. Mike offered the same greeting back to them as he stepped out of the truck.

"I won't keep you fellows long, I'm just out looking for new business."

"Looks like you work for the co-op."

Mike nodded in the affirmative and asked, "You ever do any business with us?"

"No we haven't, we're not farming this land, we're just renting the barn for the winter."

Mike was surprised at this answer. It didn't leave him any room to question further, but he asked, "Are you businessmen?"

"No, we are artists and have come to the country for inspiration and to get away from the city for a while. We appreciate you stopping but the landowner is wintering in Florida, you will need to talk to him to discuss his farming operation."

Mike smiled and extended his hand. "Okay then, nice to meet you gentleman, good luck with your work."

They smiled and shook his hand. Mike turned to leave, he did his best not to show any emotion or reaction to any of their conversation. Inside he was boiling. Artists my ass, you are two young boys wanting to kill your fellow Americans. Mike found this worse than the foreign terrorists who sneak into the country to do the same.

He made the trip back to Roy's farm, left the key on the front seat and not seeing Roy's truck anywhere headed for home.

Russell County

Chris walked back to the barn with his friend. They entered and were immediately asked what that was about. Their Middle Eastern brothers were more tense dealing with the locals.

"It was just a salesman for the local co-op. He said he sells supplies to local farmers, and was out looking for business. No big deal," Chris said.

"Anytime someone sees us it's a big deal," one said.

Chris shrugged his shoulders and headed into the RV. Chris sat by himself at the table, he was pleased he had time to think. He always did his best to keep up with the local news. The others were not interested. If they had been more aware, they might have realized that local co-op salesman was Mike Baker. The Mike Baker who had just lost his wife to a terrorist bomber in Greenville. There are coincidences in life but there is no way that Mike

Baker who lives over two counties away just pulled up in front of this remote barn to sell him fertilizer. How in the hell did Mike Baker know where they were?

Chris had not had contact with Moe Keane in months. This was the way it had to be for Chris to stay alive. He wondered if Moe Keane would be involved with Mike Baker, he had to be. Attacks like the ones that had happened in Indiana would certainly involve Keane. Could Keane have sent Mike Baker to look for Chris? He surely wouldn't have sent a citizen; he would have sent a trained operative. He had to admit Mike Baker had guts because if the others had recognized him they would have wanted to either take him or kill him.

Chris wanted to make another contact with Bisma while there was still time. Something would happen soon, and he was running out of time. Chris grew up in Iowa and loved to hunt and fish. He was comfortable with a gun and a bow. He preferred camouflage to khakis but liked a good pair of jeans. Chris enjoyed physical sports, he was a good defensive back on the high school football team and ran track each spring. His real sport was wrestling; he was as scrappy as they come. He was good enough to earn a scholarship to a Division III school and was happy to have help with his education. The military was always in the back of his mind and he'd talked to several recruiters over the years. Nothing sounded like what he was looking for, but he impressed more than one recruiter.

Young men and women like this were not forgotten by the recruiters. All branches kept their eyes open for people who might be suited to serve their country in other ways. Special ways that came about after the attacks of 9/11. Chris Powell's name made it on a list that ended up on Moe Keane's desk five years ago.

Mr. Keane showed up at his apartment late one September afternoon and introduced himself as an officer from Homeland Security.

Chris raised his eyebrows, "Am I in trouble?" Mr. Keane.

"Not at all, I'd like to have a private conversation."

"Ok but I'd prefer a public place, I'm not getting in your car."

This quick awareness and bold answer impressed Moe. This kid can stand up for himself, he thought.

"Let's walk somewhere we can get a bite to eat, your choice."

Chris grabbed his jacket, and they headed for the student union. They ordered burgers and coffee and talked for over an hour. Moe spelled out enough details of what he was looking for and Chris was intrigued. Moe told him this was all confidential and any talk of it to anyone else would nullify any future possibilities. There would be substantial vetting before he could move forward, he now needed to think. They agreed to talk again in three days and Moe gave him a secure number to call.

Moe paid the bill, they shook hands and Moe was on his way. Chris took the long way back to his apartment. Looks like his life had taken a big turn as of today.

Chris made the call after lunch on day two. He wanted to talk more but had decided to serve his country. He asked to complete the semester.

Moe said, "Yes but I need you to fly to Washington on your fall break in two weeks."

"Sure."

"Flight information will be in your email; you print your boarding pass."

"You need my email?"

"I have it."

"If you need anything between now and then call this number, do not respond to the email."

"Yes sir, see you in two weeks."

The line went dead. This would be interesting, man of few words. Looks like he was leaving Waverly, Iowa behind as of Christmas break.

Five years later he was living in an RV in a barn with people who wanted to kill innocent Americans and he'd do whatever it would take to stop that from happening. He knew Bisma had information about cell members further up the food chain and he wanted that information.

He had given her the GPS coordinates of the cell location. This had not been authorized by Hazaq but Chris knew Bisma was an important player for the Chicago jihadists. He was working on dreaming up a reason to call her. To be honest, it was to see what more he could learn plus he would enjoy time with her. There had been no time for personal thoughts since this operation began. These guys were very focused and only interested in the virgins promised after becoming a martyr. Chris was more practical.

Chapter Thirty-Three

Missouri

Janet's quick return home had happened as fast as she left. Her mind was numb. She was astounded and not sure who to be mad at. She was pissed at Homeland Security and the FBI for violating her rights, she was also pissed at her brother. They had worked hard to amass a fortune of investments and real estate. She really didn't care about the farmland like Roger did, but she wanted it to be a source of income and good diversification for her security portfolio. The bottom line was she would do anything to keep her assets. If Roger had done things to endanger this, she had no use for him.

She would contact him, travel to Indiana, and see what she could find out. Keane had provided her with questions and encouraged her to make them her own. He didn't care how she asked them, but he wanted answers. She was at a point where she wanted those answers as well. She was also damned scared of the answers she might get.

Elm Grove

Roger read the email from his sister and smiled to himself. Another visit from Janet. How exciting, these visits never ended well. There was always a problem, something she didn't like. She needs to stay in Missouri. He responded and asked if the visit was necessary. That would not go over well.

He had his answer in ten minutes, she'd be here tomorrow afternoon.

Greenville

Mike knew he had to decide on his next move. There was really no decision to make, he had to tell Nat Jackson what he knew. He wanted to try something though. It would be stupid, but he was at that time when things did not have to make sense. He wanted to hit back for the American people. He wanted to hit the enemy like our government would not do, at least not on our soil. Our troops could attack an enemy base in a war zone. This was Russell County, Indiana. The enemy was actively planning an attack based out of a barn on a farm. Mike liked old barns, had been known to photograph them. Terrorists making bombs and planning an attack out of an old barn pissed him off even more.

Indianapolis

Bisma had not heard from Mike Baker or Chris in two weeks. She knew each day brought them closer to whatever attack was being planned next. She decided she would contact Chris to ask if she could help in any way. Any information he would give her could be something to give Mike Baker to secure her future freedom. She had the cell number for Chris and sent him a text.

"Hello from your tour guide in Indianapolis, can you meet me this afternoon at our favorite Starbucks?"

Chris felt his phone vibrate in his pocket. He pulled it out to see the text and gave a small smile. He would sure as hell like to get away for a few hours. Each day the tension seemed to grow within the group of jihadists.

"Sure, what time?" he answered.

Bisma was happy at the quick response.

"3:00 PM."

"See you then."

She had the rest of the day to figure out how to get information. Her plan was no more than wanting to know if there was anything they needed. Hazaq had not asked her to do this and he would not be pleased with her when he found out, she thought it was worth the risk.

Russell County

Joel was stepping out of the RV as Chris walked into the barn.

"I got a text from our contact in Indianapolis, she told me to meet her in Indianapolis this afternoon."

"What is that about?"

"No idea, but I told her I would be there."

"Ok I'll go with you."

"No, she asked for me to come alone."

"Why would she---?"

"I'm not sure Joel but I won't go against them, I'll go alone."

Joel didn't like it, he also wanted to get away from this farm for a while. Chris seemed to have gained more power over the last few weeks with their middle-eastern brethren, and Joel didn't like being his second.

Chris had not gotten the visit from Mike Baker off his mind. This meant something, he had dreamed up about two dozen scenarios of what that might be. Bisma would know Mike Baker, would there be any harm in telling her of his visit? The only harm may be in Bisma wondering how Chris knew of Mike Baker, but he would tell her about seeing his picture in the Indianapolis newspaper after the attack in Hampton County when his wife was killed. This was no stretch; it was the truth.

Elm Grove

Roger left work early to make sure he was home before Janet arrived. He got home to see nothing needed to be cleaned, it was immaculate. He poured some bourbon to get himself ready. She arrived ten minutes earlier than she told him and he met her at the door. She carried a small overnight bag telling him this would be a short visit, the best kind.

"How was your trip?" Roger asked.

"Boring."

"Okay, well come on in."

Roger knew this would probably be a short visit, but not a sweet visit. No surprise.

Janet asked, "Have you eaten?"

"No I was waiting for you. Care if we order Chinese?"

"That sounds fine, will they deliver?"

"Sure."

Roger pulled up the menu and let Janet give it a look. She made a quick decision, and he ordered and paid.

"It says delivery in 25 minutes."

"Pour me some bourbon," Janet said.

Roger poured one for each and made it three fingers.

"Ice?" he asked.

"Yes."

Roger got ice for them both and they sat to talk.

Janet had the desire to interrogate Roger like what she went through in Washington. If only a part of what they implied was true, he deserved to be squeezed. She had played this conversation over in her mind many times. He may have jeopardized everything for both of them. With one last little fidget of her special necklace from Moe Keane she started the conversation.

"How are things going with the farm ground?"

"As you know I get monthly reports from the holding company. The current state of agriculture is not great but has improved in the last two years. Land values have fallen a little but again not enough to cause us worry. The farmer employees have done a great job, many are customers of my bank."

"That all sounds positive. We need those farmers," Janet said.

"Agreed."

Janet then dialed in a little closer to the questions she wanted answered but decided it might be best to let the bourbon do its work on him. When the doorbell rang Roger stood to answer. Janet got up and headed to the kitchen to get a glass of water.

They ate in silence and continued the conversation after dinner. She could not let her questioning give him any idea of what she was after. After clearing dishes and loading the dishwasher more bourbon was poured, and they walked in to sit by the fireplace.

"Roger is there anything I need to know about everything that has happened over the last few years?"

He gave her a quizzical look.

"Is there anything you can tell me for our protection?"

"Not that I can think of. Agriculture went to hell a few years ago, and we were able to take advantage of it. I don't feel one bit of remorse for buying farm ground and then allowing the poor jerks who lost it continue to farm it and pay us."

Janet was ruthless when it came to her own business but this gave her some chill. He did not give a damn about anyone else. She was silly to think he would say anything to implicate himself to her. Let him have a few hours in an orange jumpsuit with Keane across the table. As much as she would like that she also didn't want that. If he were guilty, then she would go down with him. No, it would be better if Roger never sat down with Keane.

"I am heading for bed, I'm tired. Thank you for dinner and letting me come on short notice."

"You're welcome. Janet are you ok?"

"Yes, I'm fine. I wanted to get an update and sit down to talk."

"Well I'm glad you came, sleep well."

"Thanks."

"Will you be staying tomorrow?"

"No, I'm off in the morning."

With that she was off to bed and Roger was a little stunned how uncontentious this visit had been. As was his way it unsettled him a little. As she said she was up and ready to leave the next morning before Roger was ready to leave.

Missouri

Janet took the next two days to think after making the six-hour drive back home. She knew she would hear from Keane's people with nothing to report to them. She knew all along that Roger would not tell her things that had been implied while she was being questioned. She was inwardly happy he hadn't told her all the things he'd probably done. Janet had nothing to tell or to weigh on her own conscience. She knew Keane would not be happy that she hadn't pressed her brother more. There were no instructions when she would hear from them. The only thing that kept coming to her was she did not want Roger to reveal his past history.

Chapter Thirty-Four

Indianapolis

Mike was at a point where he was about to burst. He wanted revenge. He had played scenarios over and over in his mind about how he could attack the cell and kill them all. Shortly after this daydream he had the vision where he fell into a trap and they took him captive. With no one knowing where he was this turned out bleak and he tried not to let himself imagine what they might do to him. He was confident they would not kill an infidel easily and especially if they had any idea he was the one who stopped their attack on the school.

Mike jumped in his truck and made his way to the interstate. He was heading for Nat Jackson's office. He called her cell; she answered on the second ring.

"Hey Mike, what's up?"

"I need to see you right away."

"You okay?"

"Yeah, I'm fine mostly, but I have to see you."

"When do you want to meet?"

"I'm heading to your office, I'm almost there."

"Okay it must be important then, you know the drill at the entrance."

"Yes I do."

"See you in a few minutes," Nat said.

Mike clicked off and was feeling better already. He knew he was in for something in between a butt-chewing and a tongue lashing, whatever the hell that meant.

He pulled into the lot and found visitor parking and headed into the building. Mike showed his driver's license and was told to wait for Agent Jackson. Nat was waving to him within two minutes to follow her up. She closed the door behind them and turned to face Mike.

"This sounded urgent," she said.

"I guess this is a story you need to hear and a confession for me."

"I'm all ears."

Mike tore into the story of his children being threatened by someone in a letter. He was told not to go to the authorities and after careful consideration he did not. He told her how he and David decided upon a plan to track whoever was sending him letters. She was not trying to hide any emotion and knew her face was getting flushed. He told her how they tracked the woman and then confronted her. They had forced her into his vehicle and took her to a nearby park to question her. Nat's head was nodding side to side by this time.

"Do you have any idea how wrong that stunt could have gone?"

"We thought we did, but probably not."

"Go on," she said.

He told Nat about getting information on the terrorist cell and GPS coordinates of their location. He ended by telling her he had driven to the farm and talked to two men who came out to his truck.

"Jesus Mike, it's a wonder you're standing here! Those animals could have cut your throat or something worse."

"I know, it all crossed my mind many times. I told them I worked for the local co-op and was looking for new business. I told them there were several of us in the area calling on farmers."

"That probably caused them to not want to be a part of a search for a missing salesman, but it was still a damn stupid thing to do."

"I agree and that's why I'm here now."

"Mike, you need to sit down and I need to think. I need to get this information to Moe Keane. You've told me there is a terrorist cell outside of Indianapolis living in a barn and planning an attack that could happen at any moment. He will be pissed beyond measure when he finds out you were withholding this information costing us valuable time."

Mike nodded and sat down by her desk.

Nat walked over and made the call to Moe Keane. She gave him a short version of the story but made sure he knew there was an active terrorist cell close by.

"Stay by your phone," Moe said and clicked off.

"He pissed?" Mike asked.

"Be glad he's 600 miles from here. My guess is we'll be seeing him this afternoon."

"Tell me about the two men who came out to the truck."

Mike described them both. He could see them as if they were in the room with him now. Nat was surprised to learn they were both Caucasian. This was profiling, but it surprised her. The enemy recruiting from within our borders was no surprise but this... Her phone rang.

"Meet me at the Indianapolis Executive Airport at 2:30 and bring Baker with you."

"Will do." Before she finished do, he had clicked off.

"Picking him up at 2:30 north of Indy and he wants you to be there."

"Ok," Mike said.

Ice tea and a Reuben sandwich calmed Mike's nerves before they left to pick up Keane. Mike knew this airport; he'd been driving past it since he was a kid. They arrived early and pulled into the lot. Nat had barely spoken since leaving the FBI building on the northeast side of Indianapolis.

"I advise you to answer his questions carefully Mike, it will be all business."

They sat in silence watching for the small turbo jet. All flights arrive from north to south and it was not long until they saw the small jet. A smooth landing was followed by a quick turn and taxiing back to the hangar area. No sooner than the jet came to a stop and the engines were spooling down, the door opened and Moe Keane was coming down the stairs with a small *bug out* bag he always kept in his office. He walked to the passenger side of the black SUV and opened the back door.

"Back to your office Agent Jackson."

Before Nat could say a word, Keane started on Baker.

"Mr. Baker I have great respect for what you and your family have endured at the hands of terrorists. I cannot blame you for wanting to hit back and here comes the but, but this is not the way to get revenge. If this group hits a target before we can get to them, you know it is bad. Hell, it's bad on every level. Every government agency is put under a microscope by everyone in America when something terrible happens. Everyone wonders "why didn't you stop this?" I have read and seen enough about you to know you understand exactly what I'm saying. So enough of this, let's get to work."

Mike was trying not to let them see the deep breath he was currently sucking into his lungs. He hadn't taken a breath for most of that short speech and he had lived through it. He was relieved to have this in the proper hands for himself and his kids.

"Agent Jackson I have spoken to my contact at the FBI and an assault team is being assembled. You and I will accompany the team and we will go in tonight. Mr. Baker you will give us a detailed description of the farm, everything you can think of including what you noticed about the barn. We will access satellite photos using the GPS coordinates you were given. We will also plan a raid to pick up the contact you made in Indianapolis."

At this point Mike thought he had to interrupt.

"Mr. Keane I made promises to this lady. Her name is Bisma. She is wanting to help us."

"Mr. Baker you made promises you couldn't keep."

"Maybe so, but I put my ass out there to try to make a difference and I'd at least like your consideration when you've had time to think it through."

Moe was a little taken aback with this and in his way liked it.

"Okay I want to know more, I want to know everything and maybe we can turn her to our side."

They were pulling into the FBI parking lot at this point and everyone was ready for some fresh air.

Chris pulled into the Starbucks and saw Bisma right off. Chris smiled as he approached her and held the door as they went in. She was not used to this treatment from the men in her life and she liked it. They approached the counter, ordered their coffees and walked to the end of the counter to wait. The smell of the coffeehouse made Chris long for days when he wasn't living in an RV in a barn with jihadists who's only goal was to blow themselves up. Chris followed Bisma to a table in the corner and he sat with his back to the wall. He hoped his basic spy craft was not noticeable to her since he had to squeeze past her to get that choice seat.

"How are you doing?" she asked.

"It's getting more tense as each day goes by. We've prepared everything that needs to be prepared and now we're just waiting."

"Any word from our friend in Chicago?"

"Not heard a thing."

Bisma stared into her cup. "Second thoughts about any of this Chris?"

This surprised him and he let her see that in his face. Was she testing him? Was she testing him for Hazaq?

"No. No second thoughts at all. We want to get on with it. The waiting and not knowing is intense. I have always believed my part will be to live to be a part of future plans."

Bisma knew what he meant. He was talking in generalities to not alarm anyone in earshot. Chris was not the suicide bomber type. He was a soldier who would do what he was told, but he did not plan to end his life with this mission. Bisma knew he was not like the rest of the men who were jihadists. She also knew he was the only one she could have a comfortable conversation with. He seemed to genuinely like her. She couldn't remember how long it had been since she had someone like this to talk to, this was what she wanted for her life.

Chris's phone vibrated on the table, he looked down to see a text.

"What is it?" Bisma asked.

Chris looked at the short message for several seconds before he replied.

"Chicago wants us to move out this evening. Joel and I are to take the camper to a campground outside of Indianapolis where a reservation has been made. The other three brothers are to go to your apartment."

Chris looked at Bisma, "Does he know we were meeting?"

"Not from me," Bisma said.

"Not from me either. Wow this timing is weird, but it's a good thing we're together. I was hoping for a longer time to talk."

"Me too," Bisma said.

"I need to run something by you. We had a visitor stop by the farm the other day. Joel and I went out to meet the man. He said he was selling fertilizer for the county co-op. I know enough about farming to know this was entirely possible."

"What did you tell him?" she asked.

"I told him we were artists and not the landowner, told him he should contact the landowner and he left."

"That all sounds innocent enough."

"It does until I tell you this was the man from Greenville who lost his wife in the attack, Mike Baker."

Bisma stared at him in silence until she said, "How do you know it was Baker?"

"He's been in the newspapers Bisma. I have tried to keep up on local things as best I can and I had read about the attack in Greenville. It was him."

"You are what, about 70 miles from Greenville?"

"At least," Chris said.

"This cannot be good," Bisma said. "Have you told our friends in Chicago?"

"No."

"Why not?"

"I wasn't sure what to do."

Bisma was staring into her coffee again deep in thought. She knew how Mike Baker knew where to find the barn. She had given him the GPS coordinates. Why the hell had Baker gone to the farm on his own and why hadn't he shared this with her? He must have decided to go it alone; this would get him killed. He is out of his league on this one. She was glad Chris had just gotten orders to move, it might save Mike Baker's life.

"You'd better go Chris, you have work to do. I will contact you again."

With this Bisma stood to leave. Chris reached for her arm.

"I want to see you again."

"I'll be in touch, now go."

She was out the door and he was crossing the parking lot for his pickup.

Russell County

Chris called Joel as he started up his truck.

"We are moving as soon as I get back."

"We'll be ready," he said to Chris and clicked off.

Joel gathered the other men and told them to pack everything up as they planned. Nothing would be left behind. They had planned for this time and everyone went into action.

Chapter Thirty-Five

Indianapolis

Members of the assault team were quickly gathering in the conference room in the FBI building. This team was comprised of FBI agents, specially trained SWAT members of the Indianapolis Police Department and trained snipers from various local agencies who always stood on call for an emergency they hoped would never happen. To the man these people were all former military.

Moe Keane would address the group at 1800 hours. Still in Nat's office he asked her to leave so he could talk to Mike Baker in private. Jackson found that odd, but excused herself and closed the door. Moe turned to reach for his bag. He came out with a manila envelope and pulled out a photograph. He put it on the table in front of Mike. Mike looked at it and raised his gaze to meet Keanes.

"I've seen him," Mike said.

"At the barn?" Moe asked.

"He was the first man who came out to my truck. How do you have this picture?"

"He works for me."

Russell County

As Chris came up the long lane to the barn, activity was going strong. The barn doors were opened, and he backed the truck up to the hitch. All weapons were hidden in the travel trailer and would stay in the trailer until it was time for their use. Joel would stay with Chris in the trailer while the other three men would go to Bisma's apartment.

They pulled out and traveled north to the Interstate to head west. Chris was following the speed limits and driving very focused.

"How many times you going to check that side mirror?" Joel asked.

Chris gave him a look that said, "Don't ask again."

Indianapolis

The buzz in the FBI conference room quickly lowered as Keane and Mike Baker entered the room. Keane introduced Mike Baker even though he was well known to the local law enforcement community after driving the school bus away from the school saving dozens of students and families and then again when he lost his wife in another terrorist attack months later.

Keane immediately explained the mission. The opportunity to round up a terrorist cell in their own backyard was crucial and time critical.

"Our priority is to take these jihadists alive. I want them for whatever intelligence we can gather. Behind me you will see a picture of a man who must not be harmed. He is one of our agents who has been imbedded with this cell for many months. We have not had contact with him for over a year, he is one of us and he must be protected."

This was a surprise to everyone in the room. No one including Natalie Jackson had any idea that Homeland Security had an agent in a terrorist cell. There were a lot of glances all around, this seemed to be good news and bad news. Bad news because having one person in a place you planned to take by force upped the *things that can go wrong* list dramatically.

"We leave at 2200 hours, it will be a 45-minute drive to the rally point. We must assume the grounds will be secured with trip wires or possible mines. We will move in military formation, infantry style. Night vision goggles will be used by all. Everyone will have throat mics and we will use hand signals as we get closer. Any guard will have to be immobilized. If the guard is our agent, he will surrender himself knowing we are friendlies."

"Questions?"

There were none.

"Everyone get something to eat and get some rest."

Food was brought in and set up for a walk-through meal. There was small chatter around the room, this was a group who wanted to get to the business at hand. They had about three hours to wait before moving out. The vehicles were prepared for the team. Everyone busied themselves checking and rechecking weapons for the rest of the evening. At 9:45 twelve agents made their way into three SUVs and one FBI tactical vehicle with communications equipment. The last trailing vehicle would be for prisoners and casualties. The thirteenth person traveling with the group got into the same vehicle with Keane and Jackson. This would be a night Mike Baker would not soon forget.

"Mike, you will stay in this vehicle. You will hear our communications. Understand?"

"Yes sir."

They rode mostly in silence. Traffic was light on the state highway and they were soon traveling on paved county roads. Moe Keane's mind was on Chris. This operation had to work, and they had to get Chris in one piece.

"This is our last turn, we will be on the road for the farm," Mike said.

They had picked a stopping point with adequate cover plus a direct way to the barn. Everyone unloaded, checked weapons and equipment and left. Mike was amazed at the precision. He was not sure how long he would be there. He opened the door to get some cool night air. The van with the communications equipment was parked about 5o yards away. He was told there would be one agent monitoring the equipment in that truck. One other agent was waiting in the ambulance/prisoner van. Mike had been sitting about twenty minutes when he felt his phone vibrate. He reached in his pocket to look at the number. It was not a number he was used to, but one he knew.

"Baker," he answered.

"Can you talk?"

"Yes, what do you want?"

"I have information you must get to the authorities. Can you do that?"

Mike was amazed at her timing. Hell, he was sitting in the middle of a round-up of the terrorist cell.

"I can do that. What do you want me to tell them?"

Bisma knew this was no turning back time. If she tipped the authorities as to what was happening tonight Hazaq would have to know it came from her. She would have to go into hiding.

"Tell them the group at the farm is moving tonight. They'll come to my apartment."

"Moving tonight?"

"Yes, please tell the authorities. Please tell them to not hurt me when they come."

Before he could answer she was gone. Mike was dumbstruck. He sat a few moments and decided he would tell the agent in the communications truck to connect him with Keane. He ran to the truck and knocked on the side door. The door slid open.

"What do you want?"

"I have to get a message to Moe Keane."

"Impossible, he is…"

"I just received a call with information these terrorists are on the move. It may put our people in more danger."

The agent shook his head and said, "Get in here."

He keyed a microphone and said, "Agent Keane."

"Keane."

"Baker has information for you."

"Baker is supposed to be waiting."

Mike was reaching for the mic, the agent handed it to him while shaking his head.

"Keane, I received a phone call from the woman I told you about. She said the cell is moving tonight. They are moving to her apartment."

"She called you?"

"Yes, it's happening now."

"Ok, you stay put. I will notify the team of this possibility. This may be misdirection or a trap."

Mike looked at the agent, he was still shaking his head but not as hard.

Keane quietly told the others that the cell may have left this property. They would proceed with the same caution until they could verify.

Nat Jackson was wondering what could have happened, was their timing that bad?

Twenty-three minutes later they were within 100 yards of the barn. There were no lights anywhere. The only illumination came from a quarter moon. The night vision goggles showed the barn lot. No movement could be seen. Two agents moved forward toward the barn and stopped at the front corners. They slowly moved towards the big sliding door. One agent slid a wire under the door and could look inside. He watched for nearly a minute with no movement. Satisfied it was empty he radioed this information to the others. The rest moved forward. While this was happening the second agent was making his way around the barn and using another camera wire in back with the same result. It was empty. Everyone was on edge with the prospect of any booby traps left behind. They would leave two agents behind to watch overnight before a team moved in tomorrow morning to search for any clues left behind.

For safety's sake, they walked out the way they walked in.

When they arrived at the vehicles Keane and Jackson went directly to Mike Baker.

"What did she say?" Keane asked.

Mike relayed the conversation almost word for word.

"You've got better intel than the Federal Government," Keane said. "And you know where she lives, correct?"

Mike shook his head in the affirmative. Keane looked at him and smiled. He keyed his mic to rally the other agents around for a new briefing. Only he and Jackson knew of Baker's involvement with the woman named Bisma and it was not time to share that information.

"We have a tip where this group has gone. I'm not happy we're moving from a rural setting to downtown Indianapolis. We are going to a parking garage on Michigan Street. We will meet there and begin surveillance."

Chris and Joel arrived at the campground and checked in. They asked to see the map of what was available and picked a spot as remote as possible. The attendant who checked them in seemed as disinterested as they'd hoped. They paid cash and were on their way. Joel got out to help guide Chris, and they were parked in no time. Chris was getting good at this. They unhitched and hooked up to the electrical box and were on their way to find something to eat. When they got their food, Chris sent Hazaq a text to tell him they'd moved and settled in.

Bisma was watching for the three men. She saw their car and came down to meet them at the door. She was not at all happy about this. There was a lot more downside for her than upside, but maybe she could still work this in her favor. Her main concern was that she did not get hurt.

Hazaq confirmed the receipt of the text from Chris. He knew they were now exposed and was happy they had split into two groups. He was not happy the three men were with Bisma, he didn't trust Bisma. Hazaq had never trusted Bisma, but she had performed as expected in the past. It was time to make the next attack happen. All weapons were ready to go, and this risked exposure.

Bisma got the men up to the apartment. They were traveling light, each carried a backpack with few clothes. She could tell they needed to find a laundry for what they were wearing, they smelled like men who had been living in a barn. She fixed them something to eat and could see they were quiet and focused.

Keane reconvened the team in the parking garage. Local authorities were alerted and asked to cordon off a four-block area without stopping traffic. They did not want to raise suspicion with anyone including local news teams. Mike had given them the location of the apartment building where Bisma lived. It was all student housing meaning the population of the building were late nighters. They didn't know which apartment belonged to Bisma or what floor she lived on for that matter. Keane had been thinking how to play this. The only connection was that Mike Baker had her cell phone number. They would use local technology to ping her phone for the exact location. This would be much easier if they could get her to answer a call or send a text. Knowing she had Mike's cell number was their only way to her.

Bisma was looking around her apartment as the three men were talking to Haris, to see that her best weapon against them was a pair of adjustable tongs. She figured if she could pinch four guys to death she'd have the upper hand, she'd start with their testicles. Her phone vibrated in her pocket, she carefully pulled it out to see a text message asking if she'd like to have a pizza delivered? She recognized Mike Baker's number. What would these guys think? She had fed them little, so this was not a stretch even though they would not approve. She immediately called after deleting the text.

Mike was a little surprised as his phone buzzed. Keane nodded and said, "Put it on speaker."

"Yes, thank you, I would like delivery. I'd like one large with extra cheese and one large with pepperoni. How soon can I expect you?"

Keane mouthed thirty minutes to Mike.

"We'll be there in thirty minutes. Your address please?"

"I'm in student housing at the corner of Vermont and 5th Street. I'll meet you at the front door of the apartment building," Bisma said and immediately clicked off.

Mike looked at Keane to see the frown on his face.

"She does not want us to come to her apartment door. We must assume they'll be watching us. How do we know this is not a trap?"

"I trust her," Mike said.

"I understand you trust her Mike, but in all fairness, you are involved in something here that you've not been trained for."

"Understood," was all he could say.

"Where are you going?" Keane asked Jackson.

"To get pizza."

With that Nat was gone, and they were left standing to think. The balance of the assault team was brought up to speed by Keane and everyone looked at their watches. They were due at the apartment door in 26 minutes.

"Everyone make ready." Keane said. I need time to think. He walked away. With nine minutes to spare Natalie arrived back with two pizza boxes.

"I can't believe I'm actually hungry," Mike said.

Nat smiled at him and said, "Too late, you should have placed your order 15 minutes ago."

Mike smiled as he saw Keane walking to them, the smile faded.

"All right. Agent Jackson you are my first choice to meet her at the door, but with you being local I don't want to take the chance of you being recognized by anyone who may accompany her to the door."

"But..."

"No buts. Agent Perry is the youngest looking one of this group. I want Agent Perry to take the pizzas to the door of the apartment."

"Perry, I want you to hand her the pizzas and ask for twenty bucks. When she hands it to you, ask if she's having a party."

"Party?"

"Just keep her talking, we have to know her apartment number. Ask her if you can stop by later, ask her apartment number. Improvise and make sure no one is there with her. If someone is with her, then she must get you info somehow. She called us to start this. She wants this over with."

"Understood."

"Good luck son, go."

Perry pulled up the collar on his jacket, grabbed the two pizzas and took off. He walked the fifty yards to the corner and walked toward the building to round the corner closest to her door. He approached the door and walked up to pull the handle when the door opened toward him.

"Two pizzas."

"Yes, for apartment 312, thank you. How much?"

"Twenty."

"Here you go," Bisma handed him two bills.

"You havin' a party in 312?"

"Yeah, me and four friends. You wanna' come over?"

"Maybe later when I get off work, how about midnight? Is that too late?"

"No, that'd be fine."

Bisma turned and walked away. That was weird as hell Perry thought to himself. It could be a setup for all he knew. All he could do at this point was to report back to Keane. He turned and hurried away. He made the five-minute walk in four minutes.

"Tell it all," Keane said.

"I walked up, and she met me at the door. I said two pizzas, and she said yes for apartment 312, how much. I said twenty, and she handed me two bills. I asked if she's having a party and she said yes with four others. She asked if I wanted to come and I said yes when I get off work at midnight and asked if that was too late. She said no that would be fine."

"Ok we cannot raid this apartment in a building full of students. We have no idea how they're armed or if they have explosives in the room. We'll get our technology in place to look in the room from the outside. We have thermal imagining to see heat signatures. We'll have a helluva time keeping this quiet in a place where young people stay up all hours of the night."

Nat said, "Since this is student housing let's get the university to tell us the occupants in the adjoining rooms. We can at least get them out as soon as possible."

"That's a good idea. The first thing we'll do is get eyes on the building and make sure these four or five occupants of apartment 312 do not leave. We know where they are and we'll not let them walk out to carry out an attack."

Keane pointed to two members of his team and told them to set up surveillance on all doors and to report when they were in position. He then told Nat to take another agent to decide where the thermal imaging camera could be set up. The closer the better. They were on their way and knew to report back as soon as possible.

Keane looked at Mike Baker, "You stay with me. If we decide to contact your friend inside, you will make the call or text." Mike understood and followed Keane as they left the parking garage.

Chris and Joel were not eager to return to the campground. It seemed they'd had enough of life in a trailer in a barn and needed some city life for a while. A couple beers with some country music and girls wearing cowboy boots and short skirts seemed like a great idea. They chose a place on the north side of Indy and found a seat. Chris contacted Bisma to make sure all was ok. He sent a text and Bisma answered within a minute to say the three guests had arrived and settled in for the night.

"Our three brothers arrived safely," Chris told Joel.

"Good, now we wait."

"How you doin'?" Chris asked.

"I'm nervous, no need to lie about it. All we planned is upon us. The thought of being a suicide bomber sounds exciting and to the heart of the cause until you're hours from having it happen. I'm not saying I won't do it, I'm just saying it's getting damn real at this point."

"Let's have some good bourbon to steel our nerves."

Joel smiled and ordered his on ice, Chris asked for his neat with a glass of ice water. Joel didn't know Chris wasn't on the suicide mission. Chris would continue to fight another day and do his best to make sure Joel's vest and the weapons of the others hurt no one.

Chris was glad to see Joel out on the dance floor for a couple songs. He needed to relax a little, and the bourbon seemed to help. Chris nursed his drink along. Joel was encouraging him to drink up, but Chris let him know he wanted to get them back to the campground without being pulled over by the authorities. Joel appreciated his designated driver with another strong one on ice.

After a couple hours and the time to head back approaching, Chris looked at his phone to see a text. He was surprised it was this soon but then again he knew Hazaq was ready to put his plan into action. The change of venue with the team being split put them at risk for exposure. The next text would happen at 0600 according to Hazaq.

"Ok we got word we are a go, next info at 0600. Let's head out."

Joel drained his glass and set it on the bar with a thud knowing full well this would be the last time that would happen.

On the way back to the campground Chris pulled into a liquor store to buy more bourbon. Joel offered no resistance.

Joel said, "Need more liquid courage?"

"Can't hurt," Chris said without giving him a look.

Chapter Thirty-Six

Indianapolis

Indianapolis seemed to love a good GenCon. This conference had an assortment of vendors and attendees that made for some fun news stories over the four days when they were in town. The economic effect for the city was very important, and they had welcomed the conference for many years now. Attendees would often come dressed for their favorite video game or book genre or board game. They were serious and eccentric and not at all bashful. This made for some interesting security concerns when Star Wars Storm Troopers were marching down Market Street to the Circle.

Asis had all the research he needed to plan the attack. Maps, schedules and the past year's news stories were a great help. This was not a conference of meetings and speakers, but a packed Convention Center of gamers that lasted well into each night. It had moved from summer to winter and this fit perfectly.

Chris received the encrypted email at 0600 and read it with disdain. This attack would cause carnage of innocent people including mostly young adults and teenagers. He knew Bisma had received the same email and would plan for the three cell members at her apartment.

Bisma was up early to fix breakfast for her guests. She had little to say until she glanced at her laptop to see the new email. She could see this had gone to Chris as well. The email was short; it gave today's date, a time of 4:00 PM and five different entrances to the Indianapolis Convention Center. There was a tracking number for a package to be delivered to her this morning.

As the three cell members sat at her small kitchen table, she told them today was the day for their commitment to Allah. Three blank stares greeted her with small nods. These men had nothing inside as far as she could tell, they were as blank as their stares. All awareness brainwashed from them, it was scary to see.

"Eat and get more rest brothers," she said.

This was her make or break day. If she allowed this to happen, she was finished. She would either be in an American Federal prison for life or killed by her own people if it did not happen. Bisma needed the help of Mike Baker and she had no time to waste. She couldn't be assured her cell phone wasn't compromised by Hazaq. She fully expected her door to be broken down last night at midnight. When that didn't happen, she had no idea if help would come her way.

At 10:20 AM her doorbell rang nearly bringing her out of her skin. She peeked to see a delivery man holding a box. She opened the door and saw two more packages at his feet. He asked to step inside and she moved back to let him in. He placed all three packages inside the door and turned to leave without a word.

She locked the door behind him and opened the packages. She found participant entry badges, five different sets of clothing, costumes really. Masks were included. The three men were watching with interest and wondering what this was about. Bisma explained the best she could about GenCon and though still amazed at the event they understood how these costumes would help them blend in and get into the venue.

Bisma excused herself to the bathroom. She quickly wrote, *GenCon 4PM!* and sent it to Mike Baker.

Keane and Baker were rapidly growing restless. Their eyes had been on the apartment building all night along with about a dozen other spotters. Normal traffic of students coming and going did not give them any cause for concern. The only spark of interest had been the box truck with the man delivering three boxes to someone inside. This truck was now being followed by two FBI agents.

Mike Baker's phone buzzed with a text message. He looked at it and saw the message from Bisma and held his phone for Moe to see.

Moe looked at Mike and said, "Answer, understood."

Mike nodded and sent the message. Moe looked at him and said we've got a huge issue here but at least we know where to look.

"Do you think we can trust her? Is there any way she is sending us in the wrong direction?"

"How the hell do we know; I think she wants out of this Moe. She hopes this is her way out."

Moe said, "We've got to pursue this, she has to know we are watching her and can protect her."

Moe dialed Nat Jackson and gave her the GenCon message. A brief exchange of trusting the source happened between them and she said she would plan coverage.

Mike asked, "Are you still ok with me going to see my friends at the fairgrounds?"

"I'd prefer it, get you out of harm's way. I want your phone Mike. If Bisma wants to make contact I want it to be to me."

Mike handed Moe Keane his phone and was led to a car to make the fifteen-minute trip north.

Bisma got the return text within seconds and erased it. Now all she could do was hope this was enough. She left her phone on vibrate and put it back in her pocket.

The three jihadists were taking their pick of the costumes, all three different. They were packaged separately so there was no mixing and matching. It appeared to be carefully scripted. All allowed for nice concealment of their suicide vests which would be coming from Chris and Joel.

Brent Nielson, Head of Security for the Indiana State Fairgrounds didn't like cold weather events when people were wearing coats. That made their job much harder. Protocol was to search bags and purses but he imagined all kinds of things that could be hidden in a big winter coat, male or female. His requests to have trained canine units at the doors to this event were nixed due to budgetary constraints and the number of units available. The GenCon crowd that was overflowing downtown Indianapolis seemed to be more in need of security than this gathering of the Purdue agricultural alumni.

Charles Summers drove Dr. Sutherlin and Mrs. Sutherlin down from West Lafayette this morning. They were glad to have time together and had things to discuss on the one-hour trip down Interstate 65.

"It will be good to see Brian and Pam Miller, it's been a while," Dr. Sutherlin said.

As Charlie pulled in to find a parking spot, they saw Brian and Pam walking to the south doors of the Pavilion. Charlie parked and they made their way to where Brian and Pam were waiting.

"Hello Millers!"

"Good morning to the honored guests," Brian said.

Dr. Sutherlin waved that off as he shook his head.

"You were there Brian. They think we're heroes, but truly we were just glad to get our asses back home in one piece!"

Brian smiled and shook his head.

"Nice day for early February," Pam said.

They all agreed and made their way into the Pavilion to look for old friends and acquaintances. It didn't take long for them to spot Mike Baker. Mike had already found three fraternity brothers and as usual they had immediately ventured into telling stories from their college days. Mike saw the Boiler Club approaching and introductions were made. His three buddies all knew Dr. Sutherlin, and one of the three was from the same county as Doc Summers.

"Have you found our table yet?" Dr. Sutherlin asked.

"No, I've not make it into the main room yet. Let's go find our seats."

Mike said his goodbyes to his buddies and followed the rest of the group to their table. Many others were already at their tables with new friends being made everywhere you looked. The bond of Purdue agriculture made for easy conversation and the three tough years they had just experienced gave everyone the need to prop each other up emotionally.

Charlie sat down beside Mike and asked, "How you doin' Mike?"

"Not bad Charlie, how bout you?"

"Not bad, but I'll tell you, the hair on the back on my neck is standing up. I feel something in the air."

Mike sat back in his chair and gave him a look.

"What?" Charlie asked.

Mike just shook his head.

A Purdue representative asked everyone to find their seats and the festivities would get started in five minutes. When this group was called to order it meant the food would be served shortly, and that was enough to get people in their seats! There would be a few serious speakers this afternoon, but the best part of this annual gathering was food and fun. It seemed the humor usually involved Indiana University and political candidates.

All ages attended this event. There were people who walked with a cane and many current students. Many students were recruited to help but the servers of the meal were all employees from the School of Agriculture including many Professors. Most of the attendees had been in their classes. This made for a lot of good-natured fun. Mike was enjoying his meal but on edge. He'd picked out three young men sitting two tables to his right. These young men for some reason gave him cause to keep his eyes on them. They seemed to keep to themselves, not talking much or making eye contact with anyone else and had not removed their winter coats.

Brent Nielson was having lunch in the office he was using off the main entrance of the huge banquet room. He had a bank of monitors in front of him that covered the entire main room of the Pavilion. The tall ceiling made for adequate coverage but not as close as he would have liked for looking at individuals. Even though it was winter, the room gained temperature from over a thousand people gathered inside. The men at the table near the front of the room still wearing their winter coats caught his eye.

He continued to scan from one monitor to another but kept coming back to that one table. These were the only people he felt looked out of place. He immediately stood when one young man stood and turned to walk between tables. Brent was out of his office and easily found him moving towards the back of the room. He saw him turn and head for the restroom on the east end of the conference room. Brent made his way across the back of the room and quietly entered the men's room. He immediately heard the young man getting sick in a stall.

"Are you ok?" Nielson asked.

"Yes."

"You don't sound ok."

"I'll be fine; I just need a minute. Something didn't agree with me."

"All right, take care."

Nielson opened the bathroom door and let it close with a thud while standing absolutely still inside. No one else was in the bathroom as far as he could tell. It was about a minute later when the stall door opened and the young man stepped out to see him standing there. The young man had not zipped his coat up all the way and Nielson saw enough to know his worries were well founded. As he reached for his radio, the young man reached into his coat pocket. Brent Nielson never had time to warn anyone before the flash, fire and blast hit him.

Mike had also taken notice when the young man got up, he watched him go through the crowd to a bathroom. He kept watching the other two, they were keeping their eyes toward the bathroom watching for their friend. They seemed to take special notice when they saw another man crossing the back of the room at a quicker than normal pace who entered the bathroom.

The rumble from the explosion and the sound of the explosion happened instantaneously. The block wall construction of the bathroom walls kept whatever happened inside mostly contained except for smoke cascading out of the door that was blown off its hinges.

Mike's eyes went from the bathroom door back to the two young men as several screams rang out and more than one table was overturned as a shocked crowd began to move.

Mike stood as the two young men stood up. The taller of the two dropped his water glass and reached for his pocket. He distinctly heard him scream, "Allah Akbar!" as Mike shot him at the base of his skull. As he crumpled to the floor, the other man turned toward him. Mike's shot hit him in the right shoulder. As he instinctively reached for the source of pain others wrestled him to the ground and held his arms. Mike was on him in five seconds and ripped open his coat to expose the vest underneath.

"Don't let him move!" he told three farmers who had no problem pinning him down hard. Mike went to the first man to make sure he was incapacitated to a point where he could not move a finger to detonate a bomb. He pushed him from his side to his back and unzipped his coat to see the same vest. This one felt nothing as the .40 caliber bullet severed enough of his spinal cord to stop his attack. Mike pulled his arms to the sides to make sure he was not close to a detonator.

Charlie and Brian were kneeling by Mike at this point.

"You okay?"

Mike looked at them and shook his head yes.

"How did you know?" Brian said.

"I've been watching them since we all sat down. They never took off their coats, and they seemed on edge. They had me on edge, and my stomach in a knot. I immediately looked at them when we all heard the explosion in the restroom and heard him scream Allah something."

"You saved us Mike, they would've killed dozens of us."

No sooner did Brian finish his comment when two Indiana State Police Troopers grabbed Mike Baker and told him to drop his weapon. He dropped it at his feet. Charlie and Brian told them they had the wrong man but Mike said, "No it's all right, let them do their job. Brian call Moe Keane, he has my phone."

They turned to walk him out as the EMS team came up along with other State Troopers. They quickly turned their attention to the man with the bullet in his shoulder. He was stabilized and wheeled out. All the while people were standing and watching.

Another officer went to the podium to ask for people to exit the pavilion. They were being moved into the next building to the west. No one could keep a coat on and everyone was quickly searched.

As they were walking out with everyone else Brian called Moe Keane to tell him what had happened. Moe listened without asking a question, told Brian to stay in touch and clicked off. He decided they should raid the apartment knowing full well they could walk into an ambush but decided the middle of the day should have the fewest residents inside. This attack at the Indiana State Fairgrounds was likely not only an attack but a diversion to the planned attack downtown. Agents took up positions that had already been planned and breached the door in a show of force to incapacitate the people in the apartment. They cleared the small apartment in seconds to find no one except Bisma. She was lying in the bathtub with blood everywhere. Her throat had been cut, but she still had a faint pulse. No one else was there. Medical help was already stationed outside and they were in the apartment within a minute. They stabilized her as best they could, started fluids and had her into an ambulance on the way to the hospital only five blocks away.

Western Indiana

After receiving the email to abort from Hazaq, Chris was given instructions to drive the trailer to a rest park west of Indianapolis. He relayed the change to Joel and got a, "What the hell is going on?"

"I don't understand but we are moving out and going west."

They prepared the trailer and were on the road in less than fifteen minutes. Traffic was light, and they arrived in about an hour. After a quick bathroom break they were surprised to see the other three brothers from their cell approaching the trailer. They quickly got into the trailer and were back on the road. Chris wondered what kind of video capabilities the authorities had at a rest park. They would need one stop for fuel before returning to the Chicago suburbs.

It was a sunny, cold day as they pulled onto the Interstate; Chris' mind was going a mile a minute.

"Turn on the radio, I want to hear local news," he said to Joel.

Joel found a station that was beginning its top of the hour news update and they heard about an attack at the Indiana State Fairgrounds. Details were sketchy, but it was suspected to be terrorists with suicide vests. They promised more details as they were available.

"I don't understand. Was this us or another group we don't know about operating in Indianapolis?"

Chris shook his head, "I have no idea, but for us to be called off at the last minute and this happening, it has to be us."

"That makes sense, it cannot just be a coincidence."

Joel turned the radio down so they could still hear anything new and they drove in silence for the next hour. Chris pulled off and filled the tank and they were again on their way back to Chicago. Chris was feeling a growing dread to be back in the company of Hazaq. Had he been compromised in any way? Would Bisma have turned Hazaq on him?

As Mike sat alone waiting for the detectives to return he replayed over and over the events at the fairgrounds. He wasn't sure how much trouble he was in, but it was likely considerable. He was hoping Brian was able to reach Moe Keane. He also kept replaying how his fingers had gone for the handle of his Beretta. He had it holstered inside the waistband on his left side. His right hand had gone instinctively it seemed to the handle. He could feel the tacky bite of the grip as he brought it out and up to aim at the base of the man's neck. He knew it was the right thing to do, he saved lives.

When Moe Keane and Nat Jackson stepped into his room late that afternoon he felt relief. He could tell they were all business.

"Let's go Mike," Moe said.

Mike followed Moe and Nat followed behind as they took with them the long gazes of a roomful of Indianapolis law enforcement personnel. The buzz in the room was the knowledge this was the same guy who stopped the bus attack and lost his wife in the restaurant suicide attack.

"He's either a hero or the unluckiest bastard I've ever seen," one Detective said to his partner.

Chapter Thirty-Seven

Indianapolis

Bisma was in shock when she arrived at the hospital, the initial prognosis gave her less than a 30% chance of survival. Blood loss was significant, but the good news was the wound to her neck had not lacerated her carotid artery. The wound was not as deep as they originally suspected considering the loss of blood.

Police detectives would later say this wound was caused by someone who didn't have the stomach for cutting someone's throat. Someone with more rage or vengeance would have made it much worse. Someone who knew what they were doing would have succeeded. The good news was she was alive and after a few days it appeared she would make a full recovery. Her heart had never stopped beating and her brain had never been starved for oxygen. She appeared to be someone who was a fighter and a survivor.

Hospital staff had kept her isolated in a small part of the hospital where important people go to recover. People like Indy car drivers who need to be out of the spotlight of the media for a while. Moe Keane had plans for Bisma after talking with Mike Baker and Nat Jackson. She may well be an important asset for them. She had expressed remorse over things that had happened in Indiana over the last several months and told all of them she wanted out of this life.

On day six the doctors said she could be moved. She was being treated one floor down from where the Lifeline helicopter landed and took off. She was loaded onto the helicopter during the night hours and flown to a federal government jet at Indianapolis International. Her trip to Washington DC happened without a hitch and she was ready to continue her recovery at a safe house.

Forensic teams worked Bisma's apartment and the fairgrounds to link the men involved. Days of testing raised no evidence it was the same men. They had little to go on in her apartment. More DNA was available at the fairgrounds along with the surviving member of the terrorist team who was not cooperating. This lack of cooperation was quickly becoming the fact he had little to share. He knew the two other men but not well. It seemed they had been put together by someone in charge who was very good at keeping operations compartmentalized.

Interviews with all other residents of Bisma's apartment building gleaned little information. Photos were taken of all residents and then compared to every surveillance camera in the area. It appeared the three men most likely left during the day at different times and through different exits. All kept their faces concealed so they couldn't be identified. The number of male residents in the building was reconciled against the number of males leaving the building that day. All residents were questioned concerning their movements that day.

The day after the attacks the FBI released information that Bisma had been killed in her apartment. Attempts to save her had been unsuccessful. They released one grisly photo of the crime scene showing her in a pool of blood. There had been disagreement on this, but Moe Keane wanted the world to know she was dead. They also showed a picture of three costumes found at the scene. It seemed clear these costumes were the kind hundreds of people were wearing to the GenCon gathering at the Convention Center this week. The FBI spokesperson said it seems clear an attack on GenCon had been stopped.

Chicago

Hazaq carefully orchestrated how Chris would learn of the death of Bisma. He had the news story on the DVR and the three cell members who were at her apartment were all sitting with Chris and Joel when he told them he had news to share. He pressed play and closely watched Chris as the FBI agent told of Bisma's death at the news conference.

One of the three men from her apartment said, "Inshallah," as the FBI spokesmen ended his comments. It was all Chris could do to not slit their throats as they had done to Bisma. Chris said nothing and used all his training to not reveal a shred of emotion. As much as he wanted to question Hazaq on a few things, he knew it would only raise more suspicion so he kept his mouth shut. The bolder of the three cell members asked if the other attack was brothers from their cell?

Hazaq said, "There are others, yes."

Chris wondered if all the planning that led up to the GenCon attack was just a test or a way to expose Bisma or him. If so it was one elaborate and dangerous plan. He knew Bisma was fearful of Hazaq. She had been very careful with her words to Chris, but he knew. Maybe this was just his way to get her out of the team. She had proven useful and this may have been too much for Hazaq to handle.

Later that evening Hazaq wrote up his report on the evening and hit send. Asis would have it first thing next morning. It had always been Asis' idea to bring young Caucasians into the jihad. To Hazaq an infidel was an infidel, racial profiling goes both ways. Hazaq understood the Americans could be an enormous help to get cell members into places where they could go unnoticed. It also allowed them to transact business under the radar that was set up to monitor young Muslim men of Middle-Eastern descent.

Washington

In the days and weeks that followed Bisma recovered fully and told Moe Keane everything she knew about Hazaq and the Chicago cell. Keane kept Nat Jackson and Steve Bradshaw in the loop with everything, they also spent time with her during the debriefings. Information on how she had tried to shanghai Mike Baker also came out. She told them how Mike and his son David had found and confronted her. Even though they already knew this from Mike, it made them again realize how this reckless action by Baker had been a huge breakthrough.

There was also discussion on Mike Baker and how he'd saved many lives at the State Fairgrounds. His actions were downplayed by law enforcement due to the fact he probably should face prosecution for several things but he saved many more lives than the one he took. He was a hero who could not be recognized as a hero. He understood this and wanted no recognition. He wanted to forget the entire thing.

Bisma had told her story as best she could in chronological order. She came to the part where she had met a new cell member named Chris. How he seemed different. Keane let her talk about him for a long time as he decided what he would tell Bisma.

"The two times we met I found myself either drawn to him or scared of him," Bisma said.

"What do you mean by that?"

"He was just so natural. He was born and raised here and did not seem like someone who would want to kill innocent Americans."

This was good and bad as far as Moe was concerned. It seems Chris had let his guard down a little with Bisma. If he did this with the wrong person, he would end up tortured and killed. He was an invaluable part of the Chicago cell, but maybe it was time to get him out. Moe wanted to get the person in London. As far as Bisma knew the London person was behind the USS South Carolina tragedy and Alberto Mulina. Moe elected not to tell Bisma about Chris now, it seemed a later time might be useful to get her further cooperation.

Moe Keane had been thinking for a long time about restitution for the farm families who had been damaged by Roger Knight and his bank. Some of the problems were just poor luck with the weather, but Knight had done everything possible to make matters worse for customers of his own bank. Keane felt all White Oak Holding Company assets should go back to their original owners. The Bank should shoulder the responsibility and liability to get things back to the way they had been before this all unraveled. The government was also considering levying fines against the bank to help pay for the court proceedings and legal fees.

Keane felt all of Roger Knight's personal assets should be seized and distributed to all the customers and farmers he damaged. Knight's conspiracy with terrorists and terrorism would make this happen. The legal community would sort this out.

Moe had friends in the Department of Justice who would help get the process started. He also had friends in the Treasury Department and Federal Deposit Insurance Corporation who would like to make things right with these citizens and bank customers who had been wronged. It would all become much more political than he wanted, but he wanted justice. He put together the pertinent details and sent them to each department and asked them to get back to him.

Knight would protest vehemently because his assets and farm ground were all he cared about. This was his empire that would be unwound and given back to its rightful owners. "*Screw Knight,*" Moe said to himself. He thought he was getting off easy. He should be looking at a table with a needle in his arm for what he had done. Moe also had little regard for Janet Knight in all of this. She was not as implicit as her brother, but she knew most of what was going on.

It was decided to closely monitor Roger Knight for the time being. He was not a concern for public safety by himself, he was a slight concern as a flight risk but wouldn't leave all his empire.

The possibility he might lead them to the London connection was his real value.

Chicago

Chris was growing more and more irritable being with these people. Nothing was happening. They were basically just laying low for a while. He believed Hazaq was planning more attacks but nothing was being shared with the group. They never left the apartment. Chris lifted weights and worked out at a furious pace and read everything he could get his hands on. Hazaq controlled their internet use and no cell phones were used in the apartment.

Chris had time to think. Think through events like Mike Baker coming to their farm safe house. Only one person knew the location of that farm besides Hazaq, that was Bisma. Could Bisma have been working with Mike Baker and/or the authorities? She was part of the planning that killed Baker's wife! Had they caught her and turned her? If that was the case, Chris hoped Moe Keane was involved. Keane would put two and two together and know he was embedded with the Chicago cell. But Bisma was now dead, how much would they have learned from her before these animals killed her? He had all questions, no answers.

London

Asis was pleased with the attacks that had been perpetrated on the infidels. Not all had gone according to plan but his jihad had enjoyed success and was getting better at recruitment. Hazaq

had proven himself as a leader plus he seemed to be good at reading people. These small cell attacks were a good way to hit them
and it was proven by other attacks in Europe over the last few
years that small groups could do a lot of damage. It was Hazaq
who had noticed Dr. Sutherlin from Purdue was being recognized
during the gathering of Indiana farmers that happened each February. As much as they would have liked to hit the infidels at the
GenCon, hitting them at the award ceremony was better. It was
also Hazaq who had kept Bisma out of the loop of the change in
plans. Hazaq would never come out and say he didn't like her,
but Asis could tell he didn't like sharing any glory with a woman.
Her death at the hands of the other cell members was Hazaq
alone.

Chapter Thirty-Eight

Greenville

Mike and Sarah had attended David's graduation last weekend and were so happy for him. Now Mike was glad to see David coming up the lane with his car loaded. He was excited for David and nervous about his next step. Mike helped him carry things in the house and got two cold beers. It seemed right to drink a cold one together.

David and Mike got ready to fire up the grill. Mike had put a rub on the steaks earlier that afternoon, they'd be ready for a short ride on the grill. Neither he nor David wanted them burned. Mike carried out the steaks and put them on.

"Dad, let's just get this out now and then we can get to important stuff like dinner."

"Go ahead."

"I leave for basic training in two weeks, I'll be in North Carolina."

"I knew it was coming. I couldn't be prouder and more scared. I don't mean it bad saying I'm scared, just being honest."

"I'd be lying if I said I wasn't a little scared too," David said.

Mike held out his beer and David said, "Cheers."

Steaks were smelling great and ready to eat. Father and son sat down to enjoy each other.

As they finished dinner, talk turned to Sarah.

"How's she doing Dad?"

"She'll be home tomorrow so you can see for yourself. I think she's doing fine, but who knows? She lost her mother to violence. She's growing into a young woman without her mom."

"I never know what to say to her Dad. I want to give her encouragement."

"Not sure there's much else we can do son. Honestly it doesn't feel right for me to say that's it's going to be okay or it's going to be fine. It's not okay or fine. We've got a huge gaping hole in the middle of us."

David said, "They say time heals and I hope that's true, but I can't imagine how long that'll take."

"Me either."

"Let's take her to a state park and hike."

"We always liked to do that as a family, didn't we?"

"Sure did."

Sarah pulled in the next day. Mike and David were out to meet her and began carrying her college things into the house. Mike could sense she slowed just a step as she entered the house. She walked into the kitchen and put her drink on the counter.

"I see her everywhere," Sarah said.

Mike nodded and put his arms around her for a long hug. She looked up at him with a deep sadness. She turned and gave David a hug and then headed for her room.

Five minutes later she was back out and asked, "You do okay on final grades, I guess they did let you graduate?"

David answered, "Pretty good actually. You?"

"Probably kicked your butt, big bro."

This got a smile out of David and she was probably right.

"Tell me your next step," she asked.

"I leave for basic training in North Carolina in two weeks."

Sarah just nodded. She hadn't said much about David's decision, to him or her father.

"Is this because of Mom?"

"Partly, I'd like to help fight back."

Sarah just looked at him and then turned to her dad.

"Tell me more about the woman you followed, what was she like?"

Mike answered, "Not like I expected. I thought she'd be some kind of monster, American hating terrorist. She was scared. She'd lost her father to war when she was young and her mother had gotten her out of the Middle East. I truly felt she wanted out."

"But she'd helped kill Mom."

"Yes, and we'll never know to what extent she was involved. We do know she was living in an apartment with the man who did it."

"Makes her guilty in my eyes," Sarah said.

"They killed her and left her behind. That's who were dealing with," Mike said.

Washington

Moe wanted to talk to Nat Jackson and Steve Bradshaw while they could sit down under secure conditions. He emailed both to meet at 1:00 PM.

"Have a seat you two," Keane said. "Let me start with an update on Mike Baker. You know his ass should be in a big sling but in my mind he is a hero who stepped up and saved countless lives. It's already been determined there will be no prosecution, he deserves an award but he won't get one because we're just going to keep this quiet and I feel confident that will be fine with our farmer friend. Damn fine shooting for a civilian."

Smiles and nods and head shaking came from both.

"Next, I need good people like the both of you here, but we want to cut off the monster's head and I think that head is based in London. Steve has gathered enough intel along with information we have received from Bisma to tell me the leader in London must be stopped. For this reason, I'm sending both of you to Great Britain to hunt the terrorist working from that location. This has already been coordinated with British intelligence and the CIA, you will have the full cooperation of the local authorities including computers," as he looked at Steve.

"I have spoken to both of your superiors and have their cooperation as well. I have only taken these steps due to the extreme level these attacks have reached on our soil. Both of you come to this fight from different backgrounds that we want to fully utilize. You're the tip of the spear."

Jackson and Bradshaw listened intently and then gave each other a quick glance. They were both ready to battle terrorism either here or wherever they needed to go to take the fight to them.

"How soon do we leave?" Nat asked.

"I would like for you both to be prepared to leave in about ten days. I want you to schedule a meeting with the Boiler Club for a debriefing. Further arrangements will be made for your trip to Great Britain in the meantime."

Steve thought to himself this would be the final straw in his marriage which was already on rocky ground due to his work schedule. It was weird, this was almost a relief.

Nat asked Keane, "Will Bisma be a help to us for the person in Great Britain?"

"I am confident she knows little about the person in London, she will be a much greater help to fight the cell in Chicago. She has good information about them and has even lived there for a time. We know they may have moved since then, that lead is being tracked down now."

"Lastly, we have not received any intel of value from Janet Knight. Her meeting with her brother did not turn up anything. I have watched and listened to the meeting and she did a poor job of questioning him. I'll be encouraging her to pay him another visit very soon with a more aggressive line of questioning. She's got so much on the line here she is afraid what she may turn up. In other words, I don't expect much."

Keane said, "If there are no more questions you both need to head home, get rested and plan to be back here in 10 days to make final preparations. Get things taken care of at your homes and be ready for an extended deployment abroad."

They all stood and Moe shook hands with each.

"The Division of Homeland Security thanks you in advance for your service."

They turned and headed for the elevator.

As they were leaving the building Steve said, "How about dinner?"

"That sounds fine, I don't fly out until morning."

"How bout I pick you up at 7 o'clock and we go to the place we went last time?"

"See you at 7:00."

Steve drove back to his office for a couple hours of checking emails and to see if anything came through the search programs he was running. Finding nothing new he gave his wife a call to say he'd be working that evening and got a "What else is new?" as the line went dead.

Steve learned long ago to keep fresh clothes in the locker room at his office. He grabbed a quick shower, clean shirt and sport coat and took off in plenty of time to get to Natalie's hotel. She was waiting for him in the lobby. They got in his car and made the short drive to the restaurant.

Dinner talk centered on London, the time of year and the weather to expect. What kind of packing they would need to do. It was a little strange and stressed between them not knowing what the future would hold overseas. Steve wanted to tell her but decided not to share his problems at home. Steve would like nothing more than to take her back to the hotel and spend the night with her but he knew this was not the time.

He dropped her off with a handshake and said, "I'll see you in 10 days, we'll go catch bad guys!"

She gave him a smile and said, "See you soon."

Natalie was sure the next few months would be very interesting. Interesting for their careers and their personal lives. She looked forward to the challenge of hunting down people who wanted to hurt Americans.

Chapter Thirty-Nine

Indianapolis

Natalie Jackson emailed all members of the Boiler Club. She said she wanted to give them a debriefing of events. Responses came back agreeing on a meeting at Mike's home. Pam Miller coordinated and planned a meal for all involved. According to unwritten Indiana doctrine they all agreed to a pitch-in because the group was like family. They set a date, and all confirmed to be there. Mike emailed Nat and asked if his two kids could be there? Nat responded saying she would rather they not attend and added it should be Mike telling them the pertinent information. Mike reluctantly agreed.

To make sure everyone was on the same page she would tell the entire story even though some of this was being rehashed for different ones of the group. She made her notes and was pre-pared. This would be an evening of emotions even though most of it was already known.

Greenville

It was the day of the meeting and everyone began to arrive at Baker's home. Dr. Sutherlin and Doc Summers had not seen

Mike Baker and Brian Miller since the day of the Purdue Ag Alumni Fish Fry and were very happy to reconnect. It was decided everyone was ready to eat then get down to business afterward. Dinner conversation centered on Mike's children, Pam's Cheesy Potato recipe and Purdue's football chances next fall.

After the meal Nat thanked them all for coming and asked if anyone had a question before she began. Mike asked if they could take notes or if she would give them handouts.

"Great question, I would begin by telling you that information this evening should be kept within this group due to the ongoing investigation."

They all agreed, they wanted everyone involved to be prosecuted fully and they would not want to do anything to impede that process.

"Honestly, I'm surprised you're doing this for us," Mike said.

"It was Moe Keane's idea, he feels you've earned it and know most of it anyway. This may connect a few more dots."

Nat started by telling them the story about the downed airliner and how someone from London had recruited Alberto Mulina to help. She went through the story of Mulina's brother the pilot and how he was sick and couldn't get insurance and he agreed to down the jet for money for his daughter.

She then moved into how this was a diversion to get search parties into a certain area off the coast of Chile including the United States submarine. She told them of the jihadist on the submarine under deep cover, how he was a nuclear engineer by training and he was able to cause the explosion. Mulina had confirmed this was the plan of the terrorist group from London. She then went into territory that would be very sensitive to Mike Baker. She explained they had learned Roger Knight had funneled money to the terrorist organization to make this all happen. She could see the immediate realization in Mike's face that Roger Knight had been part of the group that had killed his brother.

"I am very sorry Mike," Nat said.

Mike lowered his head as this soaked in. The others were also processing this information. Tension in the room ramped up as looks of bewilderment and anger were shared.

"That piece of shit helped kill my brother. Nat why in hell was Roger Knight working with a terrorist group in London?"

Nat said, "This will be unbelievable to you all but Roger Knight had a plan to change the weather to hurt farmers in the Midwest."

More bewildered looks.

"Knight hoped the explosion of the nuclear reactor in the submarine would expend enough heat energy to raise the ocean temperature one or two degrees to magnify the upcoming El Nino that had been forecasted."

This information was incredulous to Dr. Sutherlin, he could not believe someone thought it would work and said so.

Nat said, "We have studied this after learning the plan and it didn't work, not even close. The El Nino effect on its own was enough to cause the weather problems we experienced in the last three years."

Heads were shaking all around the room.

"While we're on Knight, he also funneled money to the terrorist organization for his back-up plan which was to poison the

Red Tanager birds in Brazil to bring back the virus to kill live-stock. You all know about this already, but what you didn't know and what we believe Knight didn't know is that the terrorist organization had increased the poison effect to hopefully kill thousands of United States citizens. This was also a failure except for a couple dozen citizens. The livestock deaths occurred in alarming numbers as you all know. When questioned by Mr. Keane, Janet Knight showed her surprise when she learned she could easily have died along with thousands of other citizens. We cannot be 100% positive her brother didn't know, but we're 99% sure."

Mike said, "His greed sure had him in bed with the devil. Sounds like he'd go to any length to get what he wants."

Nat shook her head and said, "Pure evil."

This was a lot for the group to digest, even though they knew a lot of this information or the pieces. Having it all put together into a diabolical plan which they had been a part of, hit them hard. They pressed Nat to go on.

She then transitioned into the formation of the White Oak Holding Company in Illinois that was set up to buy farm ground at auctions. They knew a glut of land at auction would quickly deplete the price of land and the holding company would continue to buy at depressed levels. This information was also known by Mike but was hard to hear knowing he had lost his family farm and the stress of this whole business ended his father's life sooner than it should have. Knowing his Dad died due to the stress was another reason to want to have Knight end up in a terrible place. Knight had killed his brother and father as far as he was concerned. He had feelings in the back of his mind he never thought he could have. His eyes met Nat Jackson's eyes, and he wondered if she could read what he was thinking, it gave him a shiver. Pre-meditated murder was a ticket to death row, no matter how good the reason.

Another piece of all this tragedy was the attempt to blow up the school. Mike knew more about this part than he ever wanted to know, but he was glad he could stop this deed. It would have been another Oklahoma City situation with many people and children left dead. Losing the two sheriff deputies and four Federal Agents had left the county and state in mourning. Thank God this did not include hundreds of other families in the county.

It was time for Nat to go into an area that would devastate Mike Baker. She wanted to have this conversation with him in private but couldn't make in happen in the time when she learned it from Bisma's debrief and now.

"Our newest information comes from a female named Bisma. Mike has met her."

He shook his head as eyes moved to him.

"Mike, I wanted to share this with you before tonight, but it may be best for you to be surrounded by your friends and family."

His look of "what is it?" was on his face.

"We have learned from this new source that Roger Knight requested the Chicago cell target the restaurant and specifically Sandy."

No one was sure what would happen next. Mike's hands reached for the arms of his chair and all could see he was raw emotion.

"She told us Knight asked for her to be kidnapped and not killed, but the cell members decided to send in a suicide bomber that night."

"What the hell more does he want from my family? The bastard killed my wife, killed my brother and killed my father and for good measure he took our family farm. Agent Jackson he is still walking the streets and living in his fancy home."

"Not for long Mike. The special prosecutor appointed by the Justice Department is putting the final preparations on his case. Roger Knight will spend the rest of his life in a Federal Penitentiary."

"That's too good for that piece of shit," Brian said.

Nat Jackson couldn't agree more, but it's the best they had. There were a few questions but not many. This group looked like she had run them through the wringer. Mike and Nat had agreed with Moe Keane that no mention would be made of Chris Powell. He was still embedded within the terrorist organization putting him in danger of discovery.

"I also want to share with the group something Mike already knows."

All eyes landed on him again.

"Mike should not have been carrying a weapon at the fairgrounds but we are all happy he was. He will face no charges. Many of us believe he should be treated as a hero but this will only happen with this group."

A round of applause broke out. Mike shook his head and said, "It could've gone wrong in many ways."

"In about a week Steve Bradshaw and I will travel to Great Britain to track down the London connection."

"We'll hope to see you there!" Brian said.

"You're traveling to Great Britain?" Mike asked.

"Yes, Pam and I are going on a birding trip to the United Kingdom for some new additions to my life list."

"Have you shared this with anyone else?" Nat asked.

"No why?"

"Just for your safety."

"Pam and I will be fine," Brian shrugged her off.

"You and Dr. Sutherlin were targeted and taken hostage in Brazil. You are known to them Brian. Don't you think they'd like to get their hands on you again?"

This was said in a forceful enough manner to leave everyone sitting quietly for a few moments.

"I apologize to you all, but…"

Brian cut her off. "We all know you care about us and our families and it shows. We'll be happy to comply with your request and send Mr. Keane our itinerary."

All understood the situation and that Natalie Jackson was very personally involved. People gathered up their belongings and Corning Ware dishes and gave hugs until the next gathering. Mike offered a prayer for safe travel and safety for Nat and Steve Bradshaw, everyone appreciated this send-off. They left with the knowledge the Federal Government would do everything in its power to prosecute Knight and Mulina; continue trying to find the terrorists who attacked the school and restaurant, and lastly find the persons in London who had masterminded all these attacks. Times like this hit Mike hard when everyone left, and he was alone without Sandy.

Mike sat by himself at their kitchen table later that night and reflected on feelings he had as a kid. Americans had lived in fear of nuclear war. He used to think how the average Russian father just wanted to come home to his family at the end of each day to be with the ones he loved and loved him. He had no personal animosity towards the average American family, but he did have a problem with the American government who could send missiles to end their way of life. Any American father felt the same about the Russian government sending missiles raining down on his country. So it should be with the jihadists or terrorists or whatever they wanted to be called. Why did they come after average people? He could think on it until his head exploded and he would never figure it out.

Mike was not a vindictive man. He believed in forgiveness but also knew it was easier said than done. As far as he was concerned all of this had taken his father from him much sooner than he should have gone. He knew for sure his wife and his brother were gone because of the terrorists. He knew he did not have the resources to hunt these people down, but he wanted to help in any way he could. He also had to wonder what he would do if he ever had the chance for revenge. What would he do if he had this London terrorist in his sights? Or Roger Knight twenty miles away?

Elm Grove

Janet couldn't care less who saw her back out of Roger's driveway and squeal her tires a little as she raced down his quiet street. Let his neighbors wonder what is going on. He really had no idea of what he was facing, and he'd made it crystal clear he didn't care about his sister.

Roger decided to pour some bourbon and take it out to the patio. He could enjoy looking at the pool as the sun went down and he got himself a little buzzed on the bourbon. The angle of his Adirondack chair was just right for him and the thick cushion made it about as comfortable as you could be. He took a mouthful and let the burn settle down his chest.

Janet had just been to see him again. Her surprise visits were not welcome; she'd gone from meddling to being a big pain in the ass. Problem was, she was probably right to be worried, but what could he do? They were both in deep. At least he had his best friend, bourbon over ice, sitting in his lap. He'd never seen her so mad. She accused him of risking everything by his reckless ideas. She left with no goodbye.

His head was back and his eyes were closed when he heard the faint noise. His hands shot up to clutch his throat when the searing pain hit. His eyes were now wide open as he struggled to move. No scream would come as much as he tried. No movement would come because he was stuck and he couldn't figure out why. His hands were fumbling with something smooth that was now coming out of his throat. The terror set in deeper when he realized he was not getting a breath as his chest heaved for one. Searing pain was now coming from the area where the smooth protrusion was between his fingers. The wet feel came from his own blood beginning to drown him. It was just a couple of horrific minutes until the shock, blood loss or lack of oxygen took his life. It seemed like forever. He wondered to himself who the person was he was seeing come out of the shrubs twenty feet away. It was a woman...

The hunters' cam she'd installed a couple weeks ago had worked perfectly, she now placed it in her backpack. She could do surveillance on the front of the house easily from several places on the street but this camera let her know when the time was right for this part of the plan. His sister's visit and abrupt exit was exactly what she was hoping for. A gunshot that was muffled would have been more than she would have dared in this neighborhood. The whistle of the arrow from a crossbow was something he never saw coming. She thought putting the arrow through his Adam's apple would be a way to crush his larynx as well as impale him to the chair. He could make no noise and hopefully experience the torture of his last couple minutes. They would find no fingerprints on the steel shaft of the arrow and he would be telling no one what he saw before he left this world.

She knew this decision would haunt her over the years. Roger Knight let nothing get in his way to seek revenge for wrongs he thought had been perpetrated on his family. He had no regard for the pain and suffering he'd caused to hundreds of innocent Americans. Her revenge was swift and just and not directed to anyone except him. Yes, she may be haunted in years to come; but the punishment she delivered felt right. He did not see it coming, but neither did her mother in the restaurant that night.

Made in the USA
Monee, IL
17 October 2020

45162611R00215